The Strange Vanguard

A FANTASIA

By

ARNOLD BENNETT

CASSELL AND COMPANY, LTD
London, Toronto, Melbourne and Sydney

First Published   1928
3/6 Edition *January* 1930

Printed in Great Britain

CONTENTS

CONTENTS

THE STRANGE VANGUARD

CHAPTER I

THE SPLENDIDE

MR. SUTHERLAND rang the bell once, in his private sitting-room at the Hotel Splendide, and expected the prompt arrival of the waiter. Mr. Sutherland was a man of fifty, clean-shaven, spare, rather austere, with the responsible and slightly harassed demeanour which comes of having married young and remained married, and the thin lips and logical jaw which usually develop on the faces of men who have been called to the Bar. Brown-grey hair that might soon, but not yet, be described as scanty. Pale blue eyes, whose glance denoted a certain mild self-complacency on the part of Mr. Sutherland. The reasons for the self-complacency were various and sound.

In the first place, Mr. Sutherland was a seventh child: to be which is always a mystical asset in life, and further, his parents had indicated his ordinal position in their family by christening him, not Septimus, which is banal, but Septimius, which is rare and distinguished. That extra "i" had virtue for Mr. Sutherland.

In the second place, Mr. Sutherland some thirty years earlier had stroked the Cambridge boat. Nobody, in

I

giving an account of Mr. Sutherland to people who were unacquainted with him, ever omitted to mention this fact, and only cynical or malign persons would mention also that he had not stroked Cambridge to victory.

The third reason for self-complacency was that Mr. Sutherland was, and knew himself to be, an organizer. He organized everything in his existence; and when, as now, he was enjoying for a space the absence of his delicious, disorganizing wife and girls, and of a devoted, incompetent valet, he would organize with abandonment and utterly revel in his talent for organizing.

The apartment gave evidences of organization. Mr. Sutherland was leaving the city that evening by train. The receipted bill, much stamped, for his sojourn at the Splendide lay open on the centre-table. His suitcase lay open on a side-table, with a couple of books all ready to slip into it. The suitcase was labelled with two labels, one adhesive, the other attached by string. In the bedroom lay Mr. Sutherland's flat American trunk, still open, lest Mr. Sutherland might have forgotten something. It could be snapped to in a second. Hanging over the raised lid of the trunk (which had three labels) was Mr. Sutherland's rug, conveniently folded, and on an adjacent chair were his hat, overcoat and gloves. The spectacle of all this organized order gave pleasure to Mr. Sutherland.

The bell was not answered. Mr. Sutherland's organization, however, was not disconcerted by the delay. He always allowed a margin for the imperfections of mankind and the malice of heaven; and now he utilized this margin by systematically opening every drawer in the sitting-room, bedroom, and bathroom, and demonstrating to himself, for the second time, that he had forgotten nothing. Thereupon he shut the American trunk.

Still the bell was not answered. And now Mr. Sutherland began to have a new and dark idea about the organization of the Hotel Splendide, which organization he had hitherto admired without reserve. The Splendide was the best hotel in the city. There were four other leading and in every way first-class hotels—the Majestic, the Belvidere, the Royal Palace, and the Grand Miramar, and according to advertisement each of these four was also the best hotel in the city. The Splendide, however, had two advantages over its rivals—due to two discoveries made by its designers. The first discovery was that the visitor does not care to overhear everything that passes, by word or action, in the rooms adjoining his own, or even in the corridor; and the second was that the visitor finds little pleasure in the continual sounding of a bell—once for the waiter, twice for the chambermaid, and thrice for the valet—especially when the rung bell is situate, as it always is, just outside his bedroom door. Hence the designers of the Splendide had established double doors between adjoining rooms and between rooms and corridor, and had entirely done away with the sound of bells. When you pushed the button at the Splendide—the top one for the waiter, the middle one for the chambermaid, and the lower one for the valet—a white, a green, or a red light shone in the corridor above your door and kept on shining until the waiter, the chambermaid, or the valet (duly warned by a bell far, far out of hearing of the visitor) came and extinguished it. Thus, if you closed your double windows, you could live at the Splendide as in the isolated silence and select privacy of the grave, until you died from steam-heat and lack of ventilation.

It was all most ingenious, and Mr. Sutherland had loved it all. But now he perceived a psychological flaw

3

in this organization. The visitor, having rung without getting a reply, could not be sure whether or not the apparatus was in order. Supposing the distant bell was for some reason not functioning! A terrible thought! Mr. Sutherland, after a further pause, opened the double doors into the corridor and looked forth. Yes, the white light, symbolic of his desire for the waiter, was burning over his door and burning brightly, steadily, patiently, waiting for the waiter. But had the bell rung? Mr. Sutherland could not and did not know. He did not even know where the bell was to be found. Silence and solitude in the long corridor! Dozens of doors, and only one of them illuminated, Mr. Sutherland's!

Septimius felt himself to be a victim, and yet somehow guilty; the white light seemed to accuse him of something. He was at a loss. He knew not what to do. His great gift for organizing had been rendered futile. He hesitated, most absurdly, to step out into the hostile wilderness of the corridor. At last he did step out, and it was as though he had gone over the top in battle. Then Mr. Sutherland saw a waiter in the distance, and stepped back into the ambush of the doorway and halted the waiter at the moment of passing the door. The waiter, startled out of his professional self-control, gave Septimius a look of murderous hatred. The glance covered perhaps the tenth of a second, and was instantaneously succeeded by the conventional acquiescent smile of his calling; but Septimius had noted it, and was afraid in his heart, for the glance seemed to symbolize and lay bare the awful secret antagonism which divides the servers from the served—seed of revolutions. Septimius even feared for his life, for he was in a strange and sinister city, where lives were worth much less than in London, and some people might possibly find their advantage in the sudden death of Septimius . . . Pooh! Ridiculous!

"Please bring me the menu," Mr. Sutherland, speaking in English, addressed the waiter, whom he had never seen before. And he carefully spoke as one man to another, in order to indicate his belief in the dogma that all men are equal before heaven. "I shall dine here in my room. And when you serve the dinner let me have the bill with it—receipted. You understand. I'm leaving to-night."

The waiter smiled charmingly to indicate his belief in the dogma that the least wish of a visitor is a law to the waiter. He smiled, bowed, and departed. He had understood only two words, 'menu' and 'bill.'

Mr. Sutherland felt reassured, though he had had a shock.

After a brief delay the waiter returned, without the menu, and made quite a long foreign speech to Mr. Sutherland, not a word of which did Mr. Sutherland comprehend. The black-coated fellow was one of those waiters, prevalent in the splendid hotels of distant and picturesque lands, who can speak no language but their own, and sometimes not even that. Ten key-words of English or French may suffice a waiter for the common affair of human nature's daily food, but in a crisis they quickly prove inadequate.

Mr. Sutherland saw that this was a crisis. He could speak Sutherland-French, slowly, and he now did so. But the waiter's face was an amiable blank before the persuasions of Sutherland-French.

"Menu, menu, menu! Carte, carte, carte!" Mr. Sutherland repeated firmly and kindly, but foolishly.

The waiter shook his head. At last Mr. Sutherland in blank despair waved him from the room.

"Is it conceivable," thought Septimius, "that in a

hotel with the pretentions of the Splendide, they should place you at the mercy of servants with whom it is impossible to communicate?" He saw that it was conceivable, and sighed.

There was only one thing to do—namely to adventure forth into the general publicity and promiscuity of the vast hotel. The necessity for so doing oppressed Mr. Sutherland strangely.

CHAPTER II

THE STRIKE

THE two principal public rooms of the Splendide were the lounge and the restaurant. They lay side by side, separated by a wall of glass, and they were both vast and both ultra- or super-gorgeous. Every square foot of their walls and ceilings was decorated with the last extreme of ornateness in either oils, fresco, mosaic, porphyry, gilt, or bronze. On the ceiling alone, of the lounge, were depicted, in various mediums, over seventy slim and beautiful young women in a high state of physical development and chiefly in the fashion of Eden, perilously tasting the dubious society of thirty or forty fauns and satyrs whose moral code seemed to illustrate the joyous effrontery of a past age and who had no preoccupations about rates, taxes, bad weather, or class-warfare. The colours of this ideal world were rich, fresh, and brilliant, for it was only in the previous year that the designers had finished spending two million lire in the creation of the Splendide: which was meant to respond, and indeed did respond, to the secret aspirations of the élite of Cincinnati, Leeds, Buenos Ayres, Philadelphia, Bath and Boston (Mass).

From the lounge, through the gilded crystal partition, could be seen the equally opulent restaurant, full of tables richly set with napery, cutlery, glass and flowers, and perambulated by many restless waiters. And not one diner

7

at any of the tables, though the hour was after half-past eight!

While the forlorn restaurant held waiters but no guests, the lounge held guests but no waiters. Twenty-three guests were congregated together in the middle of the huge parqueted floor upon which, on normal evenings, they were accustomed to dance. A small number for so large an hotel; but the season had scarcely started; moreover, the Splendide much depended for its customers upon the arrival and departure of Transatlantic and Transmediterranean steamers, and no important boat had arrived or departed now for several days. The present guests were chiefly not mere migrants but steady supporters of the hotel and the city, whose purpose was to stay, and see, and leave quantities of good money behind them. Of the twenty-three, fifteen were American, five English, and the rest of doubtful origin; seventeen were women and the rest men. Their anxious and perturbed demeanour was in dismal contrast with that of the gaudy, carefree inhabitants of the ceiling-kingdom overhead.

Alone among them a tall, dark, massive, romantic gentleman of forty years or so seemed to be enjoying life. He was fat, and it might have been said that the pores of his stretched skin, being open, exuded gaiety, and that gaiety escaped frothing from his lips. As, lightly, with little mincing steps of his small toes, he moved about gesticulating and chatting with an inner group of ladies, he had the air of being continuously animated by a private and particular zest of his own. His manner was easy and affable to the point of patronage, for he knew that he was adored. Suddenly this gentleman noticed afar off, in one of the arched entrances to the great lounge, a solitary hesitant individual in a tweed suit.

"Ha!" exclaimed the gentleman of zest. "Ha!" he called out, more loudly, smiling as it were secretly to himself.

And all the company turned and gazed at the individual under the arch, inimically and yet with respect. His tweed suit, exhibited at such an hour in such a place as the lounge of the Splendide, of course offended the sense of propriety of every swallow-tail, dinner-jacket and evening frock on the floor. Also, the company beheld a man who, during the fortnight of his mysterious stay in the hotel, had systematically, by the blank repudiating look on his superior face, discouraged the advances of those visitors who liked to be sociable and who resented a repudiating look. The man, indeed, had not exchanged a word with a single soul in the hotel, servants excepted. Why was he in the hotel at all? He seemed never to indulge in any of the usual and proper sight-seeing excursions. Who was he? Nobody knew anything about him beyond his name. What justification had he for being so stand-offish? . . . Nevertheless the company had respect for the man, if only because he was so strictly loyal to the dying British tradition of keeping oneself to oneself. And further, the company somewhat pitied him for the shyness and diffidence which obviously were mingled with his amazing self-complacency.

The man thus criticized was Septimius, who had been to the managerial offices and found them deserted. The gaze of the crowd certainly incommoded him and made him wish for the gift of invisibility. Like most persons, however, Septimius had not one mind but quite a number of minds. And while in one of his minds he felt abashed, in another of his minds he was saying: "What an ignorant lot they are. They don't guess that I once stroked Cambridge. They don't guess that I was once called to the

Bar. They haven't a suspicion in their silly heads that I am *the* Sutherland, Septimius Sutherland, who abandoned the Bar for finance and became something of a power in the City and richer and more important than anybody else in this hotel, I lay. Probably they've never heard of Septimius Sutherland. It hasn't occurred to them that I'm here on what's called 'big business'—indeed the biggest, and that I've been taking risks that would frighten the boldest of 'em. And won! And won! Well, it amuses me—their ignorance does. And it amuses me to look a bit bashful and awkward. What do I care, really? Fact is, I rather like being taken for a nobody by nobodies."

And still another of his minds held the thought: "I may be the great Septimius Sutherland, but I am also a perfect ass! It's a holy nuisance to be self-conscious like this."

He kept a tactical silence.

"You know what's happened, of course?" the gentleman of zest proceeded.

"I do not," Mr. Sutherland replied, bland, amiable, and now rather less self-conscious under the bombarding stares. After all, he was not unaccustomed to handling shareholders of limited companies at annual meetings.

Because he did not care to talk across a great empty space of floor he unwillingly advanced towards the crowd in the centre of the lounge. The gentleman of zest went to meet him. Mr. Sutherland had on previous occasions taken this individual for a foreigner, but his English was impeccably that of Kensington.

"A strike in the kitchens!" explained the gentleman of zest, and his zest seemed to ooze forth from him. Apparently he saw in the situation a rich and juicy humour that he thought nobody else could see. He paused and looked humorously at the floor, as if sharing the joke with the parquetry. Then: "Or perhaps not a strike, because strikes are forbidden by law in this country. But at any rate an omission to work. Some trouble with the management. Plenty of cold food in the kitchens, but the waiters will not serve it. Sympathetic inaction no doubt. Hence we are all hungry, with no prospect of a dinner. I am Count Veruda."

Septimius felt a great relief. He had been vaguely suspecting, upstairs, some kind of a machination against himself, a powerful man whom unprincipled opponents might find it convenient to put away. He now saw that the machination, if any, was directed against all the guests equally. Moreover, the performance of the incomprehensible floor-waiter upstairs stood explained. Septimius pleasantly savoured the situation.

"I see," said Septimius, almost at ease. "Where is the manager?"

"Ha!" said Count Veruda. "The manager has prudently disappeared."

"I see," Septimius repeated, quite at ease. "Now supposing we went into the kitchens and fetched this food for ourselves?" Already he had began to scheme out the organization of such a raid.

"I am told by the mâitre d'hôtel, who is entirely on our side, that that might cause really serious complications."

"I see," said Septimius, for the third time. "But there are restaurants in the city."

"Not a good one. And we could hardly go in a body to any one restaurant. We should burst it. And as for going separately, many single ladies would not care to venture on such a course—in a town like this." The Count smiled within and without, and his body seemed to vibrate with rich fun.

"There are other hotels."

"If we went to another hotel, the fact would be instantly known, and the kitchen staff there might adopt the same tactics as the kitchen staff here. Solidarity! Solidarity!" The Count had completed his case very happily.

Mr. Sutherland had frequently noticed the word 'solidarity' in newspaper accounts of altercations between labour and capital, and now for the first time really understood its significance. He glanced around at the stricken faces of the well-dressed, well-fed, but hungry crowd. In every face he saw precisely what he was beginning to feel in his own heart, namely, the gradual, terrible, disturbed realization of the utter instability and insecurity of society. All had been well, and now all was ill. The members of the groups, and Septimius, had been nurtured in the beautiful, convenient theory that anything could be had by ringing bells and settling bills. They did naught for themselves, and could do naught for themselves, and were somehow proud of their helplessness. With them, to ask was to have, and to pay was the solution of all difficulties. And now they were hungry and thirsty; they were in the grip of the most powerful of human passions; and no amount of bell-ringing and bill-paying could procure their satifaction. No wonder they were perturbed. The situation was horrible. It seemed to announce blood in the streets and the downfall of kingdoms and of the entire social order.

"But," said Count Veruda, triumphant in his sense of the dramatic, "I have suggested a remedy. My yacht, the *Vanguard*, has come into harbour this afternoon. I invite everybody to dinner on board. If I may say so, I think I can offer as good a dinner as could be had in any hotel in the town, if not a better . . . And the Bay of Naples! . . . By moonlight!"

This was the Count's grand climax.

"You are most hospitable," said Mr. Sutherland blandly.

"Not at all," the Count deprecatingly protested, without, however, any attempt to be convincing. "But there are ladies who hesitate. Perhaps naturally!" The Count shared his polite amusement with the parqueted floor. "I hope I may count on you, Mr.——?"

"Sutherland."

"Mr. Sutherland, to give me your support."

"Count," called a masculine old lady imperiously, at this important juncture.

Count Veruda left Mr. Sutherland and humorously shot backward to the old lady.

A dark, youngish and stylish woman thereupon came up to Mr. Sutherland, who bowed to her smile.

"I don't think he's what we should call a real Count," murmured the dark young woman, confidentially, and with a certain assurance of manner. "Count of the Holy Roman Empire, or something like that. Official of the Papal Court. Probably when he's on duty he wears a uniform designed by Michael Angelo. He imagines he's a humorist, but he's funnier even than he thinks he is. However, even if he isn't a real Count, he has a real yacht, because I've seen it, and it's like a liner, and I don't see any reason why we shouldn't oblige him by eating his dinner. But, of course, no unattached woman will go unless all the others go, too."

"Of course not," Mr. Sutherland concurred very calmly, though he was somewhat disturbed and overset by the young woman's extraordinary directness of approach. He comprehended, however, that the strike had altered everything.

He definitely and immediately liked her. She was downright, humorous, and attractive, if not strikingly beautiful. She was young, but not too young; virginal, but not too virginal. She was not over-jewelled. The shingling of her hair fascinated him, and her tone flattered him. He found pleasure in her nearness to him. She was the finest creature in the lounge. "I might sit next to her at the dinner," he thought adventurously. He was the very pattern of propriety. He had a wife and grown-up daughters; but in that moment he suddenly grew younger than his wife, younger, even, than his daughters; and his one regret was that he had to catch the midnight train. The cynic says that all women are alike; it would be still more true to say that all men are alike, and that no man is old until he is dead.

"Then you agree?" said she.

Septimius answered with due gravity.

"I agree. I think we might quite properly accept the Count's invitation. After all, he is very generous."

"He may be an adventurer," said the young woman.

"Quite."

Count Veruda returned to Mr. Sutherland.

"Well, Mr. Sutherland?"

"I am with you, Count," said Septimius gaily, in a loud voice that all might hear.

"Hurrah!" exclaimed the dark young woman under her breath.

The whole company signified approval, and the affair was decided. Mr. Sutherland's reputation in the hotel for keeping himself to himself, together with his unmistakable air of prudent respectability, had carried the waverers.

CHAPTER III

THE YACHT

THE large, low, oval dining-saloon of the yacht *Vanguard*, with a pale stained-glass ceiling faintly lighted from above. The pale, curved walls, diversified with mirrors and with panels of mythology in the Della Robbia style. The huge, oval table, glittering white, with crested earthenware and crystal and many flowers. Stewards in blue and gold, with white gloves, circling watchfully round and round with food for the famished and the dyspeptic. The chief steward, behind Count Veruda's chair, attentive, directive, imperative, monosyllabic : exercising dominion by glance and gesture. Between the ring of stewards and the edge of the table—the guests!

Now, as regards the guests, it would seem that the yacht's dining-room must have become a mortuary and a lunatic asylum; for many of them reiterated that they were tickled to death at being aboard the yacht, and the rest reiterated that they were crazy about being aboard the yacht. The truth rather was that they were crushed, morally, by the magnificence of the spectacle and the entertainment offered to them by Count Veruda. In vain did the more brazen ones try to pretend by an off-hand demeanour that they had been familiar with such scenes from their youth up and were, therefore, quite unmoved; they failed every minute to maintain the pose. And if sus-

picions had existed in the minds of some of them concerning
the authenticity and solidity of the Count, those suspicions
were now in a fair way to be destroyed.

The process of crushing had begun as soon as the
invited horde crossed the street from the hotel portals to
the landing steps. Two great mahogany launches were
awaiting them at the steps, each manned by a blue-and-
gold crew of four. There was plenty of room for everybody in the capacious bosoms of the launches. If these
commodious craft were only the attendant launches, what
must the yacht be? Persons whose notion of a yacht and
yachting was a frail, wobbling bark, with a tin of sardines,
a cottage loaf and tea out of a tin mug, were obliged at once,
and radically, to revise that notion. The launches shot off
like torpedoes, tandem, into the dark, mysterious, balmy
bay. Up the invisible flank of Vesuvius ran a rope of
fire—the electric lamps of the funicular railway. The
shore-lights of Naples gradually spread out into two semi-
circles behind the foamy wash of the launches, and above
these tiaras rose the lighted hills of the background of the
city. A Neapolitan moon had poised itself aloft in the
deep purple sky. Then the whiteness of the yacht *Vanguard* grew plainer, and larger and still larger! Commands!
A shutting-off of engines! To the high side of the yacht
clung an illuminated stair of mahogany, teak, and shining
brass—broken mid-way by a flat space for the recuperation
of the short-winded. At the top of the stair stood officers,
who with dignified respect raised their caps in grave welcome
to the exalted guests. And lo! the guests were fairly on
board the main deck, which was lighted like Broadway or
Piccadilly Circus. No hitch! No hesitations! No delay!
A set of gongs played a tune, and in three minutes or less
the guests were at the table.

Of course the *Mauretania* or the *Majestic* was bigger; but for real style, from table-appointments to stewards, the *Vanguard* had every transatlantic liner well beaten: so much was admitted unanimously and handsomely by all Americans well experienced in marine travel.

But what crushed the spirit most effectively was not the style, nor the grandeur, nor the glitter, but simply the cost of it all. The *Vanguard* belonged to one man, not to a limited company with a capital of fifteen million pounds. The Americans had no qualms about the concentration of such a quantity of wealth in the hands of a single individual; for they knew and felt that just as every soldier of Napoleon had a field-marshal's baton in his knapsack, so every American citizen has a two-thousand-ton yacht in his capacious hip-pocket. But in the pockets of certain humble Britons were concealed misgivings as to whether all was for the best in the best of all possible worlds. These faint-hearted persons thought of the droves of unemployed in the streets and slums of their industrial towns; they even thought of the perspiring, rebellious kitchen-serfs of the Splendide desperately risking a livelihood to snatch perhaps an extra fourpence-halfpenny from the Splendide's managerial tills, while Count Veruda, owner of the *Vanguard*, spent as much on petrol in a month as would have kept seven Neapolitan families for seven years. However, as sherry followed cocktails and champagne followed sherry and port followed champagne and Chartreuse followed port, these crude sociological qualms vanished away, together with the sense of being morally crushed. A golden mist spread in the saloon, and through it gleamed the bright truth that everything positively *was* for the best in the best of all possible worlds. As of course it is.

Meanwhile, Count Veruda, with the chief steward

behind him, was modestly trying—and not without success —to look as though he were not the owner of the gorgeous *Vanguard* and a multi-millionaire. Indeed, he wore his wealth most unpompously; it was apparently naught to him.

Then a faint vibration made itself felt in the yacht and particularly in every part of the dining-saloon. The vibration grew in strength. And straightway the more alert spirits in the company began preposterously to suspect that Count Veruda was not all that he seemed to be, that he was indeed a perfidious and cunning pirate, and that the yacht's engines were being made to revolve as the first action in a plot to abduct the entire body of guests and hold them to ransom for incredible amounts in some distant, inhospitable isle hitherto uncharted on Mediterranean maps.

Dismay sat on the faces of several. The dismay spread. Glasses were no longer raised. Gratitude vanished from the hearts of the entertained. The nervous imaginative could feel the heaving of the yacht at sea.

"That is the dynamos," said Count Veruda, silently laughing. "I expect we're using rather more electricity than usual, and the Chief Engineer wishes to be on the safe side."

How absurd those slanderous suspicions !

But a few of the wary and the timid were not quite reassured. An old lady on Mr. Sutherland's left tremblingly murmured something in his ear. Mr. Sutherland, gently smiling, tranquillized her ridiculous fears with a word.

"The yacht cannot be moving," said he. "She must have had an anchor down, if not two, and in a comparatively small ship like this the anchor could not possibly have been raised without our hearing the noise of the chain." Still, the old lady was not quite at her ease, and spoke again.

Mr. Sutherland forgave her tedious insistence because he knew what old ladies were, always had been, and always would be. And not old ladies only.

A white screen was at this point let down on the after wall of the dining-saloon; and Count Veruda unassumingly announced:

"I now propose, with your permission, to show you the new Valentino film. It has been seen in London and, I think, in Paris. But nowhere else."

The whirr of cinema apparatus seemed to put an end to the vibration caused by the dynamos. The dining-saloon suddenly became dark. The effect was highly disconcerting. The unrolling of the reel started.

"I hate films," said Mr. Sutherland quietly to the dark young lady who, in the hotel, had expressed doubt as to the authenticity of the Count's title; Mr. Sutherland had contrived that she should be on his right.

"So do I," the young woman replied.

Mr. Sutherland greatly dared.

"Shall we creep out and explore the yacht a bit?"

He trembled lest she should refuse the audacious suggestion.

"Let's," said she.

Mr. Sutherland thrilled in anticipation of joy in the exclusive possession of her companionship.

The darkness hid their furtive departure from the eye of the host. They passed through the lounge into which the dining-saloon opened, and so to the deck.

CHAPTER IV

ON DECK

THEY climbed up one story and leaned speculatively side by side against the rail of the main-deck. The boat-deck, with the bridge and the captain's quarters, was above them. The warm Neapolitan gloom, relieved now by only a lamp or so at the ends of the long deck, wrapped them softly round about. Not an officer, not a deck-hand to be seen. And nothing to be heard save the faint murmur of vibration ascending monotonously from the depths of the ship. A ship of mystery, enfolded in the magic influences of the universal enigma—and those banal idiots were all sweltering in a room downstairs, watching a film!

"I say," said Mr. Sutherland, "you might tell me your name?"

He was aware of agreeable sensations. She was elegant, she was intelligent. He had made some progress with her during dinner—and she with him.

"Harriet Perkins."

"Thank you."

"Do you mean to say you didn't know?"

"How should I? I never speak to anyone in hotels."

"And quite right too! If you do, you may find yourself glued to a bore for the rest of your stay before you know where you are. What's yours?"

"My what? Christian name?"

"Of course not," she laughed. "Your size in gloves."

"Septimius."

She turned a glance on him and clapped her hands.

"I've won five hundred pounds," she said.

"A bet?"

"Yes. But only with myself."

"Oh!"

"I always knew you were the man in the City. You are, aren't you? There couldn't be two Septimius Sutherlands, could there?"

"No. I am in the City."

"Everybody knows about you—except people who stay in hotels. How thrilling!"

He was flattered, and somewhat surprised.

"Then do you read about company meetings?" he asked.

"Yes," she said. "And I read prospectuses and things."

"Well, well!"

"I only read them for fun, like divorce reports. You like divorce reports, don't you?"

"Oh, of course!" he admitted bluntly.

What he especially liked in the composition of Harriet Perkins was that you could talk to her as to a man. In his simplicity he had not grasped, or he had forgotten, that the first care of every young woman of the world is to be talked to as a man. The desire to be talked to as a woman comes later. Long ago, what he had liked in the composition of the delicious, maddeningly feminine creature who afterwards became Mrs. Sutherland was that he could talk to her as to a man. And it had not yet occurred to him that his daughters were constantly endeavouring to get themselves talked to as men by men.

"*Some* dinner!" said Miss Perkins reflectively.

"Yes," Septimius agreed. "And it was a rather wonderful effort in organization, that dinner was! Thirty people, I suppose."

"Twenty-three," Harriet casually corrected him.

"Oh!" Septimius was a little disturbed by his error of thirty per cent. in a computation. "Well, twenty-three, then. It would be reckoned a biggish dinner in any household, wouldn't it?"

"It certainly would!" Harriet eagerly assented.

"And considering that our friend the Count must have sprung it on his staff at a moment's notice! Why, I understand that at seven o'clock nothing was known of any trouble in the hotel kitchens. And there couldn't have been twenty minutes between our deciding to accept his invitation and our arrival on board, and when we got here everything was ready. I've always been interested in questions of organization, and I must say that to-night's affair is one of the finest examples of sheer, rapid organization I've yet come across."

"Have you ever had to organize a big dinner yourself?" Harriet suddenly demanded. She spoke cautiously, with respect, as though careful not to assume that he had not personally organized big dinners.

"I can't say I have."

"Because, if you had," she proceeded, with less respect now, "you'd know for certain that a big dinner like to-night's simply cannot be improvised in twenty minutes. Why, the soup we had would take at least half a day to prepare."

"Would it?"

"It would." Dogmatically.

"Do you realize, my dear Miss Perkins, that it follows

22

logically from such a statement—I don't dispute the statement for a moment—that the dinner was not improvised, that in fact it must have been all carefully prepared beforehand?"

"I realize it all right," Harriet answered quietly.

"She's no ordinary girl, and I knew she wasn't," said Mr. Sutherland to himself. And aloud: "Then how do you explain the matter?"

"I don't explain it," Miss Perkins dreamily murmured; then added with more liveliness: "The situation can't be explained till it's been explored. Suppose we explore the yacht a bit, shall we? Your idea, you know."

CHAPTER V

LUGGAGE

HER snub nose and her grey eyes seemed to challenge him to peril. He wondered fearfully what might happen to his sacred dignity if he was caught, with her, in the act of exploration. Pooh! Such challenges from female to male are always accepted, at whatever risk. They compel the male to rise gloriously above common sense.

Feeling more like a burglar than a knight, Mr. Sutherland followed her through a doorway, across the bottom of which was a thick slab of wood designed to keep out the intruding sea. Of course, as a knight, he ought to have gone first, but she had taken the lead, and he did not quite see how to wrest it from her. Now, they were in a sombre passage, and a beam of light shot slantingly up from below. An open steel gate; a hole in the solid floor; a glinting steel ladder with a thin steel handrail to it! The ladder seemed to extend downwards without end. Harriet lightly and rapidly engaged herself in the rungs of the ladder, and Mr. Sutherland, still rash, followed.

"Mind my fingers!" she warned him, for he was vertically above her on the ladder, and there was only one rung between his brown boots and her ringed hands.

"Oh!" exclaimed Mr. Sutherland in alarm, and paused for a moment.

They came to a little landing, and then to another steel ladder, apparently even longer than the first one. Harriet began the second descent. Mr. Sutherland thought of the bottom of the sea.

"Oh, how lovely!" he heard Harriet remark under him, with a voluptuous sigh of appreciation.

"This must be the engine-room," said Mr. Sutherland, as he joined her on the comparative security of a perforated steel floor.

"If it isn't the kitchen," Harriet smiled nicely, yet quizzically.

"Why did I make a banal remark like that? Naturally it's the engine-room!" thought Mr. Sutherland, disgusted with himself, but somehow happy.

The great engine was fenced in by steel hedges, as if it were an untamed and dangerous leviathan. Wheeled parts of it were slowly revolving, and pistoned parts of it moving slowly up and down and to and fro. It was like an immense cat, playing idly with itself, keeping itself in condition by means of gentle and otherwise quite futile exercise. It made very little noise. There was no escaping steam, no jar of metal against metal, no sensation of active power. Various dials and clocks showed meaningless faces; the polished brass of their forms made bright yellow spots of light in the dusky steeliness of the huge chamber.

Suddenly they both saw something move under the perforated floor beneath them. It became very clear that they had not yet arrived at the bottom of the ship, much less the bottom of the sea. Mr. Sutherland started, and he hoped that Harriet had started also, but as to this he could not be sure. He obscurely descried the shape of a man below the floor—a djinn imprisoned in the very entrails of the *Vanguard*. This man, who was middle-aged, presently climbed up to a steel gate within a couple of feet of Harriet's short skirts, unfastened the gate with a click, stepped into the engine-room, and fastened the gate with another click—a click which seemed as final as a decree of fate. He was well-dressed in blue and gold, and wore a peaked blue cap with a white cover over its crown. He politely raised the cap.

"We were just admiring your perfectly heavenly engines," said Miss Perkins, with an alluring, placatory sweetness of tone.

"Ay, miss!" the man agreed laconically. He did not smile; on the other hand he did not frown. He was evidently a most respectable and superior man, incapable of being surprised, and well accustomed to holding an impartial attitude. He said no more.

"Is this the largest yacht in the world?" asked Mr. Sutherland.

"Nay!" the man answered. "But she's the largest motor yacht in the world."

"Ah! She's a motor yacht," said Mr. Sutherland. "The Count didn't tell us that." He glanced at Harriet as if for confirmation. "Then no stokers, or anything of the kind?"

"No stokers. No coaling. A few greasers."

"And her speed?"

"Fifteen. Sixteen-and-a-half if I put her to it."

"You are the engineer, I presume."

"Chief."

"I'm sure it's all very interesting," said Mr. Sutherland, after failing to think of a more brilliant remark.

The chief then raised his cap again, and suddenly and at surprising speed climbed up the ladder which Count

Veruda's two guests had just descended. He appeared to have no objection to leaving the pair alone with his heavenly wild leviathan.

"What a *nice* man!" Miss Perkins burst out. "I think he's adorable . . . The far-away look in his blue eyes!"

Mr. Sutherland was rather astonished at this verdict. He had not even noticed that the man's eyes were blue, and in the lined, grim features he had seen naught worthy to be called nice. Still, he was pleased, because the man who had thus taken Harriet's fancy was certainly older than himself, and certainly not more handsome. Hence his own middle-age and lack of physical witchery could be no bar to her approval. And he desired her approval more than anything.

At this juncture, Septimius became aware of two matters. The first, was that in his tweed travelling suit he felt far more at home and at ease here than he had felt either in the hotel lounge or in the yacht's dining-saloon. And the second, which was somehow exquisitely contradictory of the first, was that Harriet's evening frock made a better showing in the engine-room than in environments of the character for which it had been designed. The frail white and pale green thing, with the olive-coloured fringed shawl over it, had an extraordinary piquancy amid the stern, sinister, formidable steeliness now surrounding her: which piquancy excited Mr. Sutherland.

Important changes were occurring within Mr. Sutherland—changes perhaps as important as can occur within anybody. Miss Perkins had full, luscious lips, and eyes sparkling with romantic vitality. She had a good figure. She had a rich, low voice. She was rather tall. Her hands and feet were small, her ankles and wrists thin. She had perhaps other fascinating qualities which Mr. Sutherland could not determine. But beyond all such there was something else—something which Mr. Sutherland could not define: namely, the totality of Miss Perkins. It was not this or that item in a catalogue of charms which was working the changes in Mr. Sutherland's heart; it was the whole Miss Perkins herself who was the cause of them, and the result would no doubt have been the same if her eyes, voice, lips, feet, hands, ankles, wrists, had been quite otherwise than they were.

Mr. Sutherland knew by unshakable conviction that on earth no other woman existed to compare with Miss Perkins. She possessed a unique gift. She was romance itself. Mr. Sutherland wanted to work for her, to shower presents upon her, to make her smile and laugh, to protect her from the possibility of mishap, pain, discomfort, all unhappiness. He had little hope of being able to do so. He was so humbled by her that he could discern in himself no quality capable of pleasing her. He had the sense to understand that the changes occurring in his prim, sedate, unromantic, married, fatherly soul were terrible. But he gloried in their terribleness, while fearing it. He felt that he had just begun to live, and that, until that moment, he had never lived. He sympathized with, admired, and comprehended men who had ruined their careers for the sake of a woman—men such as General Boulanger and Charles Stewart Parnell, whom, hitherto, he had frigidly despised as weakling voluptuaries.

Yes, in one of his minds Mr. Sutherland was alarmed, and in another he was gloriously ecstatic. And the entire business was astounding in the highest degree, and most probably nothing comparable to it had ever come to pass in any floating engine-room before.

The engine continued lazily to revolve and slide its parts, as if dozing.

"And how come you to know about the organizing of big dinners?" Septimius inquired, with an effort towards archness.

"Oh!" answered Harriet vaguely. "Mother . . . The old days."

The single word 'mother' reassured Mr. Sutherland. (Not that he would have admitted that on any point he needed reassurance concerning Harriet Perkins!) She came, then, of good family, family used to lavish hospitalities, solid family. They talked about organization, a subject which seemed to interest Harriet as much as it interested Septimius. Septimius always talked very well on this his favourite subject, and Harriet listened admirably and stimulatingly. They talked for ages and æons. Gone from Mr. Sutherland's mind was all thought of exploring the mysteries of the yacht! Gone also, apparently, from Harriet's mind! Mr. Sutherland saw that, despite her energy and initiative and independence, she was one of those delightful, acquiescent women . . . He had shown a wish to discuss organization, and she had charmingly concurred.

The middle-aged man, with the face that had so appealed to Harriet Perkins, came scurrying violently down the steel ladder from above, and he was followed by another and younger officer at similar speed. They both stood by. Two greasers also appeared. Mr. Sutherland and Miss Perkins, their talk thus brought to a sudden halt, both had the feeling that the moment was big with great events. They were not mistaken. A bell rang out loudly and imperatively within a yard or so of their ears. A steel arrow moved by itself on an indicator, and pointed to words which said "Stand by," though the officers were

already standing by. The younger officer sprang towards
a lever.

"Shall we go back to the deck?" Miss Perkins gently
suggested.

"I think we ought to," he answered, with an out-
ward calm at least equalling her own.

They hastened up the steel ladders; Miss Perkins again
took the lead. But now the steel gate, which had been
open when they went down, was shut, and also it was
fastened. Mr. Sutherland shook it, and Miss Perkins
shook it; and they both tried hard to manipulate the bolt;
but the gate was obstinate.

"Caught!" exclaimed Mr. Sutherland, but soundlessly
—in his heart. Nevertheless his faith in Harriet Perkins
was not a bit diminished. They heard, far below, the
renewed summons of the autocratic bell. Then there
was some enlivening change in the character of the sound
of the engine, and a moment later the whole ship began to
throb and shake in earnest. Then a deck-hand appeared
in the darkness of the corridor. He produced a key of some
sort and unfastened the gate, and Mr. Sutherland and Miss
Perkins had the freedom of the corridor. They emerged
excitedly, like a couple of children, on to the main-deck.
They saw, over the rail, a huge form rising on ropes out
of the water. It was the starboard launch. It vanished
above their heads, being swung in on to the boat-deck.
Through the windows of a deck-house they saw the
port launch similarly treated.

"The others have all gone back," said Septimius.

"Looks like it," said Harriet. "See the bedroom
windows lighted in the hotel."

And in fact many windows were now gleaming in the
façade of the Splendide across the water.

"We're left behind," said Septimius.

Harriet shrugged her shoulders.

"Why do I make these idiotic remarks?" Septimius asked himself. "Obviously we're left behind."

"We ought to have been warned," said Septimius.

"Oh!" murmured Harriet. "In the confusion . . . Two launches . . . The people in one launch would think we were in the other."

"Quite! But those engineer fellows might have told us."

"None of their business," said Harriet.

"Still—But she's moving!" cried Septimius.

"I do believe she is," Harriet agreed.

"But we must have heard the anchor chains. We couldn't possibly not have heard them," Septimius protested.

"Perhaps she wasn't anchored at all," said Harriet. "Perhaps she was only moored to one of those buoy things that you see in harbours. Then she'd only have to slip a rope hawser or whatever they call it, and off she'd go."

Septimius, silent and corrected, remembered with shame the superiority of his tone in giving marine explanations to the old lady in the dining-saloon.

"But this is simply awful!" observed Harriet, though her tone seemed to be saying that it was the greatest lark conceivable.

"It is!" Septimius concurred. "We must get the yacht stopped instantly, and be put ashore—somehow." But in his tone there was no apparent eagerness for such a course of action.

Nevertheless, he led the way aft along the deck, Harriet following. A door stood ajar, showing the faintly lit interior of a cabin. Septimius paused—he knew not why

—at the doorway and looked within. Harriet glanced over his shoulder. Lying on the floor of the cabin were a flat American trunk, a suitcase and a rug, which so remarkably resembled Septimius's trunk, suitcase and rug that he was moved to examine them. They were indeed his trunk and suitcase, duly labelled in his own City hand for London via Rome, Paris and Calais; and the rug was his rug. The presence of those three articles in the dim, rich cabin appeared absolutely magical to Septimius; but the magic of it was most sinister, and it illustrated the instability and insecurity of Society far more affrightingly than the strike at the Hotel Splendide. Mr. Sutherland saw that he must maintain his nerve, and he did maintain it. He said no word, and Harriet said no word either. But then Harriet, not being acquainted with the aspect of Septimius's luggage, perhaps had not his reasons for amazement.

"Somebody else can organize too!" thought Septimius generously.

The strange thing was that he was not furious with resentment against the mysterious and unspeakable Count Veruda. For the Count's machinations, whatever their aim, had at any rate secured to him for a time the enchanting society of Miss Perkins. This detail presented itself to Septimius as more important than anything else.

Returning to the rail, Septimius and Harriet saw very clearly the whitening wake of the yacht under the Neapolitan moon. The *Vanguard* was unquestionably gathering speed. She must be making for either Capri or the open Mediterranean. The notion of bringing to a standstill the mighty and resistless movement of the great vessel became preposterous to Septimius, and he gave it up. Besides, none of the crew seemed to be about. All the navigation was being conducted from the unseen boat-deck over head.

"Miss Perkins, please!" called a respectful voice from somewhere: not the voice of Count Veruda.

Harriet started, and then without a word to Septimius walked off and disappeared round the after end of the deck-houses. Mr. Sutherland was alone.

CHAPTER VI

LYING DOWN

MR. SUTHERLAND walked about the deck; he made a complete circuit of the dark, deserted deck-houses, and met nobody save one deck-hand, who ignored him, and whom, from pride, he ignored, though he was hungering for information on a number of important points. He could not see the mast-head navigating lights because of the intervening upper-deck. But forward, he saw the green and the red glare of the starboard and port navigating-lights, and they seemed to throw a baneful illumination upon the vast, vibrating, silent organism of the moving yacht. Never had Mr. Sutherland been caged in an environment so uncanny and oppressive.

At last he was once more in front of the cabin tenanted by his self-transporting baggage. He carefully inspected it and found therein every device of comfort and luxury; beyond it was a bathroom of equal merit. By way of experiment he turned on a tap marked 'Hot,' and the water which cascaded therefrom was more than scalding enough to satisfy the most exacting apostle of efficiency. He stood still, meditative, and falsely pretended to himself that he was not hurt by Miss Perkins's inconsiderate and off-hand departure. He thought, besides, of all that had so inexplicably happened to him; he gazed at his luggage. He then said, aloud:

"Shall I take this business lying down?"

Now Mr. Sutherland, like many persons commonly supposed to be without a sense of humour, was capable on occasion of being most queerly and disturbingly humorous. He answered his own question:

"Yes, I shall take it lying down. I'll go to bed."

And he rang the bell by the bedside. A knock quickly followed, and the chief steward entered.

It seemed odd to Mr. Sutherland that the bell of an ordinary guest-cabin in so important a yacht should be answered by so stately and majestic an individual as the chief steward. Mr. Sutherland, who was still successfully maintaining his nerve, thus coldly addressed the chief steward:

"Apparently my things have not been laid out."

"Sorry, sir."

The chief steward proceeded, with a dignity comparable to Mr. Sutherland's own, to unfasten the suitcase and lay out all necessary matters for the night: while the guest began to undress.

"Can I have something to drink?" asked Mr. Sutherland.

"Certainly, sir."

"What can I have?"

"Anything you like, sir."

"Well, I will have a cup of weak camomile-tea; very weak, not more than one flower to the cup—if it's a breakfast cup."

Mr. Sutherland often took camomile before retiring. It was in France that he had learnt the digestive and sedative qualities of properly infused camomile. People, especially relatives, had tried to laugh him out of camomile; but they had failed. He was not a man to be frightened by the absurd associations of the word 'camomile.'

The chief steward, having departed, came back.

"Very sorry, sir. We have no camomile on board."

"No consequence. No consequence," said Mr. Sutherland blandly.

"Can I get you anything else, sir?"

Mr. Sutherland reflected.

"A tot of rum?" he suggested. Not that he had the least intention of drinking the rum, but the phrase 'tot of rum' struck him as excellently marine and in keeping with the aquatic situation.

"Certainly, sir."

The chief steward disappeared and reappeared.

"Very sorry indeed, sir. We have no rum on board."

"No consequence. No consequence," said Mr. Sutherland blandly. "I regret to have troubled you. Might take that eiderdown off the bed. I think I shan't need it."

The chief steward did as he was told, and went away humbled.

It was a proud moment for Mr. Sutherland; but a moment does not last very long. Mr. Sutherland reflected with grief that he had lost his berth in the train de luxe, the costly price of which was not under any circumstances returnable, and that all his appointments in London would be broken. And when, in his white pyjamas, he had sunk down on the soft bed and turned out the lights and lay listening to the faint straining sound of elaborate woodwork due to the quivering of the yacht as her twin propellers urged her through the placid moonlit waters of the Mediterranean—then, Mr. Sutherland's mood changed quickly to one of utter dismay and apprehension. True, by the superb calm of his demeanour, and by his magnificent inactivity, he would compel his enemies and captors sooner or later to explain themselves and thus to play the first revealing move in the game about to begin. True, his brilliant tactics must have astonished and perhaps momentarily baffled them. But his predicament was none the less monstrous, incredible, unthinkable. He could discover absolutely no clue to the absurd, nightmarish enigma of it. The affair was too big to be a practical joke. On the other hand, if the affair was serious, as it positively must be, to what end had it been undertaken? His common sense forbade him to believe that he had fallen into the hands of bandits who would hold him to ransom. Such adventures did not happen to big financiers—save of course in the film studios of California. Further, his knowledge of character forbade him to believe that airy Count Veruda had wits enough to conceive and execute the enterprise of which he, Septimius, was the victim. Hence, Count Veruda could only be the agent of mysterious and invisible brains as gigantically bold as they were recklessly unscrupulous. Mr. Sutherland had sufficient wisdom to be afraid. He was afraid of the mere spirited grandeur of the plot in which he found himself entangled. He had not spent twenty-five years in the City without hearing rumours, and indeed circumstantial stories, of strange, nefarious deeds attempted and accomplished for the purposes of what was called 'big business.' But he had never heard of anything at all comparable to the present prodigious matter. And he could think of none of his own financial schemes which might be prejudiced by the enforced absence of their author from London. As a fact, all his current schemes were completed, and the last one had been definitely completed that very morning in Naples.

Then there was the question of Miss Harriet Perkins.

Was she among the conspirators? She unquestionably was. The people in authority knew that she was on board, and they knew her name; and she had answered quite calmly and obediently and shamelessly to her name. Without doubt she had been employed to keep him in the yacht while the rest of the company departed. With that aim she had inveigled him into the engine-room and by her wily arts had held him there. He had been her dupe. Men had been hoodwinked by their passions before, and he had been hoodwinked. That Harriet Perkins was a vampire was as clear as daylight to Mr. Sutherland. And yet Mr. Sutherland would not credit it. He would not because he simply could not. Harriet a vampire? Ridiculous! Harriet was the finest feminine creature he had ever seen, or would see, and she had not duped him. Still, she was plainly a vampire, an evil woman, and he was her dupe. So his thoughts ran round and monotonously round in his head, and never stopped and, therefore, never reached any conclusion.

The oddest thing of all was that he did not care whether Harriet was a vampire and a villainess or not. She might be anything she chose, provided she was the unique Harriet. It was unnecessary for her to make excuses for herself. He could make all the excuses for her. She could not sin in his eyes. Such was his principal mind. But in another of his minds he perceived dispassionately what was going on in his principal mind, and he was afraid, he was terrified, by the wonders therein. His happiness in the thought of Harriet Perkins frightened him as much as his astounding physical predicament. Awe filled him, and he trembled. Sleep was impossible . . . Then he woke up with a start, for sleep is never impossible. His ears had heard a scream followed by an outburst of apparently hysterical laughter or sobs. Harriet's scream! Harriet's laughter or sobs—perhaps the laughter or sobs of a girl overwrought by the presence of acute danger! Mr. Sutherland jumped up, switched on the light, sprang to his scarlet dressing-gown (for nothing would have induced him to appear on deck in pyjamas), and opened the cabin-door.

CHAPTER VII

THE MILLIONAIRE

Miss Harriet Perkins was invited by the gestures of a silent, timid, fair-haired young man to follow him down the stairs which led to the lower deck, where were the lounge and the dining-saloon earlier put at the disposal of the twenty-three guests from the Splendide.

The young man, whose austere dinner-jacket had no touch of the marine, switched on lights as he went forward, and then extinguished them behind himself and Miss Perkins. For this purpose he had to pass and re-pass Miss Perkins several times; it was rather as if they were playing a game for position; she smiled at him and he smiled blushingly back. She knew he was admiring her; she liked him; she judged him to be honest. But she could not help thinking how odd it was that the yacht *Vanguard* should be so sparing of its electric light, unless, indeed, it had a reason now for keeping as dark as possible.

Also she wondered that her hotel name should be known there, too. Then she decided that in this particular she was alarming herself unnecessarily. Various persons, including Mr. Sutherland, had addressed her as Miss Perkins in the hearing of various stewards. Nevertheless she was alarmed, because she had other reasons for alarm.

At the forward end of the lounge the young man murmured:

"His lordship desires the pleasure of a few minutes' conversation with you, madam."

It seemed strange to Harriet that a mere foreign Count should be referred to as 'his lordship.' For herself she determined to deal very faithfully with the foreign Count.

"Are you 'his lordship's' secretary?" she asked the young man.

"One of them," replied the youth, and revealed a further room, small, but of great richness. "Miss Perkins," he announced loudly and timidly. Harriet gave him a smile as he withdrew and shut the door behind her.

A cigar-smoking, carelessly-dressed gentleman of medium height, with a head of very considerable size, formidably glinting orbs, untidy greyish hair, and a welcoming, almost benevolent smile, sprang awkwardly out of an easy-chair, much too large for him, and advanced to grasp Harriet's hand.

She had a shock; she wanted to gasp (but of course did not gasp) at the sight of this personage, whom she at once recognized, but had never before seen. The mystery of the *Vanguard* seemed suddenly in some parts to be illuminated and yet in others to be further darkened. She thought, severely shaken:

"I'm right up against it. I must have a policy."

But no policy offered itself to her questing brain.

"Miss Perkins?" said the man, dashing away his cigar. "I believe ye *are* Miss Perkins, aren't ye?" He had a deep strong, rough voice and a Midland accent. He showed none of the marks of the public school, the University, or the best clubs. If a gentleman, which had yet to be proved, he was one of nature's . . . Not even a dinner-jacket!

"I am," said she, nervous and challenging. "But who are you? Perhaps I'm more at sea than you think."

The man laughed pleasantly at her simple wit.

"My name's Furber. Lord Furber."

This was Maidie's terrible, legendary husband. She rather liked him, while sympathizing with Maidie and resolving to stand up for Maidie with every resource at her disposal. She liked his eyes, with their occasional faint gleam of dangerous fun.

"Not the great engineer?" she exclaimed in a tone falsely tremulous, assuming both awe and fearful joy. It was as if she had said: "Dare I believe that I am actually in the presence of the prodigious Lord Furber?"

"Ye're flattering me. *Once*, I reckon, I was a bit of an engineer."

He affected to be insusceptible to flattery, but he was flattered. Harriet was confirmed in her belief that there exists on earth no man who cannot be flattered by an attractive woman. She felt his admiration descending upon her. Therefore she was at ease, and capable of concealing anything and everything except a delicious tendency towards impudence.

She went on:

"Newspaper proprietor, then, if engineer's too good for you! Capitalist! Millionaire! Yes, now I recognize you from your portrait—it's always appearing in your own newspapers, isn't it?"

His lordship laughed again, but not quite so naturally as before. She suspected that it might be perilous to affront him, but she had a certain taste for peril, and when his lordship asked her to sit down, she sat down with gusto, with excited anticipation, with a full sense of the liveliness of life, and with a queer satisfaction that the door was shut and she had him all to herself.

And all the time her brain repeated monotonously: "Imagine *him* being on board! Imagine seeing *him* here!"

Lord Furber said:

"I'm sorry ye've got carried off like this from your hotel."

"And from my luggage too," Harriet put in.

"Yer luggage too," he concurred.

"I shouldn't have minded so much if they'd carried off my luggage with me. I might have rather liked being carried off if only I'd had my luggage."

"Oversight!"

"What was an oversight? Carrying me off, or fotgetting my luggage?"

"I apologize," said Lord Furber, not answering her question.

"I should have thought it was Count Veruda's place to apologize. The yacht's his."

"Who told ye that?"

"He did."

"Well, I lent him the yacht for the evening. She isn't his and never was. I own her and I run her, and nobody else does. And she's more expensive than ten women."

Maidie had indeed mentioned a yacht, but very casually as being a matter in which she herself felt no personal interest; she had not even given its name.

"Then the Count is a liar," she said.

"Yes," Lord Furber admitted judicially. "Yes, I reckon he is. But I'm bound to say he asked my permission first, and I gave it."

"Asked your permission?"

"Veruda's my secretary."

"One of them," corrected Harriet quickly, recalling what another secretary had said.

"One of 'em. But my favourite. I picked him up because of his picturesqueness. He amuses me. He keeps me interested."

"I always felt the Count was an adventurer. And yet he looks like a rich man."

"Not he! He looks like the popular notion of a rich man. *I* look like a rich man, and I am rich—very rich." Lord Furber laughed, as if to himself. "Now, Miss Perkins, what do you want me to do?"

"About what?"

"About yeself."

"Turn back at once and put me ashore where I started from."

"Certainly. Like a shot—if you insist. But listen now; wouldn't it meet the case if I wirelessed the Splendide to have yer luggage sent on by motor to the next port we call at?"

"Where's that?"

"Depends."

"On what?"

"Circumstances."

"And my hotel bill?"

"Oh! We could fix that."

"And my clothes in the meantime? I haven't a thing except what I'm in. And even you can't make it perpetual evening, Lord Furber."

"Yes, I can. We'll stay below. The curtains shan't even be opened. Breakfast by electric light. Lunch by electric light. Every meal by electric light till your luggage arrives . . . Of course, I admit there's your reputation to think of. But that'll be all right. You needn't worry about that."

Miss Perkins hesitated, and then, as it seemed to her jumped into a deep river.

"Lord Furber," said she. "Where in heaven's name do you come from?" The challenge in her tone frightened her for a moment. But she was getting a little used to Lord Furber and, after all, he was only a man like other men.

"The Five Towns."

"You would!" she exclaimed, striking wildly out into the very middle of the river. "And you've never really left them. And perhaps that's what's the matter with you. And what's more, you're still in the nineteenth century. You can't have looked at the calendar lately, or you wouldn't talk in that antediluvian style. Do you suppose my reputation is going to suffer because you and your secretaries and things have bungled their organization? I don't need anybody to tell me not to worry about my reputation. 'My reputation to think of,' indeed! Have you any ladies on board? Or women servants?"

Lord Furber smiled, unruffled.

"One woman. I can't travel without my chief steward—he's my butler on dry land—and he can't travel without his wife. So his wife's here." He sighed.

"Then I'll see her. She'll arrange things for me for the night. And the yacht shall go back at once, and when I've had my sleep out you shall land me yourself at Naples."

Lord Furber shook his head.

"Can't."

"But you said you would."

"Yes, but I can't. I was hoping ye'd oblige me by not insisting."

"But I do insist."

"I tell ye I can't do it."

"You mean you won't."

"Have it yer own way, then. I mean I won't." He gave a short laugh, loud but grim.

Harriet murmured:

"So now we know where we are." She threw up her head and answered his laugh with a laugh light and negligent. But she was feeling by this time the strength of the current of the river. All Maidie's accounts of her husband's peculiarities had not prepared her for so curt a refusal. She saw in the man's eyes some hard glint of the force which had made a Lord Furber out of a working engineer.

"Ask me anything else and I'll do it."

"Then send for Count Veruda. I feel as if I could talk to him for his own good."

"He isn't on board. He took his guests ashore and hasn't returned . . . But you needn't be afraid," Lord Furber added kindly, protectively.

"I'm not."

"Are ye sure?"

"Yes, I'm sure. But *you're* afraid."

"I admit it," he indulged her. "Have a cigarette, will ye?"

"I don't smoke," said Harriet drily. "You're afraid because you're puzzled. It's my reasonableness that's puzzling you. If I'd made a scene you'd have felt safe. But now you can't make me out. I said we knew where we were. It isn't quite true. I know where I am, but you don't know where you are. I've got *that* advantage.

And I'll tell you another thing. Like all millionaires, you're suspicious, and because I'm keeping calm you're suspecting all sorts of things about me."

"For instance?"

"You're suspecting I got myself left behind on your yacht on purpose."

"Well, I *was*," he said bluntly. "But I don't now."

"I do smoke—but only my own."

Miss Perkins opened her bag and took out a cigarette case. Lord Furber held a lighted match.

"I'll hold it, thanks," said Miss Perkins, and when she had lighted the cigarette she carefully dropped the match on the Persian carpet. Then she looked up at him as he stood almost over her. "You're so deliciously naïve, aren't you?"

"What do you mean?" Lord Furber spoke gruffly, and stepped back.

"Perhaps that's why I like you."

"What do you mean?" he repeated. "Tell me why you think I'm naïve."

"No. You might lose your temper. You haven't got much self-restraint, and I hate scenes. If I wanted a scene I should make it myself."

"I shan't lose my temper."

"I say you might."

"What do you know about my temper?"

"Anybody can see you've got a temper."

"Tell me why you think I'm naïve. Tell me." Harriet shook her head. "Hang it all!" he went on, and threw an ash-tray violently to the floor. "Must I go on my knees to you? Tell me."

"Sit down, then." Harriet laughed. "And don't jump up again." Lord Furber sat down. Harriet could feel her heart beating. "You're naïve because you think everybody has the same kind of motives as you have yourself. You've got Machiavelli written all over your face. You love plotting, and so you imagine that everybody is plotting something against you. And because you fancy you can detect scheming everywhere you think you understand human nature. You've never grown up. Perhaps that's a reason why you're rather adorable." She deliberately dropped some ash on the Persian carpet.

A pause.

"And what plotting d' ye accuse me of being up to now?"

"Well, the whole business of the dinner was obviously a plot. There was no improvisation in it at all. It was all completely thought out beforehand. And the brains that planned it certainly didn't leave two of the guests behind by accident. Mr. Sutherland and I must have been left behind on purpose. I'm not a millionaire, but I'm not a simpleton either."

"Miss Perkins," said Lord Furber. "Just listen. I shan't ask ye to believe me, because I know I can make ye believe me. No. Don't drop yer eyes. Look right at me."

Harriet, who in fact had lowered her gaze, raised it again.

"Well?"

"I didn't know ye from Eve until ye came into this room. I'd never heard of ye. I don't want anything from ye. If ye got left behind it was yer own fault. And you can understand that, with two launches and twenty-three people, it would be easy enough for one or two to be left behind. I hear ye were seen in the engine-room with Mr. Sutherland. I suppose you and he are old friends."

"Lord Furber," said Miss Perkins. "Just listen to me. I shan't ask you to believe me, because I know you can't help believing me. Till this evening, I'd never spoken a word to Mr. Sutherland in my life. I know nothing at all about him except what everybody knows who reads the newspapers. He's naïve, like you. But he's a nice old thing, and he fell in love with me at first sight. Oh yes, in love! I wanted to be kind to him, and I went down with him into the engine-room, and I stayed talking there with him simply because I saw he was enjoying it. But——" she stopped.

"But?" Lord Furber's eyes gleamed provocatively.

"But I know very well now your people only left me quietly in the engine-room because I was with Mr. Sutherland. You didn't want to disturb him, and you couldn't disturb me without disturbing him, and so I am to share Mr. Sutherland's dreadful fate." She laughed. "It was Mr. Sutherland you wanted to capture. Once you'd got him on board you'd have kept him here somehow, whether he'd been in the engine-room or anywhere else. And to get him on board you gave a dinner to twenty-three persons, and I shouldn't be at all surprised if you even organized the hotel-strike. Nothing would surprise me. I haven't shown a great deal of surprise, but you must admit that I'm entitled to be astonished by what's happened to me since I was enticed into your two-thousand-ton yacht."

"And why d'ye settle on Mr. Sutherland as the victim of all this wonderful Machiavellianism? Don't answer if ye'd prefer not to."

"Of course I shouldn't answer if I preferred not to. But I don't a bit mind answering. His luggage! That's why I settle on Mr. Sutherland. His luggage! We discovered it together in one of the cabins. I didn't know it was his till I saw the labels."

"He might have had it sent on board himself for anything you know."

Miss Perkins rose to her feet.

"Don't be so silly," she somewhat crudely advised Lord Furber. She was shaking. The cigarette shook in her hand.

"*What ?* "

"I say don't be silly. And what are you going to do about it? Hit me? It's time somebody talked straight to you. You're a millionaire, and so everybody humours you and flatters you—and pulls you to pieces behind your back. I know you turn your home into a perfect hell with your childish tantrums."

"You know nothing about my home!" growled Lord Furber.

"I know a lot about your home. I can see your home in your face at this very moment. You're all alike, you self-made millionaires. Spoilt children, every one of you. You ought to be well smacked—and in the right place, too."

At this point Lord Furber, genuinely amazed and furious, overthrew a table. A siphon rebounded on the carpet, but did not break.

"Hell's delight!" cried he.

"There you are! I told you you hadn't got any self-restraint. Naughty little thing! Do try to be a man and don't be silly with your absurd suggestions about Mr. Sutherland having sent his luggage on board himself. I never saw anybody more staggered than Mr. Sutherland was at the sight of that luggage. He didn't say one word. He didn't know that I'd read the labels. He just kept quiet. He's got a thousand times more self-restraint than you have, and I can tell you if you're up against him you've got your work cut out and no mistake. . . ."

Harriet dropped back into her chair. She thought: "I can't keep this up any longer. It's about time I felt faint. I believe I do feel faint." And to Lord Furber in a weak voice:

"Brandy."

The cigarette fell to the carpet and began to burn a neat hole in its pricelessness. Harriet sighed because, climbing all wet up the further bank of the river, she felt safe once more.

CHAPTER VIII

HER STORY

LORD FURBER instantly became one of nature's gentlemen. From the sideboard, which seemed to contain all liqueurs and spirits (except rum), each decanter secure in a round socket, he took some 1821 brandy, and in ten seconds was holding, almost with tenderness, the glass to Harriet's languid lips. She coughed. She sighed again, shut her eyes, and opened them.

"I'm saved," she breathed.

His lordship beheld her with equal respect, humour and admiration. But she had terribly shocked the vanity of the autocrat in him and frightened the child in him. Not even Maidie, his wife, had ever, in the wildest moments of her red hair, handled him half as roughly as Harriet Perkins. Harriet had shown him to himself. He was too much of a realist to deny the truth of the picture she had drawn. He had always vaguely known, but never realized clearly, that he in fact was as she had painted him. He was too proud to sulk or to resent, and too proud to be ashamed. And in that moment he wanted more than anything to win her good opinion. He felt as though he was sitting for an examination. The ordeal occupied the whole of his brain; his millions were so useless in the test that they seemed to have been reduced to the equivalent of twopence. His sense of values was drastically altered.

In sum, his emotions were unique, and such as he had never expected at the hands of destiny.

"Oh!" said Harriet. "I smell fire."

The fire of the cigarette was steadily boring its way through the Persian carpet.

"Oh no!"

"I hope it isn't your lovely carpet."

They both looked calmly at the burning carpet.

"It's nothing," said Lord Furber. "These carpets are fire-proofed. Always have 'em like that on board, ye know."

Then he stamped on the red glow, and with dignity picked up the siphon and the overthrown table.

"Have you forgiven my remarks?" she asked coyly.

"I've forgotten," his lordship replied, and he had.

"You must excuse me nearly going off like that. But I'm not used to being spirited away in two-thousand-ton yachts and having to keep my end up against millionaires and barons and things."

"What *are* ye used to?" asked the baron eagerly, standing near her with his hands in his pockets. "Tell me what your line is. I'm very interested, and I'd like to know something about ye."

His interest was genuine, and violent. Indeed, he was coming to the conclusion previously reached by Mr. Sutherland—namely, that there was none like Harriet Perkins in the whole world. He had been dazzled, and he rejoiced in the exceeding novelty.

"I'm nothing. And you can't tell something about nothing, can you?"

"See if ye can't. Just try. And after ye've tried I'll tell ye something." His tone was very persuasive.

"About yourself?"

"No. About you. It'll be my turn. Ye've been telling me quite a lot about myself."

Harriet sat up.

"Have you ever been in a ladies' club?" she asked.

"No. I don't like clubs and clubs don't like me. Why?"

"If you'd been in a woman's club—London, I mean —you'd have seen in the dining-room at night a row of small tables and a solitary woman sitting at each table and horribly pretending to be jolly and self-sufficient. I'm one of those women. Younger than most of them, but in quite a short time I shall be older than most of them. I'm thirty, and I shall go on being thirty for years yet— only my face won't go on being thirty. It's a pleasant age while it lasts, and our business is to make it last as long as ever we can. I've no relatives, except distant ones— and the more distant they keep themselves the better I'm pleased. I've got just enough income to wear presentable frocks, but not enough to cover myself with jewels. I was never brought up to do anything: and I don't like bridge, golf, or tennis. I like dancing, but if you don't pursue bridge, golf or tennis, it isn't easy to find partners for dancing. I get asked out—more often to lunch than to dinner—because I can be bright, if I haven't got a head-ache. In fact, I have a tongue in my head. You may have noticed it. Sometimes I'm not asked twice to the same house because absurd persons think I have rather too much tongue in my head. I can produce wonderful silences at lunch-tables by some quite simple remark. Strange, isn't it?

"People wonder why I don't marry. So do I wonder. Because I can certainly arouse feeling in the male bosom. Only, the men I like don't seem to get as far as a definite proposition—I expect they're frightened of what I might say to them. And those who do get as far as a definite proposition somehow always leave me cold. And then that's that.

"When I'm sick of my flat in London and my club, I go 'abroad'—as they call it, and wander from hotel to hotel, and make heaps of acquaintances, mostly female, and I don't care for any of them, and none of them care for me. There are thousands and thousands of us wanderers, particularly in Italy. When I'm sick of 'abroad,' I go back to London and begin to hope for the best again. Yes, and then more 'abroad.' For ever and ever, Amen. I'm not physically repulsive; and I've brains and brilliance—who'd deny it?—but I'm a thoroughly unsatisfactory creature, because I don't *fit in*. And I'm growing worse every year . . . You asked me to tell you, and I've told you—I don't know why. And it's heaven's own truth that I never told anyone before."

Lord Furber ceased to be one of nature's gentlemen.

"There's only one thing the matter with you," he said, suddenly fierce. "Ye're an idler before God. You ought to work. Ye're taking from society everything ye need, and giving nowt in return."

"And what about you?"

"That's a different question. Let's keep to the point."

"How can I work? I was never taught to work. I don't know how to work."

"Anybody can learn to work."

"I'm not strong. I have headaches and backaches."

"Aches be blowed, miss. Bad health never yet stopped anybody from working that wanted to work. Think of Herbert Spencer, and Mussolini here. Bad health's

always the last refuge of the female waster." The baron's
eyes blazed, and his hands, removed from his pockets, were
gesticulating, and his feet restive.

"And there's another thing," Miss Perkins proceeded
calmly. "Why should I take the bread out of other
women's mouths. Lots of them need work and can't
get it. I don't need work."

Lord Furber clinched his teeth together, and pulled
a face, and seemed to dance about in fury.

"Great Scott!" he growled. "I thought those ideas
were dead and buried and 'd begun to stink years ago. And
here I have to stand and listen to 'em now! Of course
ye need work. Work's just what ye do need. And if ye
do honest work at a fair price ye won't be taking bread
out of anybody's mouth. On the contrary, ye'll be putting
it in. All work's to the good. Look at ye! Look at
yeself. Other people are keeping ye, making yer clothes
and cooking yer food and cleaning yer room and washing
yer fal-lals and playing music for ye. And ye do nothing
yeself except sit around and complain of headaches and
backaches. How's that, Miss Perkins?"

Lord Furber felt quite happy.

"You're rather a brutal baron, aren't you?" Harriet
fenced feebly.

"If I am, I'm taking lessons from you. I'm treating
ye as an equal. Of course, if ye want me to treat ye like
a doll again——"

"Again?"

"Yes, again. I said I'd tell ye something about
yeself. Here it is. Ye were only pretending just now
when ye nearly fainted. Ye'd got tired of fighting and
ye wanted a rest. And so ye thought ye'd play up to me
with a touch of the doll business. D'ye suppose I didn't

56

see through it? Ye thought ye were deceiving me, but I was deceiving you by pretending to be deceived. What about it?"

"What made you think I was only pretending?"

"Yer colour. It never changed. When a woman faints it's because the blood's leaving her head. So she goes pale."

Miss Perkins laughed gaily.

"Five Towns again!" she said. "You're still in them. Won't you ever get away? Haven't you ever heard of rouge? I expect not."

Lord Furber turned his back, walked away, and returned. He was frowning. Then the frown vanished and he gave a loud laugh and lifted his arms.

"Kamerad!"

"Still, I *was* pretending," said Harriet.

Lord Furber dropped his arms and stamped.

"Confound ye."

"Now, as you're so clever, tell me how to find work, and I'll find it."

Lord Furber wrestled with a wild, foolish impulse, and was thrown.

"Ye've found it."

"What d'you mean—I've found it?"

"Be my secretary."

There was a pause in which his lordship had a terrible fear that she would not refuse his offer.

"And take the bread out of Count Veruda's mouth?" she smiled blandly.

"Yes. I couldn't stick the two of ye."

"You're very adventurous, baron."

"Well, perhaps I am."

"But I don't know shorthand or typewriting or filing

E   57

or book-keeping. I did once try to learn typing, but I was beaten off with great loss."

"I don't want a clerk. I've got scores of 'em. I want a secretary."

"What should I have to do?"

"I'm an idiot. I'm an idiot. And I canna help it," said Lord Furber to himself. And aloud: "Oh! All kinds of odd jobs. Ye'd be very useful to me. Ye're tempted?"

"Who wouldn't be."

"It's agreed then. Salary doesn't matter. Start to-morrow."

"How like you!" observed Miss Perkins. "Do you imagine I'd take any post without knowing quite a lot about my employer? It's employees who ought to ask for references, not employers."

"Just listen, then. I'll tell ye about yer employer."

CHAPTER IX

THE BARON'S DEFENCE

LORD FURBER stood and then sat down. He lighted a cigar and immediately threw it away. The Titan was nervous before Harriet. He felt that he was still sitting for an examination and must pass it, if possible, with honours.

He said to her:

"I'm a self-made man—don't be afraid, I'm not going to give the details of manufacture. Now there's always something amateurish about anything ye've made yeself. I know I'm amateurish, say rough-finished, in parts. That's enough about that. I began as a mechanical inventor, and from the first my inventions brought me in a lot of money. When I say a lot, I mean a lot. I wasn't out after money, never have been, but money overtook me and I couldn't escape it. Royalties on patents, ye know. I went on inventing until I was thirty-five, and then I dried up. I suppose I'd run through the vein. Happens sometimes. You do come to the ends of things. But money rolled in just the same. Even more. One day I found all of a sudden I was worth a million in gilt-edged stuff. That was nothing. To-day if I was reduced to a million again I lay I should think myself a pauper. Ye notice I don't tell ye how much I *am* worth. No reason why I shouldn't; but it's more effective not to. If ye

59

knew the figure ye wouldn't be half as impressed as ye are
—no matter how big the figure was."

"Oh! Shouldn't I!" said Harriet, rising out of her
chair and strolling about the room.

"No, ye wouldn't! And this piling-up business is
still going on, and I can't stop it. Nothing can stop it.
I don't mind telling ye that Henry VII paid all the expenses
of governing England out of an income less than mine is.
That'll give ye a notion. People call me one of the New
Huns, because I'm so darned rich. Well, I can't help
it. What could I do? I couldn't refuse my royalties or
the interest on my investments. Silly! I couldn't burn
the money. I've been asked why I don't use my money
trying to regenerate society. Society's all wrong, but it
can't be set right by chucking money about. Silly! It can
only be set right by common sense, and common sense is a
thing money can't buy. Same with charity. I do a bit of
charity, because I'm afraid not to. But I hate it. I
don't believe in it. It only does harm. Some of the
New Huns spend their money on social schemes and charity
because they're ashamed of being rich and they want to
dope their consciences. I haven't a conscience, and if
I had one it would be a perfectly clear conscience as far
as my money's concerned. So what in Hades am I to do?
I try all I can not to let my money accumulate. This
yacht's one of my efforts in that line. My wife does her
best, too. No good." He shook his head. "Nobody
can spend more than a certain amount, and nobody's wife
can. You see the difficulty?"

"Quite."

"Then sit down. It's against nature for a woman to
be trapesing about while a man's in an easy-chair as easy
as this one. Sit down."

Miss Perkins obeyed.

"Please, may I speak?" she asked modestly.

"I haven't quite finished," said Lord Furber.

"I only wanted to remind you that I'm not your secretary yet."

"No. And if ye keep on tapping your feet like that ye never will be."

Miss Perkins arose and resumed walking.

"Well," Lord Furber continued, with a sort of deep growling sigh, "as soon as I stopped inventing I began to be bored. Rather a lark to be raised to the Peerage, and waking up the House of Lords. But I got tired of that after a few months. I had to find something to *do*. If I'd kept on doing nothing, with all my energy, I should soon ha' been doing nothing in a lunatic asylum. Then I discovered I had judgment—and financial judgment. I found that out by looking into my investments myself, just for something to occupy myself with. I'd always left 'em to stockbrokers before. I soon found stockbrokers were listening to me, instead of me to them. So I took up finance. Great pity, because it made me richer than ever. But if a man has a faculty he must use it."

"Besides," said Harriet, "on the whole, I suppose it's better to be too rich than too bored, isn't it?"

The baron gazed at her, frowning absently.

"Interested me for quite a time, finance did. But in the end I saw there was no real point to it. Ye see, it isn't creative, and doesn't get ye anywhere. Then I simply let my money stew in its own dividends. Then I thought of the press and bought a newspaper. Bought several. Before I knew where I was I'd grown into a press-lord. Imagined I should have power if I owned a few papers, and I expect it's power I'm after more than anything. Disappointing. Yes. A newspaper must pay. If it doesn't it's a toy. I hate toys. If it is to pay it must be read. But the public will only read what it wants to read. So the newspaper owner must keep his ear to the ground. It's like this. Ye find out what the public's thinking, and then ye tell 'em they must think just that, and they go on thinking just that, and ye say ye've influenced 'em—and call it power. There's nothing to it. It's not real. The world will roll on in its own way. Newspaper stunts are childish. Two o' my papers are now trying to get taxi-fares lowered in London. They may succeed. But lowering taxi-fares isn't much to sing about for a newspaper enterprise with twelve millions of capital, and charging advertisers £1,400 per insertion for a front page. No, young woman, the power of the press-lords isn't worth mentioning compared to the trouble they take and the money they make and the infernal worries they have with labour."

At this moment the bashful under-secretary, Tunnicliff, ventured timorously into the room and stood close to the door awaiting notice.

"Well, my lad?"

"If Mrs. Bumption could speak to your lordship for a moment. She says it's urgent."

"Where is she?"

"In the dining-saloon, my lord."

"All right."

Mr. Tunnicliff vanished.

"I've tried the stage," his lordship went on, very deliberately and gloomily. "A bit of a bottomless pit, that. And I never was fond of children. Nobody on the stage ever grows up. They'll spend five shillings on a telegram to tell you they haven't three halfpence to buy stamps with. They'll interview about you putting on a play that's a sure fortune, and they promise to come and read you the thing next day, and ye never hear of 'em again until ye read in the paper they've gone to New York to play an English gentleman in a French melodrama; and they don't come back for ten years. That's the stage."

He moved towards the door, thinking: "I'm doing this rather well. It's a good story. She's impressed." Then he stopped.

"There's racing. Scoundrels behind ye. Snobs in front of ye. If the jockey's to be trusted the horse isn't. Ye can have racing."

"But the cinema!" said Miss Perkins vivaciously. "Surely Providence allowed the cinema to be invented in order that a Lord Furber might exploit it."

"Young woman," the baron replied. "Yer tongue 'll get ye into mischief one day."

"It has done already. I told you."

"And sooner than ye think for, too. I've tried the cinema. I could stand the film kings, and I could stand the film stars. It was the lady continuity-writers that drove me off. They all have flaxy hair and come from Nebraska. No! Ye couldn't give me the cinema. Well, I suppose I must go and get it over with Mrs. Bumption. She's the majestic consort of my chief steward. Hell's delight!" He yawned. "I'm more bored than the prince in the fairy-tale."

"Your case is serious," said Harriet.

"It's more serious than ye think, miss."

"It couldn't be, you poor dear!" said Harriet brightly.

The baron went out. But already he was looking forward to the moment when, having pitched Mrs. Bumption overboard, he could return to Harriet. Not that he had any real hope of finding the courage to pitch Mrs. Bumption overboard.

It suddenly occurred to him that he had forgotten one point, and he went back to Harriet.

"I say. A bit ago ye had the impudence to suggest that I was like yeself, taking everything from society and giving nothing. What about my inventions?"

"My fault!" said Harriet. "Honestly, I'd never heard of them. Another grievance, I suppose."

Lord Furber slammed the door on her. And while talking to Mrs. Bumption he was thinking: "I know the wench 'll end by being my secretary, and I don't want her to be my secretary. Might as well have a catherine-wheel for a secretary. Could I safely pretend I was only joking when I offered her the job? I wonder if I have impressed her—passed my exam."

CHAPTER X

THE SNORE

"WELL," said Lord Furber, returning to the room after an absence of five minutes. "I've heard your story; ye've heard mine. My offer's still open, but it won't be open much longer."

Miss Perkins was seated.

"And what would my duties be?"

"Ye've asked me that once already."

"I suppose I should be expected to take part in conspiracies. Crimes with violence. And so on."

"Ye've got quite a crazy notion of me."

At that moment, for Harriet, Lord Furber had the wistful aspect of a child, conscious of having been naughty and trying without much hope of success to defend itself. He seemed absurd, touching, kissable, and pathetically unlike the legend of the London Titan. She was almost inclined to take his side against his wife, her old crony, Maidie, Lady Furber. "What he says is true," she thought. "He's bored—and so am I. That's why we're both restless, and why we're both going wrong."

"Still," she said judicially. "I've been the witness of one crime myself, and a victim of it, too. At any rate it would be a crime in England."

"The Sutherland business!" his lordship exclaimed in a fierce tone. "It wouldn't be a crime either in England

65

or anywhere else. I didn't bring the fellow on board. And I haven't kept him on board. If he chooses to stay after other folks go, that's his look out. I couldn't be expected to hang about the Bay of Naples till he's ready to go ashore. People who deliberately flirt in engine-rooms of sea-going yachts have darned well got to accept the consequences. And I could say a lot more for meself. Supposing I accused you and Sutherland of being stow-aways? What about that?"

He glanced at her with positive ferocity in his gleaming eyes, and then suddenly he was the erring child again.

"I don't care what you say," Harriet persisted. "You've abducted Mr. Sutherland, and well you know it."

"Now listen here, miss. Why can't women ever stick to the point? Are you going to take on the job I offer ye or aren't ye? Yes or no. There's no compulsion."

"It isn't true!" Harriet burst out in the most surprising manner.

"What isn't?"

"You! Me! This yacht! This night! Mr. Suther-land!" The fact was that she had suddenly awakened to the wonder of existence and could scarcely believe that she was not in a dream.

"It's all a bit of a lark, isn't it?" said Lord Furber in a lower voice, but brightening sympathetically.

"He understands," thought she. "And there are moments when he isn't bored—nor me, either." And aloud she said, benevolently: "I'll give my answer to-morrow morning—and not before."

He hesitated, as if undecided whether to smack her or to kneel at her feet.

"All right. Let's take a stroll on deck. It's devilish hot down here."

"Not hotter than I can stand," said Harriet.

"I was thinking of meself."

She rose, and impatiently he flung her wrap on her shoulders.

"You haven't told me about Mrs. Bumption," she said.

He grinned.

"Just had a rare fine example of Mrs. B. What d'ye think she wanted me for? It seems Mr. Sutherland has gone to bed in his cabin after ordering various drinks which they couldn't supply. She told Bumption that I ought to know about it as she hadn't received orders from me about Sutherland. Fact is, I never did give any orders about Sutherland, and it didn't occur to me that he'd go to bed. I was waiting for him to ask for me and kick up a row. Bumption, for once in a way, defied his wife. Swore he wouldn't disturb me for anything—after I'd said I wasn't to be disturbed. So she decided to disturb me herself. Said she didn't like strangers going to bed in this yacht without her getting instructions from me about them. Said she'd always supposed she was in charge of all domestic arrangements and if she wasn't she'd prefer to give notice and Bumption would give notice, too. I had to soothe her. Such is my life on board, miss. Don't ye think I need a lady-secretary?"

Miss Perkins laughed a long, quiet laugh, which died very slowly.

"So, Mr. Sutherland has gone to bed." The laugh was resuscitated.

"That's the news of the night."

"Without seeing me again! What a shame!"

"Not so much in love with ye as ye thought," said Lord Furber like lightning. There was malice in his tone. "Shaken ye up, his going to bed without consulting ye, miss!"

"And hasn't it shaken *you* up? He's a great man, Mr. Sutherland is, and I adore him. His going to bed is the most marvellous example of self-control I ever heard of. The poor man's abducted, and he just goes quietly off to bed, while you're waiting for him to come to you and make a row. Don't you wish you'd never got him on board? Aren't you afraid of him?"

"There's only two people in this yacht that I'm afraid of."

"Who are they?"

"Mrs. Bumption."

"And——"

"Come *along!* They say it's a grand night on deck."

Harriet Perkins followed the wistful, naughty child, who was now gloomy and now gay, who wanted her and didn't want her, and who was ready either to do her a violence or embrace her feet.

It was indeed a grand night. Moonshine on a smooth sea. Shore lights twinkling. The jagged shape of Capri on the port quarter. Astern the flank of huge Vesuvius no longer lighted by its electric string, rising dimly against the dark velvet sky. Vibration of twin propellers. Warm freshness of the Mediterranean evening, and yet not a breath of air—for the wind, the zephyr, was dead aft.

The pair walked side by side along the deck, past the long range of the deckhouses. The tramping of the navigating officers unseen on the bridge could be faintly heard.

Suddenly came a new sound through the open window of a cabin. Mr. Sutherland's cabin. A steady, not unmusical snore. Mr. Sutherland's snore. Mr. Sutherland, like many persons considering themselves to be the martyrized victims of insomnia, had been mistaken as to his entire wakefulness. There was something at once grotesque, comic and formidable about the noise of that snore from the nose of Harriet's admirer. Harriet tried to master her sensations, failed, screamed, and finally yielded herself, not without hysteria, to something which she had thought would be laughter, but which seemed, even to her own ears, most curiously to resemble sobbing.

CHAPTER XI

CHIVALRY

MR. SUTHERLAND, in his scarlet dressing-gown over white pyjamas, framed by an oblong of light in the doorway of the cabin, looked like the devil. He also felt like the devil (not being yet entirely awake). He saw the hand of some sinister male on Harriet's shoulder; for Lord Furber, fearing that Harriet in reaction from the stress of the scene below, had lost control of her feminine nerves, had essayed to steady her by a firm masculine touch.

The spectacle presented itself to Mr. Sutherland in such a manner as to raise instincts which, unsuspected by himself, had descended to him through perhaps hundreds of years of ancestry. Mr. Sutherland was transported by the misunderstood spectacle back into the age of chivalry.

All of a sudden he became uplifted, wildly happy, superbly reckless, in the overwhelming consciousness of a great mission in life. In the thousandth part of a second he recalled his athletic youth, and how he used to keep fit for rowing by daily bouts with the gloves against a hanging football or a fellow-oarsman. He jumped forward and, clenching his fists, hit Lord Furber violently under the point of the chin. Lord Furber, quite unprepared for the onset, was not employing his feet properly; he had the wrong stance, and he fell backwards; his head caught the end of a brass belaying-pin which transfixed the yacht's rail, and the next moment he lay a crumpled, moveless object on the deck, in the full light from Mr. Sutherland's cabin.

"He loves me!" thought Harriet Perkins, triumphantly reassured. "He may have gone to bed and to sleep without asking my permission, but he loves me and he is magnificent." And she, too, was uplifted and wildly happy.

For a space both of them forgot Lord Furber.

"What was the fellow trying to do?" Septimius demanded, breathing rather hard.

"Nothing," said Harriet feebly.

"But you screamed and he had his hand on you!" Septimius drew his dressing-gown about him.

"I—I think he must have thought I was going to faint or something, and he wanted to soothe me."

"You're sure you aren't——"

"Quite, thanks. But I'm very much obliged to you, all the same."

She was giving another brief sound between a laugh and a cry, but stopped herself.

"But—but," exclaimed Septimius, bending down a little and coldly gazing at his victim. "Surely this isn't Lord Furber? This can't be Lord Furber?"

"Yes, it is."

"What's *he* doing on board this yacht?"

"It's his yacht," Harriet answered. "Only that! It sn't Count Veruda's yacht at all. It's Lord Furber's!"

"All this seems to me somewhat unusual," observed Septimius placidly. The instincts of the primitive age were withdrawing again into his subconscious self, and he was ceasing to be a knightly defender of dames.

"Now, for goodness' sake, please don't be calm," said

Harriet sharply. "Something must be done. If you've killed him——!"

"If I've killed him, of course, there may be a certain amount of trouble," replied Septimius. He spoke grimly, not without a mild satisfaction. It occurred to him that his right arm had been actuated partly by an obscure, unrealized desire to revenge himself, upon anybody who chanced to be about, for having been abducted in the yacht.

The deck was silent. Not an officer, not a seaman in sight. Not a sound save the faint reverberation of footsteps on the bridge above. The woman's scream, the man's fall, had not been heard. The ends of the deck were dark. Only in the middle thereof was the sheet of light from Mr. Sutherland's cabin crudely displaying the stricken baron and a bending figure on either side of him. The faces of the two watchers were as pale as that of the victim.

"Anyway, I seem to have knocked him out for the time being. I'd no idea I could do it. But he's breathing."

"Are you sure?"

"Yes. Why did you scream?"

"It was your funny snoring."

"I never snore," Septimius protested frigidly.

"Don't you think you'd better do something, Mr. Sutherland?"

"Yes. But what am I to do? I haven't the least idea. He'll come round soon. Perhaps we'd better put him on my bed. Will you take his legs?"

In a moment, the body of Lord Furber was lying on Mr. Sutherland's disordered bed. Neither Septimius nor Harriet noticed a faint trail of red spots on the deck and the floor of the cabin.

"You run and fetch someone," Mr. Sutherland suggested.

Harriet, herself a little breathless, disappeared to obey. Septimius looked inquiringly at the white, senseless countenance and inert hands. It seemed to him that now he was on the very edge of understanding why he and his luggage had been carried off in the yacht. The name of Count Veruda conveyed naught to him, but the name of Furber, a terrific adventurer in the City of finance, inspired him with all sorts of fearsome notions. Hearing quick footsteps on the deck, he shut and bolted the cabin door.

"One minute," he called out when Harriet tried and failed to open the door. "One moment, *if* you please."

He had taken off the red dressing-gown, and was summarily putting on a suit over the pyjamas. The fact was that he could not bear any longer to be seen in a dressing-gown. His self-consciousness was stronger than his humanity. The baron might expire from neglect, but Mr. Sutherland's modesty must be preserved from further outrage. He hastily tied a muffler round his neck and opened the door, praying that he did not look too much like a burglar or a worse criminal.

Bumption, the chief steward, stout and impassive, followed Miss Perkins into the cabin.

"Lord Furber has apparently had a fall and fainted," Mr. Sutherland blandly explained.

Bumption glanced at his master and instantly his fat cheek blanched. A spot of blood was showing on the pillow to the left of the baron's head, and it was spreading, spreading. Bumption ran away. In a few moments, Mrs. Bumption sourly appeared. Bumption stood in the doorway behind her. Mrs. Bumption weighed as much as any two other persons present. Her ageing features

F   73

had for years past been fixed in a permanent expression of hostility to all mankind and all mundane phenomena, for owing to a slothful liver she flourished on grievances, which she would create faster than kind fate could destroy. Even Bumption's perverse passion for her was a grievance.

"What's this, miss? What *is* this, sir?" she asked.

"His lordship's had a fall. He fell on the back of his head. Cut himself on something." This from a laconic Septimius.

"His lordship must have fallen on his chin too," said Mrs. Bumption acidly.

The baron's chin showed an excrescence, which seemed magically to grow larger and darker every second. Mrs. Bumption, who had resource, took a spent match from the ash-tray by the bedside and with it tickled the baron's nostrils. The baron unclosed his eyes and beheld Mrs. Bumption's stupendous bust heaving above him.

"Good Lord!" he murmured faintly, and closed his eyes again.

CHAPTER XII

THE SKIPPER

"I'm the Captain of the ship," said Captain Joseph Slapser. "I hold a master-mariner's certificate. I am responsible, and what I say goes. And I don't care who it is. There's me and there's the crew, and all the rest is passengers. The owner is a passenger, and I put him down as a passenger in the ship's papers as I gave to the harbour-master at Naples. 'The Right Hon. Lord Furber' I put, and his lordship knows it. There isn't any such person as an owner in sea-law when a ship's at sea, and no such persons as owner's friends. There's me and the crew—and passengers."

"Quite," agreed Mr. Sutherland.

"It's something chronic," said Captain Joseph Slapser, complainingly.

The skipper was a grandly-dressed, solid, ruddy figure with blue eyes, a firm chin, and a defiant expression which was designed to cover the fact that he was not what gentlemen call a gentleman. He came from the same class as his owner, and his owner was a gentleman while he himself mysteriously was not. He possessed ample knowledge, skill, and experience to navigate a ship through all the seas of the world, and yet he felt inferior to Mr. Sutherland.

He had been summoned to Mr. Sutherland's cabin by the chief steward, at the command of Mrs. Bumption,

75

and he was trying to take charge of a situation which he did not in the least understand. His remarks had followed upon the remarks of at least two people whose tongues had betrayed an imperfect appreciation of what sort of an almighty a captain is when you come down to brass tacks; people who had apparently failed to comprehend that a private yacht is merely a ship in the eyes of the Board of Trade.

The brilliantly lit cabin, with its sculptured woods, its engravings, and its furniture and upholstery, was thronged: three portly beings, and two slim ones—the latter Septimius and Harriet. Mrs. Bumption alone was not nervous. Mr. Bumption was but little nervous because, in the presence of his wife and mistress, he always felt eased of all responsibility. Mr. Sutherland was nervous and admirably concealed his nervousness. Harriet Perkins was rather agreeably nervous, and advertised the fact to the perspicacious by a too light demeanour. The most nervous of all was the Captain, and the least successful in hiding his nerves. The Captain would have preferred a gale and a lee-shore to the present quandary.

And on the bed lay the baron, his head bandaged, his chin glistening with Pond's Extract, his eyes closed, his face very pale, his hair awry, his suit disarranged, his collar and necktie unfastened: utterly inscrutable.

"*I'm* not a passenger," said Mrs Bumption, glaring fearlessly at the Captain.

"I didn't say you were. You're crew . . . And I'm Captain." The skipper glanced aside momentarily at the baron, who had an unfortunate habit of addressing him as "Joe" in the hearing of subordinates. It was as if he were saying to the helpless baron: "Put that in your pipe and smoke it; and give me the sack afterwards if you like."

Suddenly the Captain sprang to the doorway, where two men, a steward and a deck-hand, were strenuously eavesdropping.

"You get forrard," said the Captain to the deck-hand, and to the steward: "You get aft. And hurry."

No need there of any explanations concerning his precise status on board. They hurried, and their obedient haste gave confidence to the Captain.

When he turned his face again towards the interior of the cabin, Harriet Perkins was whispering to Mr. Sutherland. In the circumstances, Captain Slapser objected to any whispering, but he did not quite see how his powers could prevent it.

"Don't you think this room ought to be cleared or Lord Furber removed? The place is really too full for an ill man. Couldn't you say something?" said Miss Perkins to Mr. Sutherland, in a whisper which even in that crisis was delicious to his ears.

Miss Perkins was steadily getting less nervous, for she perceived that her rôle was that of observer only, and her chief sensation was curiosity to see how her two antagonistic heroes, the baron and Septimius, would conduct themselves in the crisis. She felt as though she were reading a serial story in which she was a character to whom no harm could possibly arrive.

Thus challenged, Mr. Sutherland was bound to play the man, and in spite of danger, squarely confront the testy skipper.

"It seems to me," said he blandly to Captain Slapser, "it seems to me that Lord Furber ought to be removed to his own apartments. What do you say, Captain?"

"I say, better leave his lordship be," the Captain replied curtly. "We don't know how bad he is: and so long as he looks comfortable——"

Miss Perkins watched expectantly her placid hero.

"I'm a little surprised you've no doctor on board a yacht like this," said Septimius.

"You may be," the Captain retorted. "Nobody wants to stop you from being surprised, sir." The 'sir' slipped from him unawares, from habit, and he regretted but could not recall it. "I've nothing to do with doctors. If an owner chooses to carry a doctor, that's all right. If he don't, there's no call for any *visitors* to complain."

"Merely a remark, sir."

"Nor remark, sir. Some folks may wish before they're much older that we did have a doctor aboard. As I said, we don't know how bad his lordship is. You and this young lady say you saw him fall, but I never noticed his lordship was one for falling about all over the decks, even in a sea, which there isn't. If I'm asked my opinion by the police or a British Consul I should say he'd had an upper cut on the jaw before he fell. I don't mind telling you as I've seen a man drop in the ring from an upper cut and never speak again, though he *did* open one eye once. And it was at San Francisco that was, and I knew his widow."

"Very sad! Very sad!" murmured Mr. Sutherland. "I've never seen a prize-fight, but I've often boxed."

"And I'm not surprised to hear it," observed the Captain, his voice charged with sinister significance.

"You made a mistake there, Seppie," Harriet inwardly reflected.

"I said too much," thought Mr. Sutherland, and remarked aloud: "Then if his lordship isn't to be moved, I venture the opinion that this cabin ought to be cleared." He glanced at Harriet for approval of the moral courage which he was exercising at her behest.

She nodded to him. He was content.

"You're right," said Captain Slapser. "And I'll thank you to go first. And you too, miss," he added, to Harriet Perkins. "I don't know who you are, either of you. His lordship never said anything to me about you."

"No. Nor to me," said Mrs. Bumption severely. "At least, not till I asked him—about Mr. Sutherland, if that's the gentleman's name. And he didn't say much then."

"I'll thank you," the Captain proceeded, "to go at once to the purser's office, you and your lady friend, and tell him who you are and everything, so as he can enter you in the ship's papers. And I don't want any hanky-panky. The purser will have to see your passports."

"Certainly," said Septimius.

"My passport's at Naples in the Hotel Splendide," said Harriet.

"Well," said the Captain, "well, miss, you can tell that tale to the next British Consul we see. I shall ask him to come on board specially. No one's going ashore off this ship till I know where I am. And if I have to call in the Italian police, I shall call 'em in, and that's all there is to it. What! This young lady has a long interview with his lordship, and this Mr. Sutherland is supposed to be asleep in his cabin. And the next thing as happens is we find his lordship knocked senseless, and blood all over the place; and then I'm told he slipped and fell down!" Captain Slapser grunted—the grunt of a man who has no doubt at all of his capacity to put two and two together.

At this juncture Lord Furber opened both eyes, as if to suggest to the company that his presence in the cabin was being rather unduly ignored. The gesture drew general attention and caused excitement. Captain Slapser and Mrs. Bumption seemed at once to feel a certain loss of

79

especially by her, was loathsome to his sensitive pride. Perhaps it was a desire to force her to admire him that led to his final remark to the Captain:

"Would you mind telling me what your sailing orders are?" he asked, in a voice superbly casual.

"My sailing orders are my affair," replied the Captain.

Mr. Sutherland, picking up a cap, went out, with a parting glance at Harriet to follow him.

The Captain said:

"You'll stop here for a bit, miss, if it's all the same to you." Evidently the Captain in his astuteness was determined that those two should not plot together on the way to the purser's office. "Mr. Bumption, show this gentleman where Mr. Antinope's room is."

Harriet Perkins, for her part, was not pitying Septimius Sutherland, and his effort to force her admiration was absurdly unnecessary. She was admiring him with all her heart—for his modesty, sangfroid, self-control, and his scrupulous respect for the authority of Captain Slapser. With the directness and the ruthless realism characteristic of a woman, and especially of a young woman, she regarded the Captain as a vain, preposterous, and bloated jack-in-office whom Septimius, had he chosen, might have morally smashed to pieces with about twenty quiet words. And she remembered every instant with pride that the whole trouble had arisen through Mr. Sutherland's mad passion for herself. She beatifically saw Harriet Perkins as the inspirer of grave men to romantic and terrible deeds. Yet she refused to credit that Mr. Sutherland's deed was terrible or might have disastrous consequences. But, if it was to have disastrous consequences, she was inclined to think that she would not care.

Her pity descended upon Lord Furber. This mighty

legend of a man, whose marvellous success in life he had himself indirectly admitted to her to be after all nothing but a gigantic failure, seemed now to be almost intolerably pathetic. So much so, that if she had continued to look at him as he lay on the bed she might well have shed tears! He was like a child with a toy, and his toy was the earth, and he was tired of his toy and wanted a fresh one and couldn't find a fresh one. He was also strangely like herself. Yet she was his mother, and she had impulses both to chastise him and to pet him.

She gazed challengingly at the Captain, and walked out of the cabin to the deck. The Captain would have given much to prevent this disobedience to his commands, but at the moment could think of no method of doing so. He limited the expression of his feelings to a grunt. Hearing the grunt behind her, Harriet turned back into the cabin and, smiling very agreeably, said to the Captain:

"Captain!"

"Miss?"

"You may grunt."

The permission to the Captain being gracefully accorded, she finally quitted the cabin.

The night was persistently exquisite in its balmy and moonlit freshness. The zephyr, now on the quarter, gently flirted with Harriet's cheek. The great yacht urged its solitary way through the calm water, masterless, without a purpose, at the mercy of a preposterous jack-in-office who was losing his head because there was no supreme authority to call him Joe and rule him. Harriet felt sorry even for the yacht. And sorriest of all, most disquieted, for herself.

"I've simply nothing to wear to-morrow morning!" she exclaimed tragically in her soul.

CHAPTER XIII

ON THE RAIL

HARRIET PERKINS, leaning over the rail, heard cautious footsteps on the after stairway leading to the boat-deck. There were four stairways of communication between the promenade-deck and the boat-deck, two forward and two aft. She turned; the nearest stairway rose almost directly behind her. Mr. Septimius Sutherland was descending it; she recognized him in the gloom by his self-possessed (some would have said self-complacent), slightly perky carriage. As he was evidently trying to achieve noiselessness, she gave no greeting. Indeed, she resumed her original position at the rail and stared into the water.

Mr. Sutherland came silently to her side, and his left elbow on the rail touched her right elbow on the rail. The dark water slid swirling far under them, apparently at a tremendous speed, to form the wake of the vessel; its swift, smooth motion had a magnetic quality to hold human vision in a spell. No reason why eyes gazing at it should not gaze at it for ever and ever!

The girl heard a pleasant murmur in her ear:

"You should put on your wrap. The temperature is falling."

The olive-coloured wrap was wound round her arm.

She thought teasingly, yet benevolently:

"'Temperature is falling'! How like him! Why

84

couldn't he say, 'It's getting a bit coldish'? Silly old dear!"

His elbow left hers, and the next moment the green wrap was unwound from her arm. She liked the untidiness of the muffler about his neck. It seemed to her to be much more romantic than a collar and tie. The cap helped the romance of the muffler. To reward his attentiveness she snuggled her shoulders into the cloak as he settled it around them.

"I understood the Bumption had marched you off to the purser," she murmured.

"So he had. But the Antinope was not in his right place, and the Bumption went off to look for him. So I decided I would look for him myself." The words of Mr. Sutherland were spoken so low as scarcely to be distinguishable, but Harriet caught them.

Mr. Sutherland continued:

"I thought I'd look for him in the cabin of the wireless operator." He emphasized the last two words, and glanced at her.

Harriet started.

"I see."

And she did see what Mr. Sutherland meant her to see. She saw also that her admiration for Mr. Sutherland's scrupulous respect for the authority of Captain Slapser had been premature. Mr. Sutherland's respect for the Captain's authority was an illusion, and now Harriet admitted that if it had not been an illusion it would have been ridiculous. Mr. Sutherland was living up to the reputation which she had made for him in her own mind.

"And did you see the wireless operator?"

"Yes. But he wouldn't do anything."

"What did you ask him to do?"

"Send a message—to Rome."

"And he wouldn't."

"Said he couldn't without the orders of either the skipper or his lordship."

"You told him Lord Furber was—ill."

"Oh! He knew about Lord Furber."

"Seems to me they're all banded together, against us," Harriet whispered.

"Yes."

"But what's the good of sending a message? What sort of a message should you have sent?"

"Well, I hadn't decided. I thought I'd find out first if a message could be sent at all. Then you and I'd have had a chat."

"D'you know where we're going to?"

"Genoa, I should imagine. By the moon we should be moving in a north-westerly direction. That lighthouse there behind ought to be on the island of Ischia. Hullo! Hullo!" These last words a little louder.

About a couple of hundred yards off, on the bow, a huge curved form rose out of the flat sea, and the moonlight glinted upon points of metal. It might have been some marine monster; but marine monsters do not usually carry a long gun on their backs.

"Submarine," said Mr. Sutherland casually. "Night manœuvres. Probably Italian. A near shave, that! If she'd come up under us . . . But she couldn't have done. They have instruments, you know. So it's all right."

He did not know that submarines had 'instruments,' but he thought that they should have, and the idea soothed the imagination and also gave him an air of being immensely informed.

The submarine produced an eerie and intimidating

effect on the watchers. It ran level with the yacht for a time, showing no lights; then slackened speed, dropped astern, and disappeared into the depths.

"Pity we couldn't communicate with her," said Harriet.

"No use! What could we have done if we did communicate with her? Submarines don't carry a doctor."

"No. But what fun!"

"Ah! . . . Fun . . . Yes." There was a certain reserve in Mr. Sutherland's tone.

Harriet said:

"You don't really think there is anything seriously wrong with Lord Furber, do you? I mean, really." She had now turned herself into an ingenuous, trustful girl appealing with confidence to the fount of all wisdom. She was atoning for her levity, in a manner to bewitch.

"I hope not. I think not. I'm almost sure not. But you can't be *quite* sure. There might be some lesion of the brain—you never know."

"However, it's not a bit probable," said Harriet, determined to be optimistic.

"No. But it's a bit possible," said Septimius solemnly, determined to be realistic. He shed gloom around him. "Naturally I'm very sorry about it all. I oughtn't to have done it. I ought to have reflected." He vaguely knew that he was blaming himself in order that he might hear her take up his defence.

"I don't think you were to blame at all," said Harriet in a most serious, solacing whisper. "In fact, it was simply splendid of you. Simply splendid! And of course you didn't realize your own strength."

These words were surpassingly sweet to Septimius; and, further, Harriet found surpassing pleasure in offering them to Septimius.

"Well, to be frank," said he, "I did not realize my own strength."

"Strong men never do," said she.

They were both uplifted into a strange bliss. Mr. Sutherland's wife and adult daughters existed no more for him. He had again that grand sensation of recklessness— so intoxicating to a middle-aged gentleman with thin lips and fixed habits.

"Besides," said Harriet, "Lord Furber brought it on himself."

"Quite. If I hadn't been kept on board——"

"Tell me," Harriet spoke very confidentially and persuasively; "why did he keep you on board? I know why I was kept on board."

"Why?"

"Because they couldn't have warned me the launches were going off without warning you as well. But *you?* Why? You must have some idea."

"I haven't," said Septimius. "Honestly. And if you'll excuse me saying so, that's not the immediate point. To my mind the point is that something ought to be done about Lord Furber."

"Well, the only way to get anything done is to go and tell the Captain that he mustn't do it. He's in such a state of dithering conceit that he'll only take suggestions by contraries."

"How well you understand people!" murmured Mr. Sutherland. His tone seemed to imply: "And how wonderfully, how nicely, you've understood me."

"I think you ought to speak to the Captain," said Harriet. "I'll go with you if you like. If we insist on his making straight for Genoa as quick as he can, he'll be sure to put back to Naples; which would be the best thing. We know the English doctor at Naples—and all my frocks are there, too."

"Excellent!" agreed Septimius. "I fancy we can deal with the Captain—prick his balloon, eh?"

Septimius stood upright in his sudden decision, and simultaneously felt a touch in the small of his back. He swung round. Harriet swung round also. A tall man faced them. Felt slippers had enabled the fellow to come right up to them soundlessly.

"I'm the purser," said the man to Septimius. "Mr. Antinope, my name is. Captain's sent me. I'll thank you to come along at once."

No 'sir'! Neither the formulæ nor the accent of respect.

Septimius raised his hand, whereupon with great swiftness Mr. Antinope seized the wrist in a terrible, flesh-lacerating clutch.

"No more o' that," said Mr. Antinope briefly.

Septimius could not move.

Harriet laid a restraining finger on Mr. Sutherland's right arm.

"Don't hurt him," she appealed to Mr. Sutherland. "Remember you didn't realize your strength. We don't want more trouble."

"Very well," said Septimius. He was ashamed of his duplicity; but he had to say just those two words, and in just that tone of lofty forbearance. And to Mr. Antinope coldly: "I am quite ready to come along."

The frightful torturing vice which Mr. Antinope carried at the end of his arm loosed its grip.

CHAPTER XIV

ON THE FLOOR

WITHOUT the society of Septimius, Miss Harriet Perkins felt lorn and chilly. But she also felt more adventurous. In a moment she decided to do some prospecting.

The majestic, curving, double companion or stairway leading down from the promenade-deck to the main-deck was lit by one tiny blue electric star. Beyond it, in the lounge which separated the dining-saloon from the owner's state sitting-room, were no lights whatever. Harriet remembered the situation of the switches used by Mr. Tunnicliff, and used them, revealing the closed door of the state sitting-room. She opened the door, and beheld the scene of her exciting interview with Lord Furber brightly illuminated. Little Mr. Tunnicliff was seated solitary therein, examining a very large sea-chart. He jumped up, blushing. The chart sank on to the carpet, waving as it fell.

"All alone?" she said, smiling.

"Yes," said Mr. Tunnicliff, modestly.

She suspected that she had put him into a delicious confusion.

"I came down because I was beginning to feel the cold," said she. "Whose is that fur-coat?" She pointed to a garment that lay on a sofa at the end of the room.

"Lord Furber's. It's always left there for him every evening in case he should want it."

90

Suddenly, perceiving a crushed cigarette-end on the carpet, Harriet knelt over it.

"Have you dropped something? Can I find it for you?"

Mr. Tunnicliff was kneeling by her side.

"No," she said. "I was only looking at the hole I burnt in the carpet to-night. Quite a good hole, isn't it? The carpet will never be the same again. But his lordship didn't seem to mind. In fact, he told me I hadn't burnt any hole. Very polite of him, wasn't it?"

"Yes, it was."

"But he always is polite, isn't he?"

Her eyes smiled. Mr. Tunnicliff's shining eyes smiled in response. He blushed again; but said naught. There he was, kneeling close by her, feeling very self-conscious, yet somehow content; but not daring to rise till she rose. They were like two domestic animals amicably and curiously surveying each other.

"How is Lord Furber now? Have you heard?" Harriet demanded.

"About the same. It seems he's quite conscious. At least he isn't unconscious. Only he doesn't hear anything, or at least he doesn't understand anything, and he can't speak."

"Dazed?"

"Yes."

"Very strange, isn't it?"

"Yes, it is." Mr. Tunnicliff coughed.

"What's that chart thing?"

Harriet padded along on her knees towards the chart, and Mr. Tunnicliff did likewise. They pored together over the chart.

"You see, it's the environs of Naples," Mr. Tunnicliff explained. "The coast, that is, and the islands."

"What are all those funny figures in the sea?"

"They're the depths, in fathoms."

"Do you know which way we're going?"

"To Genoa. Genoa isn't on this chart, of course. I think the Captain didn't like the Precida channel to-night. He's gone outside all the islands. I don't know why."

This was Mr. Tunnicliff's first volunteered remark. The emission of it seemed to give him ease and a slight confidence in himself; it certainly increased his already considerable charm in the eyes of Miss Perkins.

"Poor boy!" she thought. "I mustn't be too nice to him. It would be cruelty to children. He ought to be in his cradle." Still, she did not get up from the floor.

"Where's Rome?" she asked; her finger wandered over the chart.

"Rome's not on this sheet, either. There aren't any more sheets down here."

"Oh! But I did so want to see Rome."

"There's an atlas here," Mr. Tunnicliff said. "If that would do."

She nodded.

"Shall we look at it?"

Now the atlas was the lowest of a pile of volumes on the floor, and Mr. Tunnicliff padded on his knees towards it, and Miss Perkins padded in his wake. It was a large and heavy atlas, clearly meant to be consulted on floors by students on their hands and knees. Mr. Tunnicliff found Southern Italy and then Rome, and he pointed to the mouth of the Tiber and to the town of Ostia, and said that Ostia was the ancient port for Rome.

"What a lot you know!" observed Harriet teasingly. "Why do you look at me like that?"

Their heads were adjacent.

"I was only thinking how nice it would be for me to kiss you," said Mr. Tunnicliff, astonishingly.

Harriet had to collect herself.

"You rude little boy!" she protested, but in a tone to indicate that in her opinion they had been playing together on the carpet of a nursery.

"Well," said Mr. Tunnicliff, jumping up in sudden resentment, his cheeks now a deep crimson. "If you want to know, I'm older than I look by a long chalk, and as for little, I'm quite the average height. You're tall— for a girl."

Harriet, twisting herself, sat on the floor and raised her glance to him; but he would not meet it.

"That makes it all the worse," said she. "If you're so fearfully old, you're old enough to know better."

"You asked me why I looked at you and I told you," he sulked, his full lower lip drooping. "If you hadn't asked me I shouldn't have said anything. And now I've said it, you don't like it—or at least you pretend you don't. That's a girl all over, that is. You're all the same." He was walking about, hands in pockets.

"And here I was thinking butter wouldn't melt in your mouth!" observed Harriet, leaning back and supporting herself on her arms stretched out behind. "I suppose you've got Spanish blood in your veins."

"I haven't. I'm just as English as you are."

"Perhaps Don Juan came once to England," said Harriet.

"I dare say you think you're very funny."

"I do. But not half as funny as you are." She laughed outright.

"Oh go to blazes!" Mr. Tunnicliff shockingly exclaimed.

"Mr. Tunnicliff," she said, "I don't mind pointing out what's the matter with you. You've no sense of humour."

"Possibly not," said he, dryly.

"And I wanted you to help me."

Mr. Tunnicliff's manner immediately changed. The drooping lips lifted and he smiled.

"Of course if I can *do* anything——"

"You can, you nice *man*! What's the name of the wireless operator here?"

"Tunnicliff."

"Same as yours."

"He's my cousin. As a matter of fact I got him his job."

"How heavenly you are! Have you a visiting card? If so, just write on it what I tell you, and give it me. I expect your cousin would do simply anything for you?"

"I'm not so sure," said Mr. Tunnicliff searching his person for a card, which he found. "My cousin's a bit of a Tartar."

"All the better. Now just write this, will you? 'Please do what you can for the bearer, who is in distress.'"

"But are you?"

"Yes. Of course I'm in distress! Would I ask you to write a lie? Aren't we all in trouble, with poor Lord Furber as he is? Where does he live, your Cossack cousin? Somewhere on the top-deck, isn't it?"

"I'll go up with you, if you like."

"No. I shouldn't like. Your temper is too uncertain."

"Oh! All right, all right! Here!"

He vouchsafed the card. Harriet read on it: "The Honourable Luke John Tunnicliff."

"Ah!" she murmured. "Entertaining angels unawares, was I? And now will you officially lend me Lord Furber's fur coat. I'll bring it back, honest Injun."

She got up from the floor, and he obediently endued her into the rich, warm, and not heavy garment.

"How lovely it is!" she murmured, and looked at him. He was assuredly adorable. A baby, naturally, but his eyes at once honest and incandescent, and what delicate nostrils! As for height, their faces were on a level.

Then in a new tone, she said:

"I think on the whole you may kiss me if you want to."

Mr. Tunnicliff threw his head back.

"No thanks," he said stiffly. "I don't want to now." His face was darkly lowering again.

"Why?" Harriet showed some pique.

"I couldn't kiss any girl for the first time in cold blood," said Mr. Tunnicliff.

"Fish!" Harriet burst out. Then, controlling herself to a gentle irony. "A kiss is nothing."

"Is it!" the youth exclaimed savagely. "You wait —and you'll see."

"You ought to write your memoirs," said teasing Harriet, not so much to daunt Mr. Tunnicliff as to reassure herself by wit. For his kindled eyes were unexampled in her experience.

CHAPTER XV

HARRIET tapped at the door of the eyrie of the wireless operator on the navigating deck of the *Vanguard*. There was no answer. She knocked again. Still no answer. A proper maidenly feeling prevented her from entering without due permission, for she had heard or read somewhere that wireless operators at sea passed the whole of their lives in these mysterious shanties, sleeping and even eating in the same; and she hesitated before an indiscretion. Cousin Tunnicliff, the Tartar, might be asleep, or dead, or otherwise not in a seemly state to receive an unknown lady. As she waited, the inhospitable cabin took on a mysterious and sinister air. Her heart began to beat at the thought of what dread secrets the place might hold. At last she turned the knob and pushed open the door about an inch.

"Come in, d—n you," grunted an Oxford voice menacingly.

The greeting admirably suited Harriet. She said to herself:

"I think I can do something with a man who begins like that."

And she went into a very stuffy interior, preparing a smile for the taming of Tartars.

A young man in shirt sleeves, with a listening apparatus

which resembled a tiara and ear-ornaments clasped about his devoted head, was ensconced in an arm-chair. His position was peculiar. He leaned his back against one of the arms of the chair, and his legs dangled freely over the other. In one hand he held a ragged paper-bound book, and in the other a glass of whisky. From his thin-lipped mouth drooped a cigarette.

"Good evening," said Harriet, throwing back the plenteous folds of Lord Furber's fur overcoat.

"I'm sorry," said wireless-operator Tunnicliff, without the least sign of confusion. He squirmed himself gracefully out of the chair, dropped the book, placed the glass very carefully on a table, and removed the cigarette from his mouth. He was tall and handsome—a contrast to his cousin—and his nostrils had a delicate curve. It was at once evident that he was a member of the caste which confers a favour on the world by condescending to be born.

"Is that your usual form of welcome, Mr. Tunnicliff?" Harriet asked brightly. And she exerted charm, aware that the masculinity of the vast overcoat would increase rather than diminish her piquancy.

"I apologise. Please take a chair," said the operator coolly, if not coldly. At any rate, he was in full possession of himself. "Important people," he explained, "important people don't knock. The rest are a nuisance, and I treat them as such."

"But I'm very important. At least, I think I am," said Harriet, sitting down and arranging the coat as artistically as possible.

"No doubt," the operator agreed calmly. "Do you object to smoking?"

"Not at all."

"Excuse me," said the operator, searching for a jacket

and putting it on in a corner. The flex joining his tiara to the aerial magic followed him as he moved to and fro.

Harriet glanced at the room. It seemed to be divided into a business or professional half and a domestic half. The latter comprised a bed and bedstead, the lower part of which was a chest of drawers, a chair, a row of bottles, a rug, a pipe-rack, and (on the walls) two interesting prints cut from old numbers of *La Vie Parisienne*. Nothing was shipshape. Everything was untidy, and nearly everything was shabby. None of the drawers was quite shut, and from several of them portions of attire indecently protruded. The top corner of one of the prints had escaped from its pin and hung over triangularly. The place seemed to be defiantly protesting: "No, I am not pitiful or pathetic. This is the way my owner likes me to be, and those who don't care for it can do the other thing."

"Please look at this," said Harriet, handing the visiting card to an outstretched hand, nicotine-stained and aristocratic. "And my name is Harriet Perkins."

The operator perused the card, dropped it on the table, and resumed the glass of whisky.

"You'll pardon me just finishing my supper," said he, in the tone not of a question but of a positive assertion, and emptied the glass.

"I adore your little house here," Harriet remarked, in the way of conversation. It was true; she did.

"Oh!"

"It seems so *natural*," said she.

"Yes?"

"And it's so *male*. Women's wigwams are so frightfully prim," Harriet added.

"Are they? Never seen one."

"Are you listening to anything just now?" she asked, indicating his ear ornaments.

"No. There's nothing at the moment."

"You don't mind if I slip off this overcoat, do you? It's Lord Furber's. Such a warm night, isn't it?" She emerged from the overcoat, and, having shed it, shed also her wrap, and incidentally dropped her handbag. "I mustn't lose that," she said, picking it up. "It contains all my liquid resources. I always carry my traveller's-cheques about with me, and it's a good thing I do. I got left behind on the yacht, you know; sort of innocent stow-away, and if I hadn't had my traveller's-cheques just *think* how I should have been fixed—no clothes and no cheques—when I reached dry land again! I dare say you've heard how the yacht ran off with me."

"I did hear something. Now what's this 'distress' that Luke talks about?"

"It's this," Harriet answered, deploying all her re-sources to be ingratiating. "I haven't a rag except what you see. And I simply must have some clothes. I was wondering if you'd be so very, very kind as to send a wire-less to Count Veruda at the Splendide at Naples asking him to meet the yacht at Ostia with my trunks, and to wireless a reply that he is coming. He could get a maid to pack. Most of the trunks are packed already—I was meaning to leave Naples the day after to-morrow, anyway. You see how tremendously important it is for me . . . Would you?"

She leaned forward with bright eyes and parted lips, as if thirsting for the nectar of his affirmative response. Far from being a Tartar, he showed himself the quietest, coolest, most matter-of-fact thing imaginable.

"But the yacht isn't calling at Ostia," he said.

"No. Not as at present arranged," she said. "But of course it will call, when you receive the reply from Count Veruda."

"Well, perhaps she would," said the operator. "I should be sorry to contradict you. But it would depend on the wording of the reply."

"Oh! That could be fixed," said Harriet obscurely.

"You aren't the first person to-night to ask me to send off a message." The operator smiled.

"Really!" she exclaimed, as though the information was of immense interest. "And did you?"

"No. I couldn't oblige."

"But you'll oblige me, won't you?"

"I should love to," the operator replied placidly, unexceptionably, ruthlessly polite. "But I can't. I have my orders. And they are to send nothing out except what I receive from Lord Furber or the captain."

"But Lord Furber's ill. He's had an accident."

"So I believe," said the operator. "I'm sorry. Very sorry." He spoke with as much emotion as though he had heard the sad news that a great-aunt's favourite Pekingese had been suddenly struck down by ear-complaint.

"That leaves only the captain. Well, we all know the captain, and we know he wouldn't understand about the importance of a woman's clothes."

"Probably not. I'm very sorry."

"Do you mean you're sorry about Lord Furber's illness, or about the limitations of the captain's understanding, or about your not being able to do me this small favour?"

"About everything," said the operator, nobly and with fortitude.

CHAPTER XVI

THE VAMP

HARRIET leaned back in her chair.

"Your orders are quite definite?"

"Quite."

"Well then, of course, you can't disobey them, even for a few minutes and to do a perfectly innocent job for a poor damsel in distress?" Harriet gave him a humorous, detached, easy, friendly smile.

"I can't." The operator spoke with equal detachment.

"Anyhow, there's no harm done, is there?"

"None."

"You'll think me very curious," said Harriet. "But do you wear those things on your ears all the time—for instance—in bed?"

"Not when I'm in bed," the operator replied. He went on as judicially as if he were describing the case of a third person: "You see, it's like this. A ship is not allowed to send wireless messages while she's in port. Our voyages are generally very short. A dozen or twenty hours at the most. Few yachtsmen care for a day and a night at sea, especially owners of big yachts. They use their yachts more as hotels than ships. So when we *do* happen to be at sea, I sit up most of the time, as a rule."

"And read?"

"Yes."

"What's that book you were reading? I'm always frightfully interested in other people's lives." Harriet became eager.

"That's the Tauchnitz volume of Swinburne selections."

"How amusing! And are you an 'Honourable' like your cousin, Luke John?"

"No. How could I be?"

"No. Of course you couldn't be, unless both your fathers were peers. And it isn't often two brothers are peers, is it? How stupid of me! But you're the nephew of a peer."

"I'm sorry to say that I'm also the grandson of an earl—through my mother."

"And yet you're a wireless operator."

"Why not? I'm a product of the public school system. My family is poor on both sides. The male paupers of the aristocracy—pardon the word—are educated in such a way that they inevitably leave the university with one of two ideas in their heads. Either they mean to be engineers or to go into the City. There is nothing else. I could imagine few trades more ignoble than the City. Engineering provides at least some pleasant toys for an intelligent child. I specialized in wireless because of its mystery. And here I am. *Voilà!*"

"And Luke John got you the situation?"

"It just happened so." The operator shrugged his shoulders.

"I should have thought you would have hated to serve under the new rich."

"Quite the contrary. I rather enjoy studying the present specimen at close quarters. I'm told he's marvellous. It's quite conceivable. Nothing is inconceivable.

I admit he has a certain barbaric force. But he hasn't a notion how to live. He's unhappy and he's bored. He doesn't know what he's alive for."

"How true!" Harriet murmured with feeling.

"It's really touching to see how he loves to employ people who are better bred than himself. There's Luke and there's me. Not to mention the alleged Count Veruda. And I am told that one of his shore secretaries is the daughter of a dead Colonial Governor or something of the kind. There may be others. Yes, our present specimen is an extremely diverting study. And the point is that he doesn't know it and I do. I give him credit for wanting to stand well with me. Also for a dim, savage suspicion that I simply don't care a gooseberry for him. The fellow is not without insight."

The operator made a little noise in his nose, apparently to signify a kindly sneer.

Harriet was now beginning to understand why the other Mr. Tunnicliff had called his cousin a Tartar. He was a Tartar in a deeper and more terrifying sense than she could have previously imagined. But at the same time he was proving himself to be a Tartar such as she might utilize. She collected her faculties. She had captured Mr. Sutherland, without an effort. She had fascinated Lord Furber, without an effort. She had captured Luke John Tunnicliff, without an effort—though in a fit of childish temper the youth had broken loose and was temporarily out of hand. Surely she could capture the operator. Never had she consciously used the gifts of heaven to gain any but the most trifling social ends. She had always scorned to do so. But she was determined to use them now for an end of importance, and she had the conviction that she would be successful.

She stood up, thrilled. In the rough masculinity of the cabin she felt herself to be endowed with irresistible feminine magic. All men (she had always heard) were alike, at bottom. They would all fall like ninepins before a certain form of attack.

"You're wonderful!" she exclaimed in a voice whose calmness was contradicted by her eyes and attitude. "I don't say it to flatter you." Her voice grew almost stern in its sincerity. "But you really *are* wonderful. Now be honest with me. Don't let's fence and be conventional. Don't *you* think you're rather wonderful?" Exquisitely she seemed to be entreating him for the precious truth.

"Yes, I do," said the operator, quite simply. "That is, by comparison."

"I should have despised you if you hadn't answered just like that," she said quietly and seriously, even harshly. "I should have been terribly disappointed. Good night!" she said with sudden finality.

She picked up the enormous fur overcoat, which now she seemed scarcely able to lift.

"Let me help you."

"I won't trouble to put it on, thanks."

"You'd better. I know this cabin is horribly close. You might easily take a chill. The tramontana is beginning to blow."

"Do you think so?"

"I know it is."

He helped her with the overcoat.

"Good night again," she said over her shoulder.

"Good night."

She had reached the door when she turned back.

"My bag."

The bag was on the floor again. The operator picked it up.

"Thanks so much."

At that instant, as she was accepting the valuable bag at his hands, the whole cabin gave a lurch, and Harriet stumbled.

"She's meeting it," observed the operator, steadying Harriet by a firm touch on the shoulder.

Harriet thought: "The tramontana is helping me." And she blessed the famous wind.

"May I sit down just for a moment?" she asked. "I'm not a very good sailor."

She told this fib with the most appalling convincingness, and unsteadily, with the operator's assistance, sat down.

"Could I have something to drink?" She smiled plaintively.

"There's only one glass."

"One will be enough." She smiled bravely.

"Whisky?"

"Anything."

She drank—and tried to read the operator's mood. He had offered her the sole glass with all the grace that would naturally be expected from an earl's grandson and a baron's nephew.

"I'm better."

"I'm so glad." The operator bent over her attentively.

She sighed with relief and said:

"Mr. Tunnicliff, can you give me a bit of paper and a pencil?"

When he had supplied her want, she wrote a few words, using the volume of Swinburne as a support for the paper.

"Now, Mr. Tunnicliff," she said, "I quite see that it

would be wrong of me to urge you any more to send off any message that hasn't been authorized by the powers. And I wouldn't dream of urging you. But you've got no orders against *receiving* messages, have you?"

"Well, of course not, dear lady. I'm here to receive messages."

"Any messages?"

"Certainly. There's no choice. I don't quite understand you."

"It's very simple," said Harriet. "Will you receive this message?"

She handed him the paper, upon which he read: "*Captain, Yacht Vanguard. You are requested to anchor at mouth of Tiber and await visit from officials. Benito Mussolini, Paiazzo Chigi, Rome.*"

The operator, reading the shaky script, maintained a most meritorious impassivity.

"You wish me to write out this message and hand it to the skipper as though I had got it on the wireless?"

"Yes. Why not?" Harriet looked up at the man with an imploring, inviting smile—a smile surely irresistible.

The operator smiled to match. "Yes," thought Harriet, "he is extraordinarily handsome."

"It is you who are wonderful," he breathed softly, gazing at her. "I'm not flattering you."

She shook her head modestly, but her thought was: "So I am wonderful!" And she did not take her eyes off him. Her glance as it were melted into his.

The cabin gave another slight lurch. She put out a hand to steady herself. The operator held it.

"Of course," said he, "there's no order to prevent me from doing this."

"I've won!" thought Harriet.

"And what a lark!" the operator added.

"Yes, isn't it!" Harriet agreed. "But it's serious, too. You don't know how important it is that I should get off—I mean go ashore—as quickly as possible. I do beg you as a favour—I throw myself on your good nature —I——"

The operator squeezed her hand ever so delicately.

"A strange yacht," he seemed to be musing aloud, "where guests are forbidden to communicate with their friends ashore! . . . Come to look at it!"

"Just so!" Harriet concurred humbly.

"Had you already had this very brilliant idea when you came in to see me?" asked the operator. "Forgive my question. It's all so interesting."

"No! The idea came into my head just now."

Harriet spoke with pleased confidence. The tension of expectation was nearly over. Yes, she had captured the operator as she had captured others. The ancient wise saws of mankind about the power of woman and the weakness of wicked men were profoundly true in their estimate of human nature. She realized triumphantly that through this elegant and untidy youth she was mistress of the movements of the mighty yacht. And she laughed to herself as she waited for his formal surrender to her seductiveness.

CHAPTER XVII

THE MESSAGE

"But, dear lady," said the operator, and his voice was as winsome as Harriet's own, "you're acting rather dangerously, aren't you? I think it my duty to warn you before anything is done that can't be undone."

"How dangerously? Nobody will be able to prove that you haven't had the message. And if any trouble does arise we can always put down the message to some practical joker."

"But the Marconi offices keep records of all the messages they send out."

"I dare say they do. But what about a practical joker on some other ship? If you only knew it, you wireless operators, you've got the control of ships entirely in your hands. A secret league of wireless operators could disorganize the traffic of the whole world for their own ends."

"Quite. I agree. You have imagination. But I wasn't looking at it from my own angle at all. I'm thinking about the yacht. This is no ordinary sort of yacht. I don't mind telling you from my own knowledge that the *Vanguard* is a very peculiar sort of yacht. I could startle you if I chose. Only my lips are sealed—as they say. Anything might happen on this yacht. And remember that the owner has been assaulted and knocked senseless, and that his assailant is on board. If the Captain's instructions were to go direct to Genoa, you may depend there was an important reason for it. Your scheme might upset something that really oughtn't to be upset. And there's another point. This Mr. Sutherland, the bruiser, has to be watched. At Ostia he might get away in spite of the Captain. There's no police force worth talking about at Ostia. The port of Genoa has all the most modern developments of policing."

Harriet said easily:

"I'll take all the responsibility. After all, I'm Lord Furber's secretary."

"You're what?" Astonishment in the tone!

Harriet thought:

"He's holding my hand rather a long time."

She said:

"His lordship's confidential secretary. At, least he offered me the place only about an hour ago. I didn't accept it instantly. But, since—since things happened I have accepted it, though of course he doesn't know. So I *am* Lord Furber's secretary, and while he's ill I'm entitled to act on his behalf, seeing that I stand higher than your cousin." She thought she saw in the operator's demeanour a clear indication that he was considerably impressed.

The operator replied:

"Forgive me if I say that I doubt if you know exactly what you want, and anyhow I don't think you fully realize what you'll be doing if I carry out your suggestion about this message. For instance, when we reach the neighbourhood of Ostia, what shall you do next?"

"I'll decide that when we get to Ostia, dear Mr. Tunnicliff," Harriet murmured softly. "I admire your caution. But I repeat, I'll take the responsibility. All I ask just now is your help, and I hope you won't refuse it." Her tone said: "I'm perfectly sure you won't refuse it—can't refuse it."

The operator smiled with a chivalry almost tender, and his next words were uttered in a low, enveloping voice that surpassed even the smile.

"Just let me say this," he began. His face approached Harriet's. He paused.

"When will he loose my hand?" thought Harriet. "Really he's going rather far."

She had a horrid fear that she had been carrying seductiveness to excess, with the possibility of very disagreeable consequences to herself. And she wondered what she would do if, as a response to her tactics, the naïve young man attempted to kiss her. In other words, having asked for trouble, she objected to receiving it.

"Just let me say this," the operator recommenced, even more sweetly and ingratiatingly than before. "This Mussolini scheme of yours is merely silly. You can't play about with two-thousand-ton yachts in such a fashion as that. You had a pleasant fancy, but you're letting it run away with you. It's the fancy of a schoolgirl." His hold of her hand tightened. "Still, I don't mind that. I always expect a woman to behave like a woman. Your fancy amuses me. But I'm much more amused at your simplicity. Believe me, you aren't cut out to be a vamp. Here for the last ten minutes you've been absurdly using your absurd feminine charm to get me to do something perfectly absurd that you know I oughtn't to do even if it wasn't absurd. You can't do it. I am just as insensible to fashionable women as I am to Napoleonic multi-millionaires. You leave me cold."

He pressed her arm anew, and continued to coo at her most gently:

"I don't know what you're after with your anchoring off Ostia, and I'm pretty sure you don't know either. What I do know is that you're a simpleton. You imagined you were serving me up on toast for yourself. Well you weren't, my dear young lady . . . Sea-sick, indeed! Let me advise you to go and lie down."

During these remarks, his dulcet note and his tender admiring smile had not varied.

Harriet, magnetized for a space by amazement, snatched away her hand at last. More completely than ever did she comprehend the meaning of the word "Tartar" in Luke John Tunnicliff's dictionary.

When she got outside the cabin, and the door was shut behind her, she remained standing some time to reflect upon her strange situation. A head-wind was blowing freshly; the moon was obscured by clouds, but of diffused light there was sufficient to show the fretted surface of the sea far below. The forms of the great launches and other boats hung suspended and stayed on either side of her. A lamp in the Captain's quarters cast a beam through his starboard windows. The moving and the stationary figures of officers on the high navigating bridge were faintly silhouetted against the dark sky. She could see the mast-head lights overhead. Turning to the left she noticed that a whole galaxy and procession of lights, a few coloured, was overhauling the yacht on the port beam; some liner shifted from the Atlantic to carry tourists on a Mediterranean pleasure-cruise; the huge and formidable affair, magically afloat and urgent in the night, passed the yacht as though she had been standing still and reduced her to a trifle on the ocean. On the starboard beam some distant shore-lights feebly twinkled. In a few minutes, the liner was a mile ahead and fast dimishing to a blur on the horizon.

CHAPTER XVIII

MRS. BUMPTION AS NURSE

By the instructions of Mrs. Bumption Lord Furber had
been carried into his own sleeping cabin. It was much
larger than the one from which he had been removed, and
it had a special system of automatic ventilation, devised by
Lord Furber himself. These facts, however, had not
influenced Mrs. Bumption. She wanted his lordship to be
withdrawn more completely from the world of the yacht, so
that none might interfere with her nursing and management
of him: hence the change. Mrs. Bumption had had no experience of nursing, and in any case could not have made an
ideal nurse. But she was the only lady in the yacht with
an official position, and therefore the sufferer was her prey.

Captain Slapser had said, in the other cabin, that what
he said "went." But Mrs. Bumption really had a better
title to the boast. The Captain was a blusterer; Mrs.
Bumption was not. Mrs. Bumption's confidence in herself was complete. The Captain had consulted Bumption,
who as his lordship's butler had a prestige far surpassing that
of either the first officer or the mate—or even the chief
engineer. Bumption, of course, had consulted Mrs.
Bumption, and it was Mrs. Bumption who, through
Bumption, had decided that the wireless message should
be disregarded. Mrs. Bumption had never heard of
Mussolini, much less of Farinacci; she scorned newspapers,

politics, and all other masculine playthings. But she had learnt that Ostia was the port for Rome, and she was a strong low-church protestant. Rome was accordingly ruled out, as being a dangerous and improper place for any sensible Briton. Captain Slapser adopted her view because he misdoubted the merits of the anchorage at Ostia.

Accordingly, the yacht held her original course for Genoa and Mrs. Bumption reigned. She knew that she reigned, and everybody in the ship knew that she reigned. She had had no sleep and desired none. She sat in Lord Furber's own easy-chair and surveyed Lord Furber in his richly-ornamented bunk, and she smoothed out her white apron over her measureless hips, and drank a little of the brandy and milk which Lord Furber had refused to swallow, and she was pleasantly conscious of mastery.

Lord Furber's eyes were shut; he lay with one cheek on the pillow, so that the dressed wound at the back of his head might suffer no pressure, and his breathing was faint, though slow and regular. He had been undressed. His face was very pale, except the swollen chin, which in colour was somewhat variegated. Nothing had happened since the first great happening, and it seemed as if nothing would happen until Genoa and a doctor should be reached. Lord Furber's few audible remarks had been apparently quite senseless, and it was clear that he did not know who he was.

Mrs. Bumption could wait. Omnipotence can always wait. Deep night and a majestic silence dominated the cabin, lit by one blue-tinted lamp just over the telephone switch-board, by means of which Lord Furber (when in his right mind) could, and did communicate direct with every part of the ship. Lord Furber had always said that he would have the sleeping cabin isolated from all sound, and he had succeeded in achieving his ideal.

Mrs. Bumption thought she heard a movement of the outer of the two heavy doors which were part of the silential system of the cabin. She turned her head menacingly. She was not mistaken. The inner door slowly swung open, and Miss Harriet Perkins appeared, smiling, still swathed in the immense fur coat. Mrs. Bumption hated Harriet. She had no right reason for doing so; but she hated Harriet because Harriet was an interloper, an intruder, a pert minx, slim, youngish, stylish, and exercised charm over mankind.

Now at this moment Mrs. Bumption's solid body became strangely light, to such a degree that Mrs. Bumption had all she could do to prevent it from rising respectfully at Harriet's entry. She did, however, succeed by an intense effort of will in keeping it down in the chair. She just stared and glared fixedly at Harriet, and her hard eyes said:

"Saucebox, you know you've no business here, and for two pins I'd tear that coat off your impudent back."

"I've had a nice little nap in the lounge," Harriet remarked brightly. "I thought I'd just step in and see how his lordship was getting on."

"I'm looking after his lordship," Mrs. Bumption replied firmly and gloomily. "And what's more, this room's private."

"The devil it is!" Harriet retorted. "Considering that I'm his lordship's latest confidential secretary! . . You're the stewardess, I think."

Her tone was very kindly.

Lord Furber stirred in his bunk. Mrs. Bumption, to cover her feelings, stood up massively and gazed at her patient. She could think of nothing effective to say to Harriet, and wisely said nothing, save with her bulging eyes. She thought to herself that Harriet was a mischievous liar, and yet she thought also that Harriet spoke the truth.

Harriet approached the bunk and took a glance at Lord Furber. His appearance was pathetic to her. She felt that in trying to vamp the wireless operator and in allowing herself ever so little a nap, she had been shamefully callous towards the victim of Mr. Sutherland's passion and power.

"Aren't you Lord Furber?" she asked, seeking to restore the victim's lost memory.

"Who the 'ell's he?" Lord Furber retorted. "Me a lord! Tell us another."

"Do you know where you are?" Harriet made a fresh start.

"I'm in some bloomin' hotel," was the answer. "But I've forgotten its name. Perhaps it's the Tiger. Yes, it's the Tiger. I've run off wi' that fat wench there. Us 's skedaddled together. Her's been making love to me. They're never too old for that, ye know."

Lord Furber raised his eyelids and beheld Mrs. Bumption with a long look grimly sorrowful.

"Wouldna' think it from the size of her, would ye?" he proceeded. "But she's been after me for years. Husband's a good 'un, too." He shut his eyes.

"Mrs. Bumption!" exclaimed Harriet.

Mrs. Bumption, always crimson of face, had put on a scarlet hue. Her mouth worked over her teeth and over the void spaces where teeth once had been. Her whole head trembled. Her hands clasped and unclasped.

"He's wandering," said she glumly, and then heavily swept, with her sense of outrage and the poor remains of her reputation, from the room, and Harriet was alone with Lord Furber.

CHAPTER XIX

RUPTURE

HARRIET first of all closed the doors, both of which Mrs. Bumption had left open, and then she came to the bunk side.

"So you haven't lost your memory," she said, with a glance, soft and quizzical at the suffering baron.

"Artistic performance, wasn't it?" said he, sleepily, and not looking up at her.

"Crude, I should call it," said she.

"I say," he looked up sharply now. "What the dickens do ye mean by saying ye're my latest confidential secretary?"

"Why? You haven't engaged another one since me, have you?"

"I haven't engaged ye yet, Harriet,"

He employed her christian name quite nicely—with benevolence rather than with familiarity. So that she smiled at him.

"You offered me the post. I said I'd decide later, or something of the kind. Well, I've decided. The bargain is closed—except about salary—and so I now *am* your confidential secretary. Only, of course, you must be confidential with me—otherwise I shall resign at once. Tell me why you did it?"

"Did what?"

"Pretend to lose your memory."

"Oh! Just for a change. When they first spoke to me, after I come to, I was a bit dazed and I didn't answer. I saw at once they hadn't a notion what to do, without my orders. And all of a sudden it struck me I'd let 'em alone and see what sort of a mess they'd make of things if I left 'em to themselves. So I lost me memory, and it was such thundering fun I thought I'd keep it lost for a while. I've discovered one or two interesting things already. For instance—my skipper is a blatant ass when it comes to the point. I doubt if he'll be my skipper much longer."

"Well, it was very clever of you."

"Oh, I am clever. Ye'll soon find that out."

"Still, you're only a child. You made yourself a new toy, and you've been so interested playing with it that you've forgotten to be bored. Of course, it was easy to play with. You couldn't have pretended to be unconscious. Nobody could—I mean not to take anybody in. But anyone can pretend to have lost his memory. It's so simple."

"Yes. Only it wanted me to think of the scheme, Harriet. All the good things are simple—when they're done. It's all very well for ye to call it crude."

"I shall have to ask for three pounds a week extra if I'm expected to be always praising you, Lord Furber. And why should I praise you when you can do that so much better for yourself ? I won't praise you. I'll never praise you again. I'm sorry now I even said you were clever."

The baron smiled contentedly.

"And ye can say what ye like," he proceeded. "It was artistic of me to go back to the old Five Towns accent. My God! How I lived in those days!" He was proud of his low origin.

"Oh! Very well then. Have it your own way. You're the most brilliant man on board, or that ever lived, or ever could live. Will that satisfy you?"

"That's better. But I'll tell ye something else. Another reason why I pretended to lose my memory was that I couldn't settle on the spur of the moment what attitude I should take towards yer big City friend, Sutherland. I needed time to think it over."

"Oh! Mr. Sutherland won't mind what attitude you take towards him. He'll always keep calm."

"Mind! Him! Calm! Him! Was he keeping calm when he knocked me down without a word of warning? And why did he knock me down? That's what I've got to know. Why should he knock me down? It's a fortunate thing for him that I particularly want to keep on good terms with the fellow."

There was a faint trace of passionate feeling in the baron's voice as he uttered these last words; at the sound of which Harriet's brain began to work more eagerly and more intelligently than before.

"Then it's perhaps all to the good that he did knock you down."

"What the blazes do you mean?"

Lord Furber sat up as he savagely put the question. He looked pathetic and wistful to Harriet, probably because of his swollen chin and the dressing on the back of his disarrayed scalp. But his tone was not in the least pathetic. On the contrary it was rather frightening. Harriet enjoyed swinging between the two warring sensations which he produced in her.

She said:

"I mean he's a decent kind of a man, and I expect he feels he owes you some apology, and that'll make it easier for you to keep on good terms with him. If he hadn't knocked you down, he might have refused to discuss anything with you at all, because you'd deliberately plotted to make him a prisoner on your yacht."

"Yes," Lord Furber agreed thoughtfully. "That's an argument all right, that is. *You*'re brilliant too." Then he struck the pillow a dastardly, uncalled-for blow, and cried: "But *why* did he knock me down? Ye're a woman, and ye can't understand the feelings of a man who's been knocked down."

"Yes, I can," said Harriet. "A man who's been knocked down feels that he's been treated in a disgraceful and inexcusable manner, and his one idea is to behave in the same manner himself."

"Why did he knock me down?" the baron reiterated, and the pillow suffered a second time. He added quietly, in sudden change: "At least I suppose he knocked me down. I remember him rushing at me, but nothing else."

"If you have any doubts as to what he did, dismiss them. He certainly did knock you down. And he knocked you down because he wasn't fully awake, and I'd screamed or shrieked, and he saw your hand on me and he imagined—well, he imagined I was in serious need of defence."

"Oh! I shouldn't have thought he was that sort of a fellow."

"Well, he just is."

"Then I forgive him. Curse him, I forgive him. But he owes me an apology. And he shall pay me."

"I'm sure he'll apologize."

"Apologize be d—d. What he ought to have is one over the costard himself . . . On my own decks too! . . .

As if anybody 'ud believe his tale about my slipping and falling!"

A bell rang very modestly and discreetly in a corner of the room. Harriet started. It was as if a mouse had stirred in a corner of the room.

"What's that?" she asked, alert and apprehensive in spite of herself.

"The telephone-bell. Ye wouldn't think it would wake me up if I'm asleep. But it does. That's the sort of sleeper I am."

Lord Furber, without moving his body, took down the receiver and listened. He listened for about half a minute or more.

"I thank ye," he murmured low into the telephone, and hung up the receiver again. Silence in the room.

"Who was it?" Harriet demanded as if by right

Lord Furber made no reply.

"It's no use you pretending not to hear," said she, with sweet cajolery, as to a child. "If I'm your confidential secretary—and I *am*—you must be open with me. You must hide nothing from me. And above all you mustn't be ashamed of telling me *anything*."

"Aren't ye asking a lot?" said the baron, warningly firm.

"No confidential secretary that was worth anything would agree to work for you on any other terms."

"This is a new notion of secretaryship."

"And I'm a new sort of secretary."

"Well, it was the wireless operator telephoning, as ye're so curious."

"I'm not curious at all. I'm only being a confidential secretary. In my private capacity do you suppose I care a pin what your Tunnicliff's been saying to you? I'm only inquiring for professional purposes. If I can't know more about you than anybody else in this yacht I'll resign at once." Harriet laughed, and undid the buttons of the fur coat, which she removed.

"Well, he told me there's an Italian submarine knocking about, and he thinks she's wirelessing like anything to somebody, but he can't make out what she's saying, because of the code she's using. That satisfy you?"

"Thanks so much," said Harriet, turning her agreeable, challenging face towards his from the glass by whose aid she was restoring her complexion with instruments taken from the hand-bag.

"That's not the first time to-night you've tried this dodge of taking off my fur coat and showing yeself as ye are."

"Ah! Who told you?"

"Wireless operator."

"He's a sneak then. Perhaps you'll be interested to know that he despises you."

"Now you're being a sneak yourself," the baron said. Harriet snapped her fingers, and then snapped together the sides of the bag.

"He may despise me," said Lord Furber. "He's entitled to think for himself, even if he's entitled to nothing else. But he plays the game with me. Trust him for that. I 'phoned to ask him if he'd anything to report and he said he had, and he reported it. That was all."

"I expect he told you what I wanted him to do for me."

"He did."

"And what did you say?"

"I said he'd better receive a message from Farinacci telling the yacht to call at Ostia. Good thing Mrs. Bumption was out of the room or I couldn't have done it—not safely." The baron grinned.

Harriet openly displayed her astonishment.

"I might have guessed it," she breathed.

"But ye didn't. Didn't I say ye'd soon be finding out how clever I am?"

"And I suppose you told him as well to show me the message?"

"I did."

"Why do you want the yacht to call at Ostia? You aren't ill. You don't need a doctor. You were going to Genoa."

"I want the yacht to call at Ostia because you want her to call at Ostia."

"You're a dear!" Harriet exclaimed, approaching the bunk. "And d'you know *why* I want the yacht to call at Ostia?"

"Of course I do. Ye want to slip up to Rome to get some clothes. Ye can't wear my fur coat for ever. But I'll say this—it suits ye."

"You really *are* a dear! And I'm so sorry for you."

"Why?"

"Because I can see you've got a splitting headache, and you aren't saying anything about it."

"Yes, I have," said the baron. "And so you'd have if you'd been treated as I've been treated by your cursed City friend."

"I'll give you some aspirin, and then you must go to sleep." Harriet suddenly became a nurse.

"Mrs. Bumption wouldn't let me have any aspirin. Said it was dangerous for me."

"She would. She's the sort of woman who finds out what you want, and then finds a reason why you mustn't have it. Of course you must have aspirin. It will ease your poor head and send you off to sleep too."

"But Mrs. Bumption keeps the aspirin."

"Not all of it," said Harriet. "Because I've got some in my bag here. You don't suppose that I travel anywhere without the greatest drug in the world. It doesn't matter whether you've got nerves through flirting, or indigestion through cocktails, or whether you've been knocked down by a jealous rival, aspirin is the stuff to take, and you're going to take it. And if you like, I'll go out and tell Mrs. Bumption I've given you some."

"She'll give notice and leave. And then Bumption will leave." The baron made a humorous noise to imitate sobbing.

"She won't leave if I stay," said Harriet. "She'll never leave me alone in the field—of her own accord, I mean. Here now!" She had unscrewed the phial. "You'll want some water, won't you? You must sit up a tiny bit. Oh! What a funny millionaire and strong man you are! This yacht of yours is pitching, you know."

Harriet became more than a nurse; she became a mother to him. It was the mother that shook his pillow while he sat up; and the eyes gazing at him as he swallowed and drank were the eyes of a mother—sympathetic and sternly, sharply watchful, and superior and teasing. Her eyes were saying: "What a silly child to go and get itself knocked down!"

But the mother was shot through with the girl who had cast off the fur coat in order to display herself in an evening frock. The girl was rapidly permitting within herself an honest affection for Lord Furber. She liked him now because of his broad, generously-accepting mind. A native impudence had led her to visit him, uninvited, in his own fur coat. He had shown not the least sign of resentment at her self-possessed effrontery. He had even found pleasure in the sight of her wearing his entirely unsuitable fur coat.

And, far more important, he had not resented her inexcusable attempt to cozen the wireless operator and change the destination of the yacht. He had seen the incident simply and benevolently, ignoring her naughtiness. She had wanted to go to Rome, and he would let her go to Rome. He had imaginatively understood the force of her tremendous desire for clothes, and had decreed that she should have clothes. There was no meanness in him. He might be a brute, but he was not a mean brute. Thinking of all that her intimate old friend, his wife, had related to her, she began to suspect that there might be two sides to the disturbing story of his domestic life—such as it was. She felt happy in the singular fact that she had been carried off in the yacht.

"What was that about a jealous rival?" Lord Furber murmured the question as he lay back on the smoothed pillow, conscious of the taste of aspirin in his mouth.

"Nothing," said Harriet. "Go to sleep. Dressing comfortable?"

He seemed to snigger, magnanimously. He was not a man to pick up and critically examine every chance, impulsive word that slipped out of a woman's mouth; not he. He would treat women as women. Yes, she would simply love being his confidential secretary.

He settled himself in the bunk, while she restored the phial of aspirin to her bag. She was happy in appreciating and in being appreciated.

There was a quiet knock at the door. Harriet answered it.

"Who was that?" Lord Furber asked, when she had shut the door again. He had not heard the voices.

"Mr. Sutherland"

"Oh! I thought he always went to bed and snored in times of crisis," remarked the baron.

"He's just going to bed. But he wanted to know first how you were getting on."

"Yes, I should say he did. It's to his interest to keep me alive. If I'd gone and died on him he'd have looked a bit soft, wouldn't he? . . . Manslaughter at the best, Nobody could say he was acting in self-defence."

"No," Harriet agreed, smiling, and anxious to soothe. "Well, good night."

"I say!" the baron imperiously called her back. "Ye can do something for me now—at once. Ye know my secretaries have no hours. At least the only limit is twenty-four."

"Quite. I quite understand," said the new secretary eagerly.

"Well. Catch Sutherland before he goes to bed again."

"Yes. What about? What am I to say to him?"

"Spin him the yarn. Tell him the tale. Put him in a good temper about me. I want him to wake up well-disposed towards me to-morrow morning. Say I've treated ye throughout with the greatest respect, and never had any evil designs on ye. Say I didn't deserve to be knocked down."

"Oh! he knows that now."

"Anyhow, tell him I forgive him. No ill-will at all. Tell him I think very highly of him as a City financier. Tell him I knew nowt about his luggage being brought on board. I didn't, till it was too late. That was one of

Veruda's bits of embroidery on the bare scheme. Very pretty and thoughtful of course, but we should ha' been better if we'd left it out. Wants a bit of explaining, that luggage does. Scheme was wild enough without it. Still——"

"But what's the point?"

"Point!" cried the baron, sitting straight up with one bound of his torso. "Point! I've got to get something out o' that chap. That's why he's here. I never wanted in all me born days to get anything out of anybody as much as I want to get something out of him. I'd sooner lose every penny of all my millions than I'd fail with Sutherland. I could always make more millions, but if I fail with Sutherland, millions of money won't be any use to me. Got it?"

"Yes," Harriet softly answered.

The baron's tone was so serious, so sincere, so passionate, so startlingly violent that Harriet knew at once that she was on the very edge of the mystery of the strange proceedings of the *Vanguard*. And she thrilled with a delighted expectancy. She foresaw hours of marvellous excitation. She was happier, perhaps, than she had ever been in her life.

"And I——" the baron's voice was raised again.

She stopped him with a gesture.

"Will you please remember you've just had a dose of aspirin, and I want you to go to sleep. If you go on like this, how can you hope to go to sleep?"

"All right!" The baron was obedient to her counsel and lay back. "Run along and do as I tell ye." His voice was now tired.

"Just let me know first exactly what it is you want to get out of Mr. Sutherland," said Harriet, with an air of casualness.

"Have ye gone stark, staring mad?" the baron asked sleepily, with shut eyes.

"No; I'm only asking for information which of course I must have."

"Well, ye won't have it. Get away and carry out instructions." The baron still spoke sleepily, half-humorously.

"I'll get away," Harriet answered negligently, even superiorly. "But either you'll tell me what I ought to know, or I shan't carry out instructions. I absolutely refuse to be your confidential secretary if you won't be confidential with me."

"I shan't tell ye, and ye're nowt but an impudent wench."

"Very well. I resign my post."

Lord Furber sat tempestuously up again.

"Go to—the Five Towns!" he shouted.

She inquired, with exasperating calmness:

"Why the Five Towns?"

"Because they're worse than hell, Hull and Halifax! You're dismissed On the spot."

CHAPTER XX

THE SNACK

SEPTIMIUS SUTHERLAND rose early, and his freshness matched the freshness of the morning. For although he had had a disturbed night, he had contrived to get quite a fair amount of sleep, sleep being one of his specialties. If he was proud of being a 'blue' he was also proud of his Napoleonic skill in composing himself to slumber at nearly any suitable moment. He had slept well before knocking Lord Furber down, and, callously, he had slept well afterwards, even though his cabin was impregnated with the odour of the aseptic which had been employed upon Lord Furber's damaged head.

Further, being aboard a yacht, he had dressed for the part, as well as he could, in white flannels and shoes and the rich jacket which his University blue-ship entitled him to wear, together with a yachting cap offered to him by an eager junior steward.

The sun had lately risen upon a calmer Mediterranean, whose various shades harmonised with Septimius's jacket.

The decks of the *Vanguard* had already been swabbed down, and now many hands, in fatigue-overalls of yellow, were busy here and there polishing her endless brass. Not one of the hands seemed to be in the least preoccupied by the astonishing events of the night. Their day's programme was proceeding precisely as usual, and they were chatting quietly among themselves about the diurnal matters which constituted the main interest of their lives.

The scene mightily pleased Mr. Sutherland. He loved order, routine, tidiness, cleanliness; and it delighted him to think that whatever might happen on board, the regularity of the yacht's toilette could never be disturbed. Reflecting upon certain defects which he constantly noticed in the functioning of his own household, he wished that all house-mistresses could take a course of study in the house-keeping of a really smart yacht such as the *Vanguard*.

In short, Mr. Sutherland physically, morally and spiritually, was at his best, his most philosophic, his most sagacious. He strolled aft, on the drying promenade deck, along the mahogany façade of the deck-houses, and under cover of the boat-deck above. At the after extremity of the deck-houses the boat-deck overhung in a huge semi-circle, beneath which was the stairway leading down from the promenade deck to the main-deck, with a considerable amount of sheltered space on either hand for lounge-chairs, occasional-tables and flower-stands. Contemplatively he lit a cigarette, the heavenly, unequalled first cigarette of the day, and stared absently, as if absorbed in the manu-facture of profound wisdom, at the white wake of the yacht. In fact, he was saying to himself:

"Why have I never had a yacht? Is not a yacht the most perfect, self-contained, self-sufficient organism in the world?"

Then his thin nose detected the wonderful smell of first-rate coffee, which reminded him that he was both thirsty and hungry. The smell came from the boat-deck above. Then he heard the faint murmur of voices—not the voices of deck-hands nor even of officers, but a deep voice of civil authority and a woman's voice. Mr.

Sutherland was tempted upwards, and he was also perturbed, though pleasantly perturbed. He was a little disappointed that others had left their beds before himself, and he felt bound to prove to those others that he too could get up early and spry after any sort of a wild night. He hesitated a moment, then quitted the shelter and braced his shaven cheeks to the tonic wind of morning, and began slowly to climb the companion leading to the top-deck.

He paused, listening to some dialogue:

"Then ye aren't my confidential secretary any more?"

"No."

"Sure?"

"Of course I'm sure."   (Rather sharply.)

"Ye'll miss a lot o' fun."

"Perhaps I shall.   But what I have said I have said."

"Yes.   That's what I used to say myself once."

"I suppose you won't let me call at Rome now for clothes?"

"Well, don't ye go and suppose any such thing, Harriet. I said ye should have fal-lals from Rome, and ye shall.   I arranged all that after ye left me last night.   What's one secretary more or less to me?"   A laugh.

"Oh! Hurrah! I won't be your secretary, but I don't mind helping you a bit if you want me to very much."

It occurred to Mr. Sutherland—and not too soon— that eavesdropping was an improper pursuit for the righteous.   Also he was aware within himself of an unpleasant spasm of jealousy.   Those two above were extraordinarily friendly.   And Miss Perkins's Christian name had been used in a tone of easy intimacy which was surely unusual after an acquaintance of scarcely twelve hours.

Deciding that he must survey the scene for himself, Mr. Sutherland proceeded up the stairs.   He beheld two persons seated at a table behind the wireless cabin, from both sides of which gleaming white wind-screens had been rigged. Lord Furber, with a patch on the back of his tousled head, was wearing a more joyous dressing-gown then Septimius had ever dreamed of. Miss Perkins was still enveloped in the baronial fur coat. On the table were a silver coffee-service, cups and saucers, rolls and butter, and a box of cigarettes.

Lord Furber jumped up at the splendid sight of Mr. Sutherland.

"Morning, Sutherland," said he. "Glad to see ye looking so well. I hope ye'll be glad to hear that I'm no worse for my fall last night."

"This fellow," said Septimius to himself, "may be a millionaire, but he is a gentleman—besides being a sound actor." And aloud: "I'm immensely relieved."

"I thought ye would be," said Lord Furber with a peculiar emphasis, and glanced at Harriet, who glanced at Septimius.

"Rayner!" his lordship cried out fiercely.

A steward appeared with the magical celerity of a conjuring trick.

"'Nother cup."

"Yes, my lord."

"And a chair."

"Yes, my lord.

"Now sit down and join us," Lord Furber urged, still standing. "Have my chair. Yes, have it. I insist." He walked about. "Coffee and rolls. Rolls fresh baked on board this morning. Don't be alarmed. This isn't breakfast. This is only a preliminary snack."

Lord Furber in his walk now met Mr. Sutherland and shook his hand.

"Chin a bit wanky. Can't think how I happened to fall on it. But it's better than it was."

Then the baron forced Septimius into the chair. From the assured mastery of his tone and gestures nobody could be in any doubt as to who was the leading authority on board the *Vanguard*.

"Morning—Harriet," said Mr. Sutherland boldly but calmly.

"Good morning—Seppie," replied Miss Perkins after an infinitesimal pause.

Two stewards appeared, one with a chair and the other with a cup and saucer. Lord Furber sat down. The trio had the air of being cronies of long standing. Cronies of any standing at all, however, they were not.

Lord Furber, as usual, was absorbed in himself: which no crony in the presence of other cronies ought to be. He was thinking of the adventure just begun and about to develop in a manner which might or might not succeed in saving him from a disastrous defeat, and which at the worst had mitigated and would still further mitigate the profound secret boredom of his splendid and opulent existence.

Harriet Perkins, absorbed as usual in herself, dwelt happily, triumphantly, on the presence of two very important men both of whom had yielded to the force and the attractiveness of her individuality. She had measured her power against the renowned millionaire, and had so far beaten him; while the magnate Septimius merely adored her and was her private property.

As for Septimius, absorbed as usual in himself, he reflected that his situation in the yacht on that lovely Mediterranean morning amid circumstances extremely ideal, was due solely to some mad, audacious, imaginative, unscrupulous and entirely incomprehensible scheme of

Lord Furber's (renowned in the City for his inventive daring). He knew that he had been kidnapped, but he knew also that he could never prove it. And on the whole he rather liked the quandary in which destiny had involved him, especially as Miss Perkins was part of it. He did not admit that he was far gone in love with Miss Perkins. The dangerous word 'love' was not in his dictionary. How could it be in the respectable, bowdlerized dictionary of a middle-aged gentleman satisfactorily married and the father of two quite adult daughters? He admitted only that his joy in the nearness of Miss Perkins was extreme, and different from any other sensation of his career as a male—and that if he had not chanced to obtain the sensation free of charge, he would have been ready to pay any price for it. True, he sniffed distant peril in the air—a pleasing peril, but still a peril. The peril was connected with Miss Perkins, not with Lord Furber. He blandly considered himself to be the equal of Lord Furber in any contest of duplicity and chicane which Lord Furber might force upon him. And he was well aware that in the probably imminent affray he possessed a marked advantage in that whereas Lord Furber no doubt wanted something from him, he wanted nothing from Lord Furber.

He decided that the polite affray might as well begin at once.

"Furber," said he, at his blandest and most modestly amiable, "I really don't know how to apologize to you for my carelessness in getting myself left behind here like this. It looks as if I was forcing myself on your magnificent hospitality. And the worst of it is"—he gave a slight, half-humorous smile—"I'm enjoying it enormously. I ought to regret it, but somehow I can't."

"My dear fellow!" replied the occupant of the gorgeous

135

dressing-gown, with rough geniality, "I'm the one that ought to apologize. I can't think how it happened. Infernal carelessness of one of my chaps, of course! The one bright spot in the muddle is that through some more muddling your luggage is here. But I suppose that was the hotel people. I hear ye were leaving Naples last night——"

"How did *you* hear that?"

"Don't know," murmured the baron, after slight hesitation. "I expect it was Count Veruda who told me, or told someone who told me . . . And as ye were leaving, the hotel concierge jumped to the conclusion that you were leaving in the yacht."

"Yes, no doubt that was it. He must have forgotten to give a glance at my luggage labels. However, it *was* my intention to leave Naples last night, and apparently I did leave Naples last night. And here I am."

"Well," said the baron. "I'm glad to have ye here, and very sorry indeed if I've put ye to any inconvenience."

"Not at all. I had three rather important appointments in town for to-morrow afternoon. At least they seemed important last night, but this morning, sailing along like this, nothing seems important—except what's going on in this really wonderful yacht of yours." Mr. Sutherland's glance met that of the baron for a moment. The baron glanced aside.

"I hope ye'll stay with me as long as ye can," said the baron.

"Oh! I will, thanks very much," answered Septimius with surprising enthusiasm. "If I might be allowed to make use of your wireless."

"Sure," said Lord Furber, and yelled: "Rayner!"

Rayner appeared.

"My lord?"

"Send Mr. Tunnicliff to me."

"Yes, my lord."

"Yes," Harriet put in suddenly; "it's all very well for Mr. Sutherland. *He's* got his luggage. And don't we all know it!" She gazed as if enraptured at his fine raiment. "But poor me!"

"Yes!" laughed Lord Furber. "Poor Harriet hasn't a clout to her back, except my fur coat."

Mr. Sutherland had again a sense of disturbance. 'Harriet.' And the pair had exchanged a peculiar smile, as though they had come to some mysterious understanding in the night hours or at dawn. Mr. Sutherland did not like these phenomena at all. It immensely annoyed him that anybody at all (except of course himself) should have come to a mysterious understanding with the enchantress in the fur coat. And he hated that the fur coat she wore should belong to Lord Furber. If it had been his own fur coat he would have been happy. But then Mr. Sutherland never travelled with a fur coat. He saw that he ought to do so.

"My lord?"

The Honourable Luke John Tunnicliff had arrived on the boat-deck. Harriet offered him a delicious smile, which he received with a blush. Then Harriet looked defiantly at the baron, as if saying: "See how friendly we are, your secretary and your ex-confidential secretary."

"Tunnicliff," said Lord Furber. "Will you please tell your cousin that he is to send off any messages that Mr. Sutherland gives him." Mr. Tunnicliff gravely nodded.

"And what about me?" asked Harriet.

"And any of Miss Perkins's too—of course," Lord Furber added.

"Not that I shall have any to send off," said Harriet.

"And any of Miss Perkins's too," Lord Furber repeated.

Mr. Tunnicliff bowed again and departed.

"The wireless is yours," said Lord Furber, heartily generous, to Mr. Sutherland. "At any time."

"Oh, there's no hurry, thanks," Mr. Sutherland replied calmly. "A few hours more or less—what does it matter?"

Harriet, having lighted a cigarette, arose and leaned over the rail.

"The sea's rather yellow here, isn't it?" said she.

Mr. Sutherland arose and joined her.

"How very interesting!" said he. "All one's life one has heard of the yellow Tiber, and here it is. See! We've passed the mouth already. That must be Civita Vecchia over there." He pointed.

"Then where's Ostia?"

"Oh! Ostia must be behind us."

"Behind us!" she turned. "Lord Furber, we've passed Ostia!" Her gaze was a reproach; it was a charge of bad faith.

"Rayner!" yelled the baron.

"My lord?"

"Ask the skipper to speak to me at once."

"Yes, my lord. Afraid he's turned in, my lord. He was on the bridge most of the night."

"Get him."

"Yes, my lord."

Lord Furber sprang up and walked about, muttering to himself and to the world at large. Having regard to the vocabulary which he was employing, Harriet turned sharply back to the rail, and glanced privately, with amusement, at Mr. Sutherland. Her wish to share her malicious amusement with him gave Mr. Sutherland much satisfaction and quite extinguished his jealousy. They both continued to examine the surface of the sea with exaggerated ease, as tactful guests always will when trouble is afoot between the owner and the captain.

Captain Slapser knew his owner and came hurrying aft with as much speed as dignity would allow. Mr. Sutherland noticed out of the tail of his eye that the supreme navigating authority was very summarily clothed.

"Joe!" cried the baron, before the captain was quite near him.

The captain, gloomy, resentful, and apprehensive, said naught to this most improper greeting.

Said the owner:

"I thought we were calling at Ostia."

"No, my lord," answered the captain, with a demeanour of unconvincing surprise.

"But haven't you had an official message from Rome? I was told so."

"I did have a message. But there's nobody in Rome has the right to give orders to a British yacht—and flying the blue ensign, too. My orders from you were Genoa."

Miss Perkins joyously nudged Mr. Sutherland in the side, which gave him still further satisfaction; he permitted himself roguishly to return the nudge. At the same moment he thought, frightened, of his middle-age and of his wife.

"Why didn't you ask me?" Lord Furber fiercely inquired.

"Your lordship was ill in bed. I did mention it to Mr. Bumption, my lord, and he thought——"

"You mean Mrs. Bumption thought," Lord Furber stopped him. Something on the surface of the Mediterranean attracted the baron's attention. With lightning quickness he said: "Look here! See that?"

A submarine was emerging from the depths.

"Yes, my lord."

"Well, what d'ye think of it, Joe? It's Italian navy, that is. What d'ye think it's here for?" He put a terrible, slow sweetness into his powerful voice. "Take my advice, Joe, and put back to Ostia as fast as ye can. And try not to tell me anything more about your friend Mrs. Bumption."

"Yes, my lord."

"And I say, Joe. We aren't on the course for Genoa here. You don't hug the shore when you're going from Naples to Genoa. What's the meaning of it?"

"Well, my lord, I wasn't sure what you'd decide. So I kept her in a bit. I thought ye'd tell me."

"Well, I've told ye."

Captain Slapser, cowed and furious, went forrard to his bridge. Soon the yacht swerved as it were savagely to port.

The baron laughed aloud. His guests, reassured, answered the signal by turning round to him. The baron winked at them. The submarine was steaming north-west, ignoring the *Vanguard*.

"Well, what d'ye think of it?" asked the baron.

"We shan't say," said Harriet. "Shall we, Mr. Sutherland?"

"No, we shan't."

"Ye think I was a bit rough on the feller?"

"We shan't say."

"No, we shan't."

"Anyhow the submarine was a godsend," grinned the baron. "Hell's delight!"

And he laughed again and more loudly.

"Now, what are those?" asked Mr. Sutherland half an hour later, when the *Vanguard's* anchor chain was rattling down into ten fathoms about a mile and a half from the shore. He pointed to a procession of small motor boats which were heading for the yacht.

Lord Furber, without answering, disappeared.

CHAPTER XXI

CHIFFONS

THE motor-craft, as they approached the yacht, showed themselves to be nothing better than jack-boats with engines in them, unkempt, shabby, nondescript launches such as abound in ports and are hired out for all kinds of occasional use; manned by dirty and untidy fellows who evidently had no feeling whatever for the smartness of the sea, and who no doubt regarded the spick and span condition of the great yacht and everything appertaining to it as the vagary of incomprehensible British madmen who paraded the ocean for fun. One of the boats, the leader, was less small than the others; indeed it proved to be quite large.

An increasing number of high, excited Latin voices rose across the water from the boats to the lofty upper deck of the yacht. The arrival of the procession seemed to stir the stodgy British phlegm of the yacht's crew. A couple of officers leaned peering and smiling from the starboard end of the bridge; and seamen and stewards lolled over the rail here and there and condescendingly grinned outright at the chattering, gesticulating persons in the boats. In each boat was a pile of cargo hidden beneath ragged sail-cloths. The noisy exhausts of the three primitive engines added to the din. The boats passed along the starboard side of the yacht, skirted her stern and bore up on the port side where a gangway was dropped from the lower deck to meet them. Cries, shouts, shrieks, bursts of laughter: the whole amounting almost to hysteria; and growls from the steersmen and engineers and from the deck-hands engaged in fending the frowsy boats off the *Vanguard's* virginal white paint. It was apparent that there were quite a dozen women of various ages in the boats, that in fact the majority of the passengers were women with some pretensions to fashion, style and charm; some were beyond question lovely. The curiosity of Harriet and Mr. Sutherland was keenly aroused. But before direct communication could be established between the yacht and the boats, Lord Furber hurried back, the breakfast gong melodiously sounded, and the baron some-what forcibly led his guests downstairs towards the dining-saloon. Septimius and Harriet would both have preferred to stay where they were; they both thought that breakfast proper was following much too closely on the snack; but they could not protest; they could only furtively glance at one another. After all it is the host who settles the hours of meals in a yacht as in a house, and guests are not supposed to be inquisitive about what may be presumed to be the host's private affairs. Septimius and Harriet submitted, and the enormous cacophony was gradually lost to their ears.

But when the doors of the dining-saloon were opened at the end of the meal (which did not excite in the guests the interest that so pretentious and costly a repast deserved to excite—possibly because of the strange absence of Bumption, the head steward), the same cacophony, but perhaps still more strident, met the ears.

"Well," said Lord Furber at the doorway, "I reckon this is the best I can do for ye, Harriet."

He waved his hand, with an air of casual disdain, in the direction of the lounge, which was full of very vivacious women, with the Honourable Luke John in the midst, conducting as it were the orchestra of tongues. The Honourable Luke John made a sign and spoke in Italian and the hubbub was magically stilled, and the ladies at once put on that expression of timidity, defiance, and expectancy which is proper to the faces of the humble in the presence of the mighty, and to the faces of sellers in the presence of prospective purchasers.

Harriet gave a squeal quite Italian in intensity. Every couch and every chair in the big lounge was covered with all descriptions and varieties of feminine attire. There were day frocks, evening frocks, sports dresses, jumpers, jackets, cloaks, shawls, wraps, stoles, furs, gloves, stockings, shoes, hats, slippers, negligées, matinées, and what not and what not; together with lingerie, from *chemises de nuit* to cami-knickers, displayed with an enchanting and truly Latin shamelessness. A profusion of stuffs! An astounding multiplicity of contrasted colours. The delicate essence of the salons of a dozen couturières, modistes, furriers, and shoemakers! Dazzling! Perilous! Intoxicating! Irresistible! The sack of Rome brought up to date! Harriet's mouth happened to be open after the squeal. It remained open. She tried to speak; and could not, so complete was her realization of the inadequacy of language.

Mr. Sutherland could not conceal his jealous amaze. The baron could not conceal his pride in a unique achievement. The Honourable Luke John could not conceal his illusion that he alone had made all the clothes and was alone responsible for their presence in the lounge. The handmaidens could not conceal their glorious anticipations of vast profits to their employers and proportionate percentages to themselves. It was a scene entirely unprecedented in the history of yachting.

"How *did* you do it?" Harriet exclaimed weakly at last.

She had a wondrous sensation of happiness and exaltation. She felt as she might have felt after the finest champagne and plenty of it. Often, in the hotels of great capitals, she had caused her bedroom to be littered with tempting finery brought to her on approval by the sirens of the shops; she had known the felicity of damning the financial consequences in a debauch of buying. But this incredible maritime experience reduced all previous experiences of the kind to nothing, to less than nothing. She comprehended now that the baron really was a millionaire, a milliardaire, with a generosity of imagination worthy of his uncountable resources.

"Well," said the baron, "the fact is I wanted my fur coat for my own back. And I got busy with my correspondent in Rome and told him to get busy, and he's a man who knows what getting busy is. He must have been running around Rome pretty early this morning—the moment the shops opened in fact. It isn't twenty minutes from Rome to Ostia in a fast car; he had three or four cars waiting, and those launches waiting, too. All they had to do then was to wait for the yacht to drop anchor. It was very simple. Everything *is* very simple when the word is passed that money doesn't matter. And I never do let money matter."

"But I'm bound to let money matter," said Harriet. "I can't afford the hundredth part of these things."

"Ye needn't," replied the baron. "Ye won't get any bills."

"But I can't accept clothes from you, my friend. Surely you must see that."

"Why can't ye accept clothes from me? Of course ye

can accept clothes from me, and, by Jove, ye will too! I want my fur coat back. It's all owing to me ye haven't got any clothes. Well, here's yer clothes. Choose 'em and be hanged to ye!"

The Honourable Tunnicliff looked at the carpet. Mr. Sutherland coughed. The sirens, though they understood little or naught of the conversation, began to tremble for their percentages.

Harriet divested herself of the fur coat and Lord Furber put it on over the splendour of his dressing-gown, and then took it off again.

"You are quite right," said she, laughing. "I was being absurdly conventional. Nobody ought to be conventional with a millionaire."

And she abandoned herself to the orgy of fashion, and the sirens began to coo round about her.

CHAPTER XXII

THE QUEEN

THE chief actress, with a couple of the sirens, was hidden behind the doors of Lord Furber's private state-room, which adjoined the lounge and which was being used as a *salon d'essayage.*

Expectation in the lounge! The sirens there were either mute or whispering low to one another. One or two were busy displaying to better advantage the creations under their charge. The Honourable Tunnicliff kept an interpreter's eye upon them; for the moment they were his flock. They were all self-conscious, and little Mr. Tunnicliff himself was self-conscious, owing to the strong presence of the baron and Mr. Sutherland. And these two also were self-conscious, owing to the presence of the sirens so tittering, posing, and provocative. The baron would have given half a million not to be self-conscious, but he could not achieve the natural, and the louder he talked to Septimius, and the more peremptory he was in putting absurd questions to Mr. Tunnicliff for translation into Italian to the sirens, the further he receded from naturalness.

Both the magnates were restless; and they were bored, and inclined to place women lower than ever in the scale of reasonable beings. Already, before her disappearance, Harriet had dissipated an immense amount of time in darting about from one attraction to another like a butterfly in a meadow, glancing at everything and properly examining nothing. Apparently the brilliance and variety of the exhibition had deprived her of the power of concentration, of the sense of order, and of the maturity of her years; she had gone back again to the unreflecting, giggling gaiety of early girlhood. Even Mr. Sutherland had begun to suspect that her more solid qualities were perhaps inferior to her dazzling charm and to think that if impossibly she were his wife he might venture to offer her a few mild hints about deportment. She would still have been hovering in the lounge between shoes, furs, petticoats, sports-coats and shawls, if Lord Furber had not picked up an evening dress at random and told her abruptly to retire and get into it without further delay. The dress happened to be green. "Here! You like green!" he had said, and had thrown the dress at her. "Don't run off till you have seen me in it," she had warned the magnates. Not that they would any-how have run off, either of them. They might be bored and impatient, but they were as anxious as even Mr. Tunnicliff to see the show, and their legs would have refused to carry them out of the lounge.

Lord Furber lit a cigarette. Mr. Sutherland would not smoke. Lord Furber finished the cigarette. Lord Furber threw the cigarette-end into a copper bowl of flowers. And still the doors of the state-room did not open.

"Good God!" he cried. "At this rate we shall be lying at anchor here for a week."

"They always take twice as long as you'd think any-body could take," said Septimius mildly. "They lose the sense of time. This is the sort of thing that makes cynics say that all women are alike." But he uttered these cynical sentences with benevolence and charity.

Then the doors parted, and Harriet, stepping forward in green, was disclosed to the company. And though she was instantly the mark of every gaze, she showed not the least trace of self-consciousness. The two sirens behind her seemed to be saying to the three men: "Acknowledge that this spectacle is marvellous. Acknowledge that this moment is supreme." And Harriet, with proud, lifted chin, seemed to be saying: "I am here to be admired. Admire me. I was never more alive and enchanting than I am now. The sensations which I can inspire in you are the justification of my whole existence. And if you are not thrilled and delighted you are blocks of stone and wood, and worthy to be spurned and kicked into the sea."

The males, however, responded in a manner more than sufficiently satisfactory to save them from being kicked into the sea. Lord Furber clapped his hands. Mr. Sutherland said "Ah!" with as much fervour as though he had eaten a perfect strawberry. The Honourable Tunnicliff blushed.

And there were murmurs of approbation from sirens who were nevertheless hinting to one another criticisms of the work of a rival house. All memory of boredom and impatience was blotted out, as one sunny morning will blot out the memory of a week's rain.

"Well?" the queen on her throne demanded.

"Have it!" the baron replied.

The two attendant sirens smiled happily. The other sirens eagerly prepared to take other confections into the privacy of the state-room. But the queen on her throne would not yet budge; she desired more worship.

"You don't say a great deal," said she. No reply. "Have you ever been to a dressmaker's in all your lives?" she demanded.

CHAPTER XXIII

JEALOUSY

WHEN, after another very considerable interval, Miss
Harriet Perkins emerged once again from his lordship's
state-sitting-room into the lounge, she wore a yachting
costume of blue and white, with a trifle of a hat, and white
and blue shoes, to correspond. It was not an authentic
yachting costume; but Lord Furber had given special
wireless orders to his agent that a yachting costume should
be included in the display, and this specimen of attire was
the best imitation of a British or French yachting costume
that could be got together in half an hour in Rome, Rome
not being in the least a yachting city as, for instance, Stock-
holm, Amsterdam and Copenhagen are.

And it was a pretty good imitation. The dressmakers
of Rome, like the dressmakers of Buenos Ayres, Rio, and
New York, visit Paris once or twice a year, and they take
back with them every time the newest spirit of Paris together
with copies of the newest secret trade periodicals.

The attire was delicious upon Harriet. Few would
have noticed that a button needed shifting and a sleeve
adjusting, and nobody except Harriet herself was aware
that the shoes were too small for her feet. The second
couple of sirens, though cognisant of the faults, were
extremely enthusiastic about the total effect. They saw
the costume, as did Harriet, not as it actually was, but as

it should, could, and would be after an hour's corrective work on it. And Harriet shared their enthusiasm.

Yet the apparition from the state-room was received in the lounge with melancholy and indifference.

Harriet was no longer a queen. She was no longer exercising the supreme social function of her sex, nor demonstrating that she had a right to be alive and to be spoilt and flattered and gifted with costly gifts. She was merely someone who was trying on new clothes. All the waiting sirens showed by their weary demeanour that they were sick of the sight of clothes and would not care if they never saw another woman's frock again. Even the couple attendant on Harriet for this particular *essayage* shed their enthusiasm in a moment, while Harriet felt sadly that clothes do not after all amount to much in the mysterious equation of life. Indeed Harriet wilted and seemed to shrivel, as one who has suddenly lost friendships or prestige. She felt humiliated and resentful. The eyes of everybody seemed to be asking the eyes of everybody else: "What's the use of going on with this silly game any more?"

The explanation was that neither Lord Furber nor Mr. Sutherland happened to be in the lounge. They had deserted and left the garments in the lounge without a decent excuse. So also the Honourable Luke. The Honourable Luke, however, returned himself to the lounge after a brief interval. But his importance in the scheme of things was insufficient to produce any noticeable improvement in the lackadaisical attitude of the sirens.

"Where is Lord Furber?" Harriet asked sharply.

"In the dining-saloon, madam."

"And Mr. Sutherland?" Still more sharply.

"I think he's up in the wireless cabin, madam. Can I do anything?"

K   153

"No thanks."

Harriet was now angry. She went out of the lounge on to the deck.

The Honourable Luke's glance, following her, said:

"Well, anyhow, empress, you did offer to kiss me and I declined. So it's no use you attempting to come the cinema star over me."

She ran up to the wireless cabin, the door of which was ajar. Mr. Sutherland was within, but alone.

"What are you doing here?" she asked impetuously.

"Oh!" ejaculated Septimius, admiring, wonderstruck, at the spectacle of her in the yachting costume.

Now, Harriet had by this time actually forgotten that she was wearing the yachting costume. But Septimius's monosyllable and the liquid gaze of his blue eyes reminded her of the fact, restored her sense of sovereignty, renewed the lost conviction that she had a mission to perform in life, and determined her to be ruthless in the exercise of power. And did all these things in the fraction of a second.

"I said, what are you doing here?" she repeated more harshly than before."

"I'm going to get off some wireless messages," Septimius apologetically replied.

"Why just now? You know I wanted you to see these frocks?"

"And I do see one of them!" said Septimius with an impressive bland fervour.

"Yes. And I suppose you expect me to run after you with my frocks."

"The truth is," said Septimius, very placatory and yet dignified, "our friend suggested that I should do my wirelessing immediately. Difficult to ignore such a suggestion from one's host, you know, dear lady. Especially when one's host is in a—er—certain mood."

"When I last saw you I thought you two were on the edge of having a quarrel."

"Not at all. I have never quarrelled with anyone in my life."

"What do *you* know about Lallers?"

"Nothing."

"Nothing?"

"Well, nothing except the name, and the last balance-sheet. You see, it's a limited company, and you know that part of my professional business is to keep an eye on limited companies. Nothing else."

"I don't believe you," said Harriet, deviating some-what from maidenly politeness. "You're hiding some-thing from me. And what's this about wirelessing? You can't wireless yourself. Where's the operator?"

"I don't know. Furber said he would be here. And he isn't here. I fear the organization of this yacht is not all that it might be."

"The organization of that dressmakers' display was not too bad," said Harriet. "But perhaps you think you could have done it better."

"Not at all."

"And you said last night that the dinner was not so badly organized either."

"True. But, did you notice the breakfast just now? The eggs, for instance! The service! And the service in my cabin really leaves a lot to be desired. It was so last night, and it's the same again this morning."

"Mrs. Bumption is at the bottom of all this," said Harriet, suddenly meditative, after a pause.

"I beg your pardon, sir," said Tunnicliff the operator,

appearing in the doorway. But he spoke in a tone which signified: "You ought to beg mine." His nostrils were superbly disdainful.

"Lord Furber kindly told me that I might get some messages off with your assistance," Mr. Sutherland said.

"Won't they do a bit later, Sep? I want you downstairs now." Harriet murmured. And, her demeanour magically altering, she presented Septimius with an exquisite smile so effective that his very spine melted like a candle in the warmth of the tropic sun.

"Certainly," said Septimius with eagerness.

Harriet looked through the wireless operator as though he had been transparent, and in triumph led away her captive, who completely ignored the wireless operator.

But when the captor and the captive reached the lounge together, the former loosed her hold of the latter, and with no word of excuse to him whisked into the dining-saloon and banged the doors after her. And there was Lord Furber seated solitary at the vast oval table. The baron was staring gloomily, even glumly, at the polished surface of the table. He looked up at the invading Harriet, and then looked down again, taking no further notice of the yachting costume.

"This," said Harriet, dropping on to a chair exactly opposite the baron. "This will not do."

No reply.

She repeated:

"This will not do."

No reply. Harriet proceeded:

"And to think that you are the great Lord Furber! This is the millionaire and the engineering genius and the grand general titan and panjandrum sitting here in front of me. Not to mention my host." She spoke cheerfully, gaily, with the superior smile of a cat addressing a worm. "You put yourself to a tremendous lot of trouble, and expense—though I don't count that, with you—to get enough fal-lals, as you call them, to fit out a whole beauty chorus. It isn't as if I wanted them. I didn't. I was frightfully happy in your fur coat. I was only having them to please you. And you only took the fur coat from me because you knew I simply loved wearing it. You bring all these poor little Italian creatures here, and you make me try on, and as soon as I've tried on one dress you run off and I have to look for you everywhere! And not only that—you tell Mr. Sutherland to make himself scarce, too. I wonder you didn't clear out the little Tunnicliff as well, while you were about it. Who do you think I was trying those clothes on for? Myself? Did you imagine I'm one of the doll-women you're so fond of? You thought you'd impress me and everybody else by your display, and your power, and your will, and all the Aladdin-lamp business and so on. You only did it for that. And then after you've seen only one dress on me——"

"Ye're repeating yeself," said Lord Furber to the table.

Miss Perkins rode over him imperturbably.

"And why did you do it? Because you were vexed. Because you were jealous. Because I hadn't asked *you* if you liked the dress. Well, I did it on purpose, just to see how you'd behave, if you want to know. And see how you have behaved! I've told you before you're spoilt and impossible. And so you are. You think because you are a millionaire and a personage you are entitled to behave as you choose and nobody must say anything on pain of being frowned at by the great panjandrum. And you choose to behave like a silly boy!"

157

Said Lord Furber:

"Every man is a boy."

"Oh! Is he!"

"And every girl is a woman," Lord Furber added.

"An epigram no doubt. But listen to me, my only millionaire. You can't put it over. You simply cannot put it over."

"Is that all—for the moment?" Lord Furber inquired. "If it is, I'll just tell ye a couple o' things. The first is, I'm not fond of doll-women. That was a downright lie, and ye knew when ye'd said it it was a thumper. And the second is, I came in here, partly because I was sick of waiting for ye, but much more because Mrs. Bumption wants to see me on urgent business, she sent me word. I'm expecting her in here every moment. How's that, miss?"

Harriet shook her head.

"Were you hurt and jealous or weren't you?"

"Yes. I was. But that was only because I knew ye'd be so d—d disappointed if I wasn't. Ye wanted me to be jealous. And ye wanted Sutherland to be jealous. And young Tunnicliff, too, I bet. Ye're a woman. I'm a boy. I like that dress. How's that?"

CHAPTER XXIV

THE PILLAR

THROUGH the service door Mrs. Bumption entered the dining-saloon, and beheld a baron who seemed to be humorously defying and spurning a youngish woman who in turn was humorously spurning and defying the baron.

Mrs. Bumption had arrived with a definite aim, and she did not mean to be hindered in her purpose by the presence of any other woman whatsoever. She walked towards the end of the table like a magnificent pillar—a pillar of society and its proper conventions. Her eyes glared. Her thin, straight nose twitched. Her lips were locked together. Her stout arms were crossed upon the broad surface of the apron which covered the major and more interesting shires of her bodily kingdom. She came slowly to a standstill; at last she was definitely motionless in a massive equilibrium. And now she so imposed upon the baron and Harriet that in the mighty disturbance of her mere advent, expected and duly heralded though it was, they forgot completely the friction of their private politics in waiting for her thunder. She had put the magnate and the unillustrious globe-trotting, hotel-haunting spinster on a level.

"I wish to give notice, my lord," said Mrs. Bumption, with majesty.

"Sorry to hear this, Mrs. Bumption," said the baron. "But why? What's amiss?"

"There's nothing amiss, as you may say, my lord," the pillar replied. "But the words as your lordship remarked about me this morning, or should I say, in the night while your lordship was in bed, cannot be stood."

"Remarks!" exclaimed the baron. "What remarks?"

"Well, my lord, your lordship gave out as it were that I'd been in the 'abit of running after your lordship. And this 'ere young lady was present to hear—not that I'd asked her to come in—though I was in charge of your lordship."

"But, did I really say any such thing?" The baron put this question direct to Harriet.

"I'm afraid you did," Harriet answered solemnly. "But of course your mind was wandering at the time. In fact, Mrs. Bumption said herself you were wandering."

"His lordship may have been wandering like in his mind," said Mrs. Bumption, "and I hope and trust you was, my lord. But they do say there's no smoke without fire, and my character's my character."

She spoke seriously as a woman profoundly convinced of her power over the romantic sex. She was not obese; she was not fifty; she was not ugly; she was not exasperatingly carping—she was the girl who for twenty years and more had held Mr. Bumption fast and fast by the tremendous attraction of her femininity.

She went on:

"And as I'm here, I'll say I don't hold with this yachting. I've known yachting lead young people astray, and I don't hold with it; and there's a lot of things in this yacht as I don't like, if your lordship will excuse me."

Her titanic frame immobile, she shifted her eyes from side to side, glancing first at the baron and then at the girl, and so to and fro several times: like a statue with movable painted orbs set in a carven face.

Lord Furber and Harriet had the same thought: namely, that here was a social situation which Lord Furber ought somehow to be able to deal with in a manner at once dignified and triumphant. Mrs. Bumption was nobody at all— the wife of a butler. Lord Furber was a high figure in the world; and he had arrived at the state of being a high figure in the world by reason of his brains. Mrs. Bumption had no brains worth mentioning. In every way she was mediocre or worse than mediocre. Moreover, she was dependent, whereas Lord Furber was just about as independent as any human being could be. Again, Lord Furber was accustomed to handling, for his own profit, many different kinds of people, while Mrs. Bumption had had but little occasion for diplomacy, and indeed disdained it. All the material and intellectual and social advantages were on one side; all the disadvantages on the other.

Yet Lord Furber could think of no effective method of engaging Mrs. Bumption in battle and defeating her. Harriet being present, he wanted to shine, and he could not shine. Mrs. Bumption outglared his diminished ray. And Harriet was there to witness his affliction and his humiliation. He was a great man; he knew that he was great and that he had earned his greatness; but the great man was being exposed and thrown down, and Harriet was there to see. Already she, Harriet, had severely criticized him, and he had not answered her. Mrs. Bumption's arrival had prevented him from answering Harriet.

Like a tiger enticed into a cage, he felt that fate was unkind to him. Rage began to rise in perilous, intoxicating vapour out of the depths of his mind. He was on the brink of doing something violent and silly, when Mrs. Bumption, stately, deliberate, implacable, turned round in the similitude now not of a pillar but of a ship going about, and left the dining-saloon by the door through which she had originally entered.

Surcease of hostilities! Lord Furber's dignity and reputation for brilliant manœuvring, if not definitely saved, was at any rate reprieved. The baron laughed, loud and uncouth, and waited to counter whatever Harriet might say. Harriet said nothing. Lord Furber could not bear the silence.

"That means I've lost Bumption," said he, at length, deciding that he would stand best with Harriet by squarely facing the facts.

"What of it?" said Harriet. "Bumption is only a habit."

Dash the chit! How clever she was! She had defined the relation in a word. He forgot that he had himself previously given her the word. He privately admitted, as he had admitted before, that a habit was just what Bumption was. But he would not admit it to her.

He said gravely and grandly:

"Bumption is my butler and he is devoted. Ye can't do without a devoted butler. What would happen to the house?"

"What *has* happened to the house?" Harriet demanded quickly.

"What d'ye mean?"

"Is your house open?"

"Yes."

"Anybody living there?"

"My wife."

"Doesn't she have to manage without Bumption?"

"Bumption always goes with *me*."

"And be hanged to your house, I suppose, so long as you aren't in it! That's just like you, that is! It seems quite natural to you, of course, to be the only person whose convenience has to be consulted. It would. You've lost Bumption for your wife as well as for yourself. Your wife doesn't matter. Any butler ought to be good enough for her. And now she'll have all the worry of getting a new butler who'll suit you, and all because you think it's funny to behave like a child. Why did you go out of your way to insult Mrs. Bumption this morning? Because it amused you and you thought you were perfectly entitled to do it, because you're so rich."

"Harriet, ye're repeating yeself. I've told ye once."

He smiled easily at the impudent girl. She looked delicious in the yachting costume (which his brains and his volition had procured for her). She had barely enough to live on. She had not denied that she could do nothing in the world. She possessed wit, but no practical faculties. And there she was behaving towards him as though she held in her frail hands all the cards of life. The spectacle of her was comic—far too comic to be taken seriously.

"What are you?" Harriet said venomously. "You're only a bladder—and Mrs. Bumption has pricked you."

Suddenly the baron lost his temper, and broke into vituperation, employing the vocabulary of his Five Towns picturesque youth. He had positively meant not to lose his temper, but now that he had in fact lost it, he enjoyed the sensation—as always. Harriet stood up in exasperating, gentle glee.

"Ah!" she said. "I knew I could make you lose your temper."

From that moment the baron passed beyond mere enjoyment into something more emotional, sublime, and, to Harriet, ludicrous. Her glee became a dance. It would be rash to say that the baron would have laid hands on her, but that the table was between them cannot be denied. He shouted his uncontrolled fury. . . .

The door opened and Mr. Sutherland entered.

163

CHAPTER XXV

LALLERS

DESERTED in the lounge by Harriet, Septimius had returned to the wireless cabin and sent off his messages; and, incidentally, en route had encountered both Captain Slapser and Mr. Antinope, the tall purser, both of whom had treated him with an extreme and uneasy deference which delightfully contrasted with their demeanour towards him in the night. He had come back to the lounge only to discover that Miss Perkins was still in the dining-saloon. Therefore he had gone unasked into the dining-saloon, partly from impatience at further waiting; partly because he thought that Harriet, having forcibly brought him from the wireless cabin, should not have abandoned him for a private interview with Lord Furber; partly because he liked to spend as much time with her as possible; partly because the interview between Harriet and Lord Furber had developed on such lines that a lot of it could be heard in the scandalized lounge, and some moderating influence must clearly be needed; and partly because he feared (or rather hoped) that Harriet might be in danger (real danger this time) from which he could rescue her.

When he beheld the altercating pair on either side of the dining-table, his mind sub-divided itself into an unusually large number of minds. One of them adored Harriet; another regretted that she should have lowered herself to the level of a mere shindy; another remembered that he was a boxer and had once stroked the Cambridge boat; another remembered that he was a husband and father and quite fifty; another regretted that Lord Furber's behaviour should match so ill the splendour and loveliness and classic grace of this room and of the whole yacht (imagine a man quarrelling, and like a navvy, while environed by those exquisite Della Robbian panels of mythological subjects!); and another keenly desired to repeat the previous night's performance of felling Lord Furber with a single blow.

Harriet raised her hand.

"Sep!" she warned Mr. Sutherland. "Not again! Once was enough. I must ask you to respect his wounds." She vaguely indicated the baron's amorphous chin and plastered head.

"My dear Harriet!" Septimius blandly exclaimed. (How attractive and amusing she was, and how friendly and intimate they were together, with their tossing to and fro of christian names!) "My dear Harriet!" he repeated. "I really don't know what you mean. I heard you arguing, and the topic seemed to be one in which I might usefully join. If I'm wrong I'll go out again."

Lord Furber's mouth had remained wide open, as though the arrival of Septimius had put a petrifying spell upon him. With an effort he broke the spell, roared with laughter, and sat down.

"Take a chair, Sutherland," he said genially, and roared afresh with laughter.

And he glanced at Harriet, as it were wistfully, boyish, appealing, and yet roguish.

Harriet warmed to him instantly. As an individuality he was apt to be extremely inconvenient, but he had an art

"Be a man for once in a way, and do without a cigarette. Show Mr. Sutherland what you're really made of. I'm speaking for both him and myself."

The baron wavered and then resumed his seat.

"I should think pretty nearly everything's happened in this yacht except murder; and that 'll be happening soon," he muttered, half to himself, and made a face at Harriet. "Well, Sutherland, what is it you want?"

"I should like to know, if it's quite convenient," said Sutherland, "why Miss Perkins and myself have been abducted in this yacht of yours." He used the gentlest, calmest, most christian tone. And he amiably smiled.

"Abducted?"

"Abducted. I don't want to seem curious or impatient. I've sent off my messages to London—they are to be relayed from Milan—and I'm in no sort of hurry to leave, and I don't think Miss Perkins is in a hurry either. Your yacht makes an excellent hotel. You are very hospitable, and your society is very pleasantly exciting. But just by way of interesting information I *should* just like to know why I'm here."

There was a pause.

"But ye came to dinner, and ye stayed the night. That's all," said Lord Furber with what appeared to be an utterly candid laugh.

"I'm afraid I don't make myself clear," Mr. Sutherland went on. "You say 'that's all'! But is it all? Why am I here? I hoped you'd understand that now at last we're *talking*."

Lord Furber tattoed faintly on the table.

"Out with it, my beautiful lord!" said Harriet. "Or he'll bash your head right in this time."

"Well," said Lord Furber deliberately. "I'll tell ye.

I see no reason why I shouldn't." He went on more loudly and staccato. "I want to buy Lallers."

Mr. Sutherland raised his eyebrows.

"You mean Lallers Limited?"

"I do. At your own price."

"But I don't own Lallers. I haven't got a single share in Lallers."

"Nor a debenture?"

"Nor a debenture. But what does a man like you want with an affair like Lallers? A hundred thousand pounds ought to cover the lot of it. Millions should be more in your line."

"I'll give ye two hundred thousand then," said Lord Furber.

"But don't I tell you I've no holding in it at all?"

"Look here," said Lord Furber, facing Mr. Sutherland. "Ye say we're *talking*. I'll give ye a quarter of a million. I want Lallers, and ye needn't keep on saying ye've got no holding in it. Perhaps ye haven't. But ye've got a rare pull over them that have. Ye must have an option. If you're ready to sell, Lallers will be sold."

"That may or may not be so. But assuming that it were so, you may believe me that I shouldn't be ready to sell."

"Ye mean it?"

"I certainly do."

"Then be d—d to ye."

"Quite!" said Mr. Sutherland with undiminished blandness. "And so you had me in your yacht in order to buy Lallers—lock, stock and barrel!"

"Yes," Lord Furber agreed, "I kidnapped ye just for that and nowt else."

"Well, it's all very interesting," Mr. Sutherland com-

L   169

mented, and having exchanged a mild and utterly uncompromising stare for Lord Furber's defiant and semi-murderous glance, he rose and abruptly left the room.

Harriet was impressed and a little frightened, in spite of herself. Deeps, chasms, had somehow opened at her feet. Men might be boys, but they were rather terrifying at times. Her charming yachting costume had lost the whole of its importance in the scheme of things. Still, she had one consolation. Both her admirers, of whose admiration she was very proud, had acquitted themselves well. They had kept her respect—and something more. The pity was that, just at the moment, they were not fighting for her.

"But I'll have Lallers," the baron formidably growled. "I've got to have Lallers!"

To hear him, his life might have depended on having Lallers.

Harriet was perfectly nonplussed.

Then through the service-door Bumption entered.

CHAPTER XXVI

A GREAT WOMAN

"Oh, I beg pardon, my lord." Having made this appeal, Bumption turned away again, as if to leave the room.

"What is it, Bumption?" The baron stopped his butler with an encouraging tone.

"I was only——" The man hesitated.

Miss Perkins was struck by the contrast between his grand, assured demeanour as chief priest of the banquet on the previous evening and the apologetic, nervous, almost human air which now characterized him. Physically he was massive, like most of the personnel of the *Vanguard* (Mr. Antinope the purser being an exception as to girth); and his style could be massive also when occasion needed, but at the moment his style was no more massive than that of a leaf blown about by the wind. Miss Perkins noticed further that the baron's mien and voice had altered at the sight of the faithful servitor; the baron undoubtedly liked the idea and conception of a faithful servitor, because it symbolized for him all that his early years had not contained; the baron became suddenly benevolent.

"Ye can talk," said the baron. "Miss Perkins won't mind. Miss Perkins has been on board in an official capacity." He put a faint emphasis on the words "has been," and gave Harriet a surreptitious glance, which she richly returned.

"I only wished to apologize for the way the breakfast was served this morning, my lord."

"Quite!" said his lordship. "Don't let that trouble you. The ship's been upset a bit. Thirteens, eh?"

"Thirteens, my lord? I don't follow your lordship."

"Sixes and sevens."

Mr. Bumption produced a dutiful smile, which played fitfully over his obvious pain. The smile vanished, his hands moved a little uncertainly over the front of his impressive blue-and-gold uniform.

"I don't hardly know how to tell your lordship—I mean—I———"

"That's all right, Bumption. Ye needn't tell me. I know what ye've got for me—notice to leave. That's it. Isn't it?"

"Well, my lord, it's like this. The wife———"

He paused once more. In referring to Mrs. Bumption he usually said 'the wife,' as though there were, and could be, no other wife on earth worthy of the name of wife; or, if you choose to interpret the phrase differently, as though he possessed many wives, of whom this one was the principal or favourite.

The baron again helped him.

"She's leaving. She's just told me."

"Yes, my lord. I've explained to her it must have been all a misunderstanding. But your lordship knows how they are, even the best of 'em."

"Oh, I do!"

"I said I was sure your lordship must have been delirious at the time."

"I was. I was. I couldn't have been anything else."

"May I say how glad I am to see your lordship so much better?"

172

"Thank ye, Bumption. I'm sorry I've put ye into such an awkward position. I'm very sorry. Ye're sure it can't be mended?"

"I think not, my lord. And that's not all of it, either. The captain don't seem to hit it off very well with Daisy." Daisy was Mrs. Bumption. "Not that that matters so much. Still he don't. He told her she was 'crew' last night, and she didn't like it. I explained that to her as well, but somehow she can't swallow it."

"And so she's leaving?"

"To-day, my lord. She says if she's 'crew' she need only give twenty-four hours' notice, and she'll leave now and ask Mr. Antinope to take a day off her wages in lieu of notice. I regret it, my lord, but you see how I'm placed."

"It's all as plain as a pikestaff, Bumption. But, tell me how yer Mrs. Bumption means to leave. She's at sea, and she can't leave except in one of the yacht's boats, and supposing I won't let her use one of the yacht's boats? What then? Will she swim ashore? Has she thought of that?"

Mr. Bumption faintly smiled—a smile which disclosed a certain humorous pride in Mrs. Bumption's resourcefulness.

"Oh! She's fixed all that, my lord. She's been packing her things this morning and mine, too. And in another five minutes she'll be in one of them Italian launches that are waiting alongside. Not that she thinks your lordship would keep her aboard unwilling. No! But she says she won't be beholden to anybody. She always was very independent, my lord. If your lordship remembers, I told your lordship she was, when you engaged her for the yacht. Of course, if she'd been in service in Belgrave Square your lordship would have known. But me having a little place in Chesham Mews and going home to her every evening, your lordship couldn't be expected to know, and that was why I took the liberty of warning your lordship beforehand, if your lordship will excuse me."

"Bumption," said the baron. "Be honest. Ye gave her a very good character——"

"And so she has it, my lord."

"Ye said she'd been in service as housekeeper at the Marquis of Amberley's, and she'd been to sea in the Marquis's schooner, and she'd come to me if I really wanted her. But the only reason I engaged her was that you wouldn't leave her behind."

"No more I would, my lord. How could I? I never have left her, and she's never left me. We've always been what they call inseparable."

"Yes," said the baron leaning on his elbow and looking up at Bumption, "it's a wonderful story. But don't ye think ye ought to give her a bit of a holiday from her husband? Pleasant change for her?"

"She isn't one for holidays, my lord. I have suggested it, once or twice. For her sake. But she isn't having any."

"Try her again. Tell her I'll pay all her holiday expenses."

Bumption shook his grieved head.

"And supposing she did go off alone, which she won't, we couldn't manage aboard without her. I couldn't face it, my lord. She sees to everything—I mean in my department."

"And not only in yours, I should say," the baron put in.

"No, my lord," said Bumption firmly. "She never interferes with the navigating; I'll say that for her."

"Well, it's a lot to say, Bumption."

"It may be, my lord. But I'll say it. And your lordship can ask anybody aboard. No, my lord. I really couldn't manage without her. And what's more, I like a woman under me. There's so many things about my job that they understand better than any man could. Laundry work, for instance. And mending. And I don't know what all. And even if I could manage, I couldn't leave the poor little thing to go home from here all alone. It's a two days' journey, and all customs and frontiers and changing trains! I couldn't bear the thought of it, my lord. I've always looked after her hand and foot."

"But she needn't go, Bumption. I'm not asking her to go. She's going of her own accord."

"Yes, my lord. But she's going."

"And you're going?"

"And I'm going, my lord. And very, very sorry I am. I know how inconvenient it'll be for your lordship. And I don't expect your lordship to take me on again at Belgrave Square. Much as I shall miss it. And I don't know as I expect your lordship to give me a character. But I shouldn't be easy in my conscience if I didn't go. At once."

"Then yer wife does realize that she's making things just a bit rough for me?"

"Oh, she does, my lord!"

"Well, that's something. Has she happened to say what she thinks I ought to do in the circumstances?"

"Yes, my lord. She's one that thinks of everything. It's her opinion that your lordship's best plan would be to leave the yacht and go and stay in a hotel in Rome or somewhere handy, until you can get a new chief steward and housekeeper over from England."

Lord Furber stood up.

"Bumption," said he solemnly, "your wife is a great woman. You're right about her. There's nobody like her. You go to Mr. Antinope and tell him I say he's to pay her her full wages and twenty pounds in addition. I should like to show my admiration of your poor little Daisy. And I hope she won't refuse the money. You tell her I'm sorry I said anything in my dreams to upset her, and tell her I'll see her d—d before I leave my own yacht. You tell her I'll see her d—d first. Be sure to say d—d."

"Yes, my lord."

"And I shall take you back at Belgrave Square because I understand the position. Yes, by G—d! I understand it. That'll do. Ye can have one of my launches if ye want it."

CHAPTER XXVII

THE ANKLE

"By the way," asked Harriet, when Bumption had thankfully left the room, "what is your christian name?"

"Ralph," said Lord Furber.

"Well, Ralph, you behaved very well that time, if you don't mind my telling you. You were both a philosopher and a philanthropist for at least five minutes—I'm beginning to admire you."

Harriet spoke with faint enthusiasm. She tried not to be patronizing and the baron tried not to be patronized. Neither succeeded fully, but both were pleased with their efforts.

"Ye'd better put that in writing," said the baron.

Said Harriet:

"And I must tell you something else. He's the nicest man in the yacht, and I love him."

"Who?"

"Bumption, of course! I'd no idea."

"Ah!" said the baron. "He's always at his best with me. And I'm at my best with him. That fellow likes me, and I like him—as much as I hate his wife. More. I don't really hate her. I admire her, because she's the only one around here that doesn't care a damn for me. See me coaxing her sometimes, and her not having any! If you ask me, the explanation is that she's jealous of him being fond of me, and me being fond of him. She's the devil! but she's a great woman, and don't ye make any mistake, Harriet Perkins. She's got him under her foot, and I'm sorry for him. No, I'm not. I envy him, because he has a grand passion. He knows what he wants. I don't know what I want, and you don't know what you want, Harriet Perkins. That's where he's got the pull over us."

"I think I admire you more and more," said Harriet.

They looked at one another and kept silence for a moment.

"Well," said the baron, "I've lost him. Oh yes! I've lost him."

"And it was your own fault—now wasn't it?" said Harriet persuasively.

"No," growled the baron. "She always meant to go and she always meant him to go, too. And if she hadn't found one excuse she'd have found another. And no money could ha' bought her. That's where she knew she had me. Well, I did the best I could. Couldn't have gone further, could I?"

"Naturally you could."

"How?"

"Didn't I say I wouldn't be your secretary, but I'd help you if you needed it? And you didn't ask me, and yet you say you couldn't have gone further!"

"Ye couldn't have helped me, wench."

"Supposing you'd ask me to be housekeeper here instead of Mrs. Bumption; I'm a very good housekeeper—at least, I used to be at home. And I'm never sea-sick. I could have worked with Bumption. Who couldn't? Mrs. B. could have lived on board like a lady in her own part of the yacht. And I should have had some work to live for. I haven't any aprons here, but you could have wirelessed to Rome for a selection of aprons and had them sent down in three motor-cars, according to your usual practice with fal-lals."

"She'd never have agreed."

"Yes, she would."

"How d'ye know?"

"Because she'd have loved to stand by and see me make a mess of her job. Not that I should have made a mess of it. She'd have glared at me and never said a word. But what things she'd have said to Bumption every night! What a time she'd have had! So don't tell me she wouldn't have agreed, Ralph. If you do, you might as well admit that you don't understand women. And I *should* like you to understand women. It would be such a nice change for you, and you'd be the first man that ever did."

She smiled. He smiled . . . They looked at one another again, silently, and grew into brother and sister, and the sister was the elder of the two.

"I wonder!" the baron murmured, almost humbly, as he reflected upon the possibilities of sister's ingenious scheme.

Harriet could see in his eyes the resurrected hope of retaining the precious Bumption; and it was a sweet spectacle to her, and she was proud of herself.

"I'd like to see ye housekeeping," the baron said appreciatively.

"I'm sure you would; and, you know, you wouldn't have to be confidential with me."

The baron jumped up and rang the bell. A steward, an ordinary, nameless steward, responded.

"That bell was for Bumption," said his lordship curtly. "Ye know that."

"Bumption is busy at the moment, my lord," the steward apologetically explained.

"Get him," said his lordship, laconic and intimidating.

"Yes, my lord."

"Harriet," said the baron. "Perhaps nobody's ever told ye before, but ye're the goods."

She laughed, happily.

"But," the baron added, "I lay ye a hundred to one Mrs. B. won't give in."

Bumption entered in an obvious state of flurry.

"Bumption, listen to me——"

"Excuse me, my lord. Daisy's slipped and sprained her ankle getting into one of them greasy Italian launches. I asked her to wait for me, but she said she wasn't taking any chances and she'd wait for me in the launch. Now she can't stand, and she says her ankle's hurting her dreadful, and Mr. Antinope's giving her brandy to stop her from fainting, and what's to be done I don't know, swelp me bob—I ask your lordship's pardon."

Mr. Bumption was really excited and Lord Furber had never seen him excited before.

"She'll have to be brought back on board, Bumption," said Lord Furber, "whether she likes it or not. And I hope this'll be a lesson to both of ye."

"Yes, my lord," Bumption agreed, hasting to the door. "But how is she to come back on board? She'll never get up the steps of that gangway. And nobody could get her up. Seventeen stone, she is."

"Well, she can't go ashore with a sprained ankle."

"No, my lord." Bumption was now disappearing through the door.

"Hi! Bumption!"

"No, my lord," the man's voice sounded faintly from

outside the room . . . He had gone. Nothing, not even the sharp summons of his worshipped master, could keep him.

"Harriet, my girl," said Lord Furber, laughing with deep gusto. "Heaven's been watching over us. Ye shall be my housekeeper. There's nothing to stop it now."

The doors of the dining-saloon opened suddenly, and Mr. Sutherland burst in. Mr. Sutherland was really excited, and neither the baron nor Harriet Perkins had ever seen him excited before.

"I say," he exclaimed. "Mrs. Bumption's fallen into one of those launches and broken her leg."

"Yes," said Harriet, "and she's dead."

"Dead! Who?"

"Queen Anne, Seppie."

CHAPTER XXVIII

THE HORSE-BOX

ONLY the deepest students of human nature and of human relations are not astonished at the high percentage of people in any given population who can find leisure to witness any event that is really unusual and interesting. In the busiest industrial city, supposed to be inhabited exclusively by incessant toilers, fifty persons will immediately appear from nowhere to watch a dog-fight, five hundred to stare at a fire, and five thousand to see a wedding procession of the exalted. The news spreads, none knows how, and no physical obstacles will prevent a congregation.

Thus at Ostia that morning, the *Vanguard* was anchored fifteen cables' length from shore; no messages seemed to go from the yacht to the port, and yet very quickly, very magically, the yacht was surrounded by a ring of small boats of every description carrying sightseers of every description.

And on board the yacht a similar phenomenon existed. The ship's company consisted of about eighty immortal souls, and about seventy-seven of them were excitedly peering from one post or another over the side of the yacht. Discipline had temporarily vanished; the conspicuous presence of the owner in his remarkable dressing-gown, and with his patched cranium, had not sufficed to preserve discipline. As a fact the owner was as excited and undisciplined as anybody else, and more than some.

Four cooks in their caps, whitely imitating the headdresses of Russian priests, leaned on the rail of the maindeck, and they were flanked on either side by stewards and deckhands. Below, gazing from various apertures, were visible the grimy faces of greasers. The chief engineer and two of his important aids surveyed the scene from the bows on the main deck. And the bright-coloured sirens were all around them chattering. Lord Furber and Septimius Sutherland were on the boat-deck. The wireless operator had perched himself on the roof of the wireless cabin. And above all, on the bridge, were the skipper, the first-officer and a mate. The first-officer was directing the operation upon which the universal curiosity was centred.

So great was the concourse on the port side of the *Vanguard*, that she would have been justified in showing a distinct list to port.

And be it remembered that many of these steadfast beholders, on account of the night voyage, had been out of bed and sleepless all night. Yet they felt no fatigue.

Only Miss Perkins and the Honourable Luke John Tunnicliff were absent from the muster.

The manner of the fascinating operation thus observed had been the subject of anxious discussion, and some heated argument, among the experts. The captain himself had been torn from his cabin (where he was engaged in looking through the ship's papers preparatory to a scrutiny by the emissaries of Farinacci, for Lord Furber had not yet told him that he had been hoaxed in that matter) in order to give an unwilling opinion as to the proper mechanical procedure. In the result a couple of long booms had been lashed to the floor of the bridge, with their joint extremities sticking out far beyond the topsides. At the said extremities had been rigged a stout double tackle (used for the main halliards when the yacht happened to be assisting motor-power with sail-power). Through this tackle ran a tremendous rope, which in more normal circumstances was the sheet. Attached to one end of this rope was a kind of horse-box which the ship's carpenter had hammered together, and the other end was in the horny hands of four seamen and two stewards.

The seamen and the stewards hauled: the horse-box (carpeted with cushions) rose from the deck and was fended off with boathooks until it swung clear of the rail and over the sea, or rather over the largest of the sirens' launches.

"Hold on!" cried Lord Furber loudly, usurping the authority of the first-officer. "Where's Mr. Tunnicliff? Where is Mr. Tunnicliff?"

Everyone looked round for Mr. Tunnicliff; and in the nick of time Mr. Tunnicliff appeared carrying the film-camera, without which his lordship would have regarded the inventory of no yacht as complete. The horse-box was slowly revolving in mid-air from the four cords which fastened it to the sheet.

"Shoot it as it goes down!" ordered the baron, being acquainted with the vocabulary of the film-studios.

Mr. Tunnicliff adjusted the camera on its stand.

"Lower away!" cried the first-officer, resuming command, and Mr. Tunnicliff (whose secretarial duties were manifold) duly shot the horse-box as it disappeared downwards.

Heads and trunks were projected still further outwards over the rails, so that eyes could watch every detail of the descent.

The horse-box settled gently into the bottom of the large Italian launch. Mr. Bumption with a terrific effort raised Daisy till she could stand on her sole sound leg, and manœuvred her massive frame until she could subside on to the cushions. So established, she set her teeth and clung to the sides of the horse-box, and the ascent began. How else could she have been salved! She could not walk up the gangway steps; she could not hop up; nor could she have been carried up without serious risk of a plunge into the Mediterranean. Moreover, she would allow no one but her husband to lay hands upon her. The entire launch itself might have been hauled up on davits, but it could only have been swung in on the top-deck, and the top-deck was not Mrs. Bumption's final destination, to reach which from the top-deck she would have had to descend impossible stairs.

She might more conveniently have been hauled up on one of the falls of the davits of the yacht's port launch. But this method she had strenuously declined, stating that it was notorious that in times of need davit-tackle invariably fouled—as a rule with fatal consequences.

"Tunnicliff!" cried the baron, and then corrected himself. "No. You're busy. Rayner! Rayner! Where's Miss Perkins? Go and find her wherever she is and ask her to be good enough to come up here at once." He turned to the bridge: "Hold on there! Don't haul yet."

Rayner, hiding as well as he could his disgust at being thus forced to run the risk of missing the culmination of the show, ran off.

Soon afterwards, Harriet appeared on the top-deck. She wore a white apron over her new yachting costume, and the apron was ample enough to have asphyxiated two yachting costumes.

"Miss Vamp!" a voice hailed her from the roof of the wireless cabin as she passed. Involuntarily she turned her head. "Ha! You recognized yourself then, dear lady. Didn't I tell you this was no ordinary sort of a yacht? Look!"

The wireless operator seemed to be in the very highest spirits.

"Thank you," said Harriet pleasantly.

She looked, but saw nothing save a perpendicular rope. She passed on forward along the deck.

Septimius came to meet her, as she stopped near the film-camera.

"You look ravishing in that apron. Ravishing!" said Septimius. "We've been waiting for you." His eyes shone. Apparently he was in an ecstasy at the sight of her.

"My shoes hurt dreadfully," said she, with maidenly calmness. They did.

The Honourable Luke glanced aside at her from his camera. His eyes outshone the eyes of Septimius. Never had she met such a gaze. It thrilled and frightened her. She recalled his words on the previous night in the owner's state sitting-room: "You wait and you'll see."

She thought:

"The wireless operator is dangerous, but Luke is more dangerous. He's more dangerous even than Ralph."

She saw Lord Furber beckoning to her, and she obeyed the gesture, Septimius following.

"I'm studying my new job, Ralph," she murmured. "I can't stop long. I'm very busy."

Near by, the four deck-hands and two stewards were hauling on the halliard. They stopped.

"Go on! Higher!" said the baron to them in a low

voice. Bumption had appeared, panting, to greet his enchantress from above.

"She's level with the main-deck my lord," said one of
the deck-hands.

"Higher, I tell you!" enjoined his lordship impatiently.
The gang hauled again.

"Tunnicliff!" called the baron, and the Honourable
Luke started once more to turn the handle of the camera.

Lord Furber gazed with young rapture at Miss Perkins,
who thought how agreeable and stimulating it was to be
the only woman among all these vitalized males.

"Look!" said Lord Furber to her.

The horse-box was rising clear of the rail of the navigating deck, and therein reclined Mrs. Bumption, revolving
as the horse-box revolved, with one foot unshod and the
ankle thereof bandaged. She could be plainly seen through
the open ends of the box. Her face was stern and yet
composed. Her knuckles showed white as she clenched
her hands on the sides of the box. She went higher. She
revolved more quickly. She dominated the yacht and all
on board. The film-camera made its rapid click-click-
click. Mrs. Bumption ceased to rise, for the horse-box
was nearly touching the topmost block of the tackle.

Harriet perceived that she was not the only woman
among all those vitalized males. A greater than she glared
mountainously down upon her.

"I wouldn't sell this film for ten thousand pounds,"
said Lord Furber to Harriet. "Look at her. She's a
great woman. She was beaten, but now she's beating
me, beating all of us. Nothing can beat her."

"Viva! viva! viva!" came from the sirens with their
shrill voices. The signal was too tempting to be ignored.
The British crew cheered loudly in response. Some of

them imagined that they were taking their revenge on the yacht's formidable housekeeper. More *vivas* ascended from the launches beneath.

"Lower away!" muttered the baron, glutted with spectacular satisfaction, and Mrs. Bumption, still twisting very slowly, began to sink towards the level of the main-deck.

"We're nobodies," said Lord Furber in Harriet's ear. "She knows what she wants, and she'll have it. That's where she's got us."

"Pardon me," said Harriet, "I wanted a job, and I have it."

"Pooh!" said Lord Furber; "ye're only a parasite on a parasite."

"No," said Harriet; "I have a job and I shall do it. Au revoir." She left her employer.

"That's my apron, if *you* please," called Mrs. Bumption as she sank.

Laughter! General laughter! The cheering and the *vivas* ceased. Mr. Bumption had disappeared. A few minutes later, news came to the upper deck that Mrs. Bumption, the horse-box having been swung in on the main-deck, had hopped to a cabin there, in the arms of her husband.

CHAPTER XXIX

THE FILM

LORD FURBER and his bland guest, Mr. Septimius Sutherland, sat down to lunch in the dining-saloon which earlier had been the scene of dramatic encounters.

Reaction follows the greatest events, and reaction had followed the raising of Mrs. Bumption from the Italian launch into the bosom of the yacht. Reaction affected the atmosphere of the lunch itself, despite the benevolent cheerfulness of the chief steward (or rather the chief priest), Bumption.

And the sense of reaction was intensified by the absence from the meal of Miss Harriet Perkins. Harriet had sent word that, being extraordinarily busy upon her new duties, and indeed absorbed by them, she had no time for the frivolities of eating and of masculine society. The convert is always fanatical, and Harriet had just been converted from idleness to industry. Without being aware of the fact, she was determined that her industry should disturb the world as much as possible.

Her industry had certainly disturbed the sirens of the frocks. Harriet would have no more truck with them. She decided on the first green dress and on the yachting costume, and on a quite appreciable amount of lingerie, and would listen to no further arguments. Was she not a working maritime housekeeper? In pity, Septimius bought a frock or two, which he hoped might both suit and please his delicious absent wife. (The transaction was perhaps intended to soothe his conscience in the matter of the warmth of his regard for Harriet.) Then Lord Furber, hearing of the business, plunged into the lounge and bought twenty-three frocks in addition to many oddments of attire.

The sirens were going away happy; but they were stopped at the very gangway by order of Harriet. Harriet, the housekeeper, had caused a meal to be prepared for them. As a perfect housekeeper she naturally thought of everything. That meal the sirens had to eat, and did eat, with twittering enthusiasm.

And let no owner or guest imagine that her attention to the repast of the sirens might prejudice the lunch of the mighty in the dining-saloon! Quite the contrary. The character and plenteousness of the lunch had occasioned some friction between the new housekeeper and the chef. The new broom swept clean, and in so doing was inspiring the usual opposition and sinful sulkiness.

Hence the lunch, triumphant gastronomically, did not prove to be very successful as a social gathering. And yet both Lord Furber and Mr. Sutherland had apparently forgotten the small unpleasantness which had arisen out of the former's strange attempt to gain control of the house of Laller.

It was not until the arrival of the coffee and the final disappearance of a beaming Bumption that reaction was overcome. The baron's eye happened to catch the rolled-up cinema-screen which was suspended above the service door. The sight put an idea into his head, and he rang for the Honourable Luke, who came with a demeanour which indicated recent excitement not wholly recovered from.

"Tunnicliff," said the baron, "what about that film you took this morning? I suppose it ought to be a pretty good one. Good light and everything, eh?"

"So far as I can judge," answered Tunnicliff carefully.

"Well, you'd better get it to Rome this afternoon— take it yeself or send someone—and have it developed. Venables could fix the thing for ye. Ye know his address. 19 Piazza di Spagna."

"Yes. Only——"

"Only what?"

"Miss Perkins has got it."

"What d'ye mean, Miss Perkins has got it?"

"She asked me to explain the camera to her, and take it to pieces and so on. And she was very interested in the spool particularly, and she took it away."

"Well, go and ask her to return it, will ye?"

"I have asked her, but she won't."

"D'ye mean she refused?"

"Yes," said the Honourable Luke, somewhat curtly: he was thinking of her rudeness to him and of his rudeness to her: the glint in her eye, and the heat which he felt on his own cheek, and her tone and his tone, and the bright language they both employed in the brief altercation— from which, indeed, he had just emerged.

Lord Furber said, in soft accents which surprised his hearers:

"Oh, all right. It doesn't matter. I hope I didn't disturb yer lunch."

When the Honourable Luke had departed, the baron rang for Bumption.

"Bumption," said he; "I wish ye'd ask Miss Perkins if she can oblige Mr. Sutherland and me by coming in here for a moment, at once."

"Yes, my lord."

And in due course Harriet came in—through the service-door. She was wearing neither the yachting costume nor the apron, but a black frock which seemingly she had obtained from the sirens before their departure— a frock as simple as it was obviously costly, ornamented with a girdle and a bunch of keys.

"And now?" she demanded formally, and perhaps a little defiantly.

"Sit down, won't you?" Lord Furber suggested.

"No thanks. I'm very busy. Have you any orders?"

"We only wanted to compliment ye on the lunch," said Lord Furber. "It was the best lunch I've ever had in this yacht."

"Glad you liked it."

"We did indeed, Harriet," said Mr. Sutherland.

"I suppose ye've nobbled the chef," said Lord Furber.

"No," said Harriet, vaguely. "Anything else?"

Lord Furber shook his head and smiled appreciatively. Harriet moved away.

"I say, Harriet," he called to her as she was reaching the door; "that film we took this morning. I hear ye've taken charge of it." And he laughed.

"I did," said she. "You can't possibly have a film like that developed, much less shown, even privately."

Lord Furber's face altered.

"Why not?"

"Well, it's not nice. Mrs. Bumption would hate it."

"She won't see it."

"She'll hear of it. And think of Bumption. He'd be terribly hurt."

"Not he! He knew it was being taken—saw it being

taken, part of it. And I've never known him more cheerful than he was at lunch."

"Of course he was. But can't you guess why? He was cheerful because he knew I'd thrown the film into the sea. I'm the housekeeper."

"I don't see the connection," said Lord Furber very drily and ominously.

"Don't you? Well, it's like this. I'm the housekeeper. I'm following as well as I can in Mrs. Bumption's steps. I model myself on her. And I said to myself, 'If she had that roll of film in her hand what would Mrs. Bumption do?' I said, 'She'd throw it into the sea.' And so I threw it into the sea." She opened the door. "And," she added simply, "you ought to be glad I did. And you *will* be."

"Say, Harriet," the baron cried; "it's wonderful how servants stick together against their masters, isn't it?"

Harriet looked into the room again.

"Are you keeping your temper?" she asked.

"Ay, lass!" said the baron jovially. He was indeed.

"Well, then, I've two things to tell you. You see these keys," she flourished the keys of office. "When I'm wearing them my name isn't Harriet—it's Perkins."

"And what else, Perkins?"

"I was sorry to have to humiliate you in front of your guest. But I see you're persisting in that bad habit of yours of interviewing servants when you aren't alone with them. I hope this will be a lesson to you."

She left.

"Well," said the baron, passing a hand over his brow, "I had a near shave then."

"Of?"

"Losing my temper. I shall be getting over-righteous

if I succeed every time like that . . . See here, my friend, this yacht's no place for us."

"In any case," answered Septimius, unmoved by what he had witnessed, "I must be leaving you. You wanted to see me about Lallers. You've seen me, and that little business is over. So I'll go as soon as it's convenient. I expect I can hire a car at Ostia. You've been exceedingly hospitable." He finished on an enigmatic tone.

Lord Furber burst out expansively, amiably, persuasively:

"My dear fellow, ye can't desert me like this. I tell ye ye can't do it. You said a bit ago—this morning, that ye weren't in a hurry."

"I'm not," replied Septimius. "I got my business over at Naples three days sooner than I expected, and I've cancelled my appointments, as you know. But I don't quite see anything to stay for."

"Anything to stay for! And we aren't a dozen miles from Rome! We'll run up there together and make a night of it. If we clear out for a while, it'll give these people a chance to think a bit, especially if we don't tell 'em how soon we're coming back to 'em again."

"I'm quite willing," said Septimius, with the utmost calmness and gentleness.

"Good for ye!" the baron cried in sudden glee.

He rang the bell with considerable emphasis.

"And only last night I was thinking to myself how acquiescent she was! Good God!"

"I beg your pardon?"

"Nothing! Nowt!"

The hundred horse-power launch was ordered forthwith.

The entire yacht seemed to spring into life.

Suitcases had to be packed.   Rugs and wraps provided. And everything in the twinkling of an eye.   Amid the uproar the baron and Septimius placidly paced the deck.

"But I must change," said Septimius suddenly.   "I can't go to Rome in these clothes."

"Why not? Change in Rome."

"But I shall be cold in the car."

"Car.   There is no car.   The launch will do thirty knots.   We'll enter Rome by water, my lad, and wake up the Tiber.   New sensations for you!   New sensations!"

CHAPTER XXX

"So this is the Eternal City!" said Lord Furber thought-fully, as the launch passed the gasworks.

He stood up. Over the stern of the great mahogany craft the blue ensign of the British Naval Reserve stuck out with the stiffness of a board in the high wind caused by the craft's swiftness. Grimy workmen at the grimy gas-works, which were wreathed with fluffs of steam and smoke, gazed astonished at the speed of the launch. And indeed, the launch had aroused astonishment all the way up the yellow and featureless Tiber from the moment when a pilot-skiff, hailing it for a job, had been nearly capsized in its heedless wash. Lord Furber wanted no pilot, nor did he pay the least attention to the damage done to the banks of the sacred river by the big twin waves which the launch threw up on either side. He had soon come to the con-clusion (correct) that the Tiber presented no interest what-ever to the voyager beyond certain mechanical fishing-nets actuated by the force of the current.

In another minute the launch was within the City; Rome had begun; the Dome of St. Peter's glinted afar off in the afternoon light.

"There's a quay here, my lord," said the steersman, as they shot under the first bridge, the Palatine. "Shall we tie up?"

"Not on your life, my son," the baron replied. "You go right ahead. Ye'll see the tower of St. Angelo soon— you can't miss it, it's the biggest tower you ever saw— after that go under two bridges, and then I'll tell ye where to stop."

"I thought you'd never been to Rome," said Mr. Sutherland.

"No more I have. But I've been meaning to go for a long time now, and so I've picked up a bit about it. When ye enter Rome by water it's obvious ye must tie up at the Ripetta; where they tied up a couple o' thousand years ago. Slow her down a bit," he added to the steersman, who was the officer in charge. "There's something to see here."

The launch subdued itself to the pace of a fast-trotting horse. Bridges, trams, domes, an island, trees, tenement houses, palaces, churches, palaces, fishermen.

"Hold on!" cried the baron. "Here. This must be it. That's the Cavour Bridge ahead, isn't it, Sutherland?"

"I don't know," said Sutherland.

"Well it is, because it must be."

In a moment one of the crew was ashore with a mooring rope in his hand, and in another half-minute the man was the centre of a crowd.

"Dump that baggage here," ordered the baron, springing ashore himself, and he called into the crowd, as a sportsman shoots "into the brown," the magic word, the word which in all the languages of the world is the same: "Taxi."

Then towards the launch:

"You can go back to the yacht now."

The launch cast off, buzzed loudly, made a sharp curve into midstream, and slipped at full speed down the current. It had vanished under the Umberto Bridge before the deliberate Septimius Sutherland had fully realized what was happening to him. Septimius, as is the fate of a rich man whose duty it is to satisfy the curiosity and the demand for novelty of three idle ladies, had several times entered Rome, but never in this manner.

"You haven't told them where we're staying," he said.

"And why should I? It's none o' their business. Where *shall* we stay?"

"Oh!" said Septimius; "I suppose there's only the Paradiso."

"I suppose so," Lord Furber agreed.

Thus in a word did the two plutocrats eradicate and destroy a hundred hotels in Rome, leaving but one intact on its foundations.

By this time, four Roman citizens, by their united efforts, were carrying, unbidden, two light suitcases, and a fifth was urging the visitors to follow the suitcases. A taxi appeared.

"Paradiso!" cried Lord Furber to the driver, and paid out five five-lire notes, according to demand.

"Shan't you call to see your agent on the way?" asked Septimius.

"Why should I?" the baron retorted. "What do we want an agent for?"

"I thought he might save you some trouble."

"I'll save all the trouble myself," said the baron.

At the majestic Paradiso the tourists were informed that the hotel was practically full.

"I'm Lord Furber," said Lord Furber. "I've just come here from my yacht at Ostia."

"In that case, my lord. . . ."

Within a minute and a half the management of the full Paradiso had manufactured a perfectly unoccupied suite consisting of a sitting-room, two bedrooms and two bathrooms and placed it at the disposal of the British aristocracy.

"How much?" the baron inquired, after inspection of the accommodation.

"Twelve hundred lire, my lord."

"A day?"

"Yes, my lord."

"Grand!" said his lordship.

"Say," he questioned the head waiter in the restaurant of the Paradiso during dinner, "is there any moon to-night worth talking about?"

The omniscience of the head waiter received a shock, for the man had not seen the moon for several years. Also the idiomatic quality of his lordship's question was rather puzzling to him. The head waiter had spent the evenings and nights of a quarter of a century past either in the Paradiso or in hotels exactly like the Paradiso, and his private opinion was doubtless that no moon was worth talking about.

"I—I will inquire, my lord."

"Yes, do," Septimius cut in. "Ask in the office. They're bound to have the latest information there!"

The head waiter did not ask at the office, his situation being too exalted for such an act; but he sent somebody else to inquire at the office; and in the meantime he favoured with his presence and knowledge other tables in the crowded room. He had a great and succulent piece of information for the other tables: namely, that Lord Furber, the famous English millionaire, was staying in the Paradiso. Before he had finished his round, the entire restaurant had been made aware that Lord Furber was patronising the Paradiso, and of the precise geographical position of his lordship's table. The identity of Septimius Sutherland evoked little curiosity; for the Paradiso public the first and last pertinent point about Septimius was that he was the one who was *not* Lord Furber.

"The moon was full two days since," said the head waiter, hastening back to his lordship's table and bearing, as it were, the precious information on a silver dish with both hands.

"Ah! And is it a clear night?"

"Quite clear," said the head waiter, on the chance that he might be accurately representing the heavens hidden from mortal eye by the splendid window-curtains of the Paradiso dining-room. (Chance favoured him; the night was in fact quite clear.)

"Anything to do in Rome this evening?" Lord Furber demanded. The head waiter bristled at a question so nearly bordering on an insult to Rome, his Rome. He catalogued the opera, eight other theatres, and some sixteen cinemas, besides a music-hall, and a nocturnal ceremonial in one of the churches.

"Septimius," said the baron, "it seems to me that the Coliseum by moonlight is the stuff for to-night. I'm an innocent abroad in Rome, but I'll lay my shirt the two greatest things here are the Coliseum and St. Peter's. What do you say? Coliseum by moonshine?"

"I say it," was the calm reply.

The pair were becoming more and more intimate. They were positively enjoying one another's society. As for Septimius, he now understood why his wilful friend, in the automobile of which they had at once hired the exclusive services, had during the afternoon steadily resisted the chauffeur's keen and natural desire to display to them the Coliseum and St. Peter's. His friend had been saving these choice morsels for the future.

"Good organization that!" thought Septimius approvingly.

They immediately departed from the Paradiso, that supreme illustration of modernness, and in ten minutes, in less than ten minutes, they stood facing the supreme illustration of the wicked ancient world; and one of the desires of the chauffeur had been appeased.

Lord Furber, standing close to the façade of the Coliseum, gazed upwards up at its tremendous height, story upon story rising into the illuminated skies.

"Yes!" he murmured to himself. "Yes!"

The two grandees were like flies at the foot of a precipice. The automobile, near by, was like the microscopic carriages to which in old days seaside entertainers used to harness performing fleas.

Lord Furber examined minutely the fitting of the vast blocks of travertine of which the exterior was constructed.

"That's true enough," said he. "They did put it up too quick. Jerry-built! Jerry-built! No mistake! But it's lasted."

Then he hurried across the darkness of the immense ground-floor arcade into the interior. The moon, though it had not yet topped the curve of the vast wall, was shining brilliantly according to prediction through multitudinous arches, displaying the grass-grown arena with its mysterious pits and subterranean chambers, the gigantic granite stairways climbing here and there and ending in nothing, and the jagged silhouette of the stone summits. In the distances tiny human figures could be descried darkly moving. Desolation, majestic and unconquerable!

"Yes," said Lord Furber, not to anyone in particular; "the Wembley Stadium's bigger, but this place has

Wembley beat. This is the sort of thing I can understand." There was awe in his deep, rich voice. "How many gladiators were killed here in the first three months after it was opened, Sep? D'ye remember? I know five thousand lions and tigers were done in, but I can't remember the number of men. Fancy them having an inauguration that went on every day for three months!"

Septimius said he didn't know. With a hurrah the baron ran off like a rabbit, and up a moss-grown stairway. He was stopped by a barrier and had to return, stumbling.

"You'd better be careful," Septimius warned him. "You'll be breaking your leg before you know where you are."

The baron ignored him and ran off again: the eager child had been reborn in him. Septimius, who had the precious faculty of always reconciling himself to facts, saw that he had been cast that night for the rôle of kettle to a dog's tail, and hurried after his host. He was convinced that the child could not find a way upwards, but luck favoured the child in the maze of arcades, slopes, tunnels, and stairs. Within five minutes the richest newspaper-proprietor in Europe was perched a hundred feet above earth, his legs dangling over a wall, a Roman arch for a frame above his head, and a full view of the measureless oval of the interior in front. Septimius joined him, but instead of sitting on the wall, leaned against it. Both were puffing, not too hard considering their middle-age.

Septimius began to share the childhood of the baron. He was excited, happy, proud. He felt glad that his wife was not there to ask distracting, silly questions and complain of the cold or the danger. On the other hand, he had a vague notion that the scene was somehow incomplete

without Harriet. He turned up the collar of his overcoat
The baron unloosed his overcoat.

"And this is less than half of what it was," said Lord
Furber. "When ye think that lords and bishops and things,
carted away pieces of this place for three hundred years and
built half the palaces and churches of Rome with 'em! And
this is what's left. . . ! By G—d, Sutherland! We're
nobodies! What a crew they were! Fifty thousand free
seats! Talk about bribing the people! Well, they knew
how to do it. *We* bribe 'em with promises. This is what
they bribed 'em with. Makes ye think, what!"

"Here, my friend," said the placid Septimius—seventh
olive branch, and bearer of a Roman name—"Have a
cigarette. And button up that overcoat."

Lord Furber absently took a cigarette and lighted it
from Mr. Sutherland's in the chill air, but he would not
button his overcoat. But Septimius, cigarette between
teeth, drew the sides of the overcoat together and buttoned
them and then turned up the collar. It was a firm, friendly
act, quickly and neatly done. Lord Furber was touched.
The intimacy of the pair was continuing to develop.

They smoked. And the ascent of the moon gradually
lightened a strip of grass on the western side of the arena,
and the strip became broader and broader. One half of
the great, gaunt interior was dark, the other illuminated in
every detail. Not a sound. No rats, bats, mice, mos-
quitoes, nor winging night-moths. Then the faint, thin
accents of an American voice, and human forms moving
pigmy-like across the waste.

"Say, Sep! What are you after?" It was the baron,
reflective, who put the question.

"What am I after?"

"In life?"

"A quiet life."

They smoked.

"And you—what are you after?"

The baron threw away the end of his cigarette, and the red-glowing particle wavered downwards and was lost to view beneath.

"Hanged if I know!" A sigh. A long pause. "All I *do* know is, I'm out to win—everything."

"Well, you've won everything, my friend."

"Not with you," said the baron.

"Surely you didn't expect to win there!" said Septimius. "You didn't start right."

"Sep," the baron took him up. "Now let me tell ye, I know I didn't start right. Let me tell ye. But I thought I might—I only heard day before yesterday that you were in Naples. I heard ye were soon leaving for London, but I didn't know for certain ye meant to leave that night. I wanted to see ye. And I wanted to see ye before ye got to London. It might have been too late for me after ye'd got to London. If I had asked ye to come aboard in the ordinary way, ye might have refused. And I *had* to see ye. Of course if I hadn't heard ye were in Naples I shouldn't ha' bothered. But seeing I did know, I had to bother. Besides it was great sport—I mean all that arranging of the dinner and so on. Great sport. Chicane, Sutherland! Chicane! Perhaps that's what I'm after in life. Well, it was a biggish thing in conspiracies—I knew it. . . . And then when I'd got ye on board, ye know, ye did play into my hands. No need for me to keep ye on board in spite of yeself, though I'd fixed that, too. Ye stayed of yer own accord. All I had to do was to hurry the rest of 'em ashore. If yer luggage hadn't come, and if I hadn't stayed talking so long with that Harriet of ours, and if ye hadn't gone to bed and snored—(Sep, ye put me out of my stride when ye went to bed; nobody else on earth would ha' done it)—and if I hadn't had my hand on Harriet's shoulder, it might all ha' been a bit different to what it was . . . I'll say this, Sep, ye took it grandly. And so did I—I mean that knocking down business. But ye beat me, and there's no two ways about it. Then I was a trifle shirty with Harriet—she'd upset me—when I happened to mention Lallers to ye this morning. Yes, I didn't begin right. I owe ye an apology; and here it is. And I won't say anything about the black eye I owe ye for knocking me down."

There was something so persuasive and appealing in the baron's rather disconnected account of his performance that Mr. Sutherland's heart was touched. Could this piece of naïve youthfulness, with legs dangling over a wall on the upper works of the moonlit Coliseum, be the hard and formidable individual who had made a huge fortune by invention and was doubling and trebling it by masterly combinations in the City? Mr. Sutherland was so affected that the said performance appeared to him now to be perfectly natural and such as no reasonable being could decently resent. But then Mr. Sutherland, after all as canny as most, began to reflect:

"Why did this master of chicane offer me a hundred per cent. more for Lallers than I'd said it was worth? What does he want with Lallers, anyway? What lies beneath all this wonderful exhibition?" And he told his heart that it must cease to soften.

Then the baron gazed at him with a boyish, candid smile, and Mr. Sutherland perceived that his heart was not completely under control. He thought:

"If this fellow with his Coliseum by moonlight asks

me now to let him buy Lallers as a favour, just because he wants it and won't be happy till he gets it, I shall give in to him. I shall make him a present of Lallers, I know I shall."

And he almost trembled as the baron opened his mouth to speak again.

But at that moment a voice at some little distance behind them among the dark masonry called out, with a twang like a banjo:

"Say, you guys! Can you give me a line on this ruin? Is it the Baths of Diocletian or the Baths of Caracalla? I only made Rome this afternoon and I kind of wandered out from my hotel to-night without my wife, and had a drink, and I've lost myself."

Lord Furber coarsely and unfeelingly burst into loud laughter.

"Don't fall off the wall, my friend," murmured Mr. Sutherland placidly.

To himself, Mr. Sutherland said:

"I am saved."

And indeed the stranger had unwittingly brought down the curtain on the scene.

CHAPTER XXXI

THE DOME

MR. SEPTIMIUS SUTHERLAND had a disturbed night in the splendid accommodation so generously provided for him by his intimate friend Lord Furber in the Paradiso Hotel. He thought a great deal about Harriet Perkins. He disliked being so far away from her. He wished that she could have joined the excursion—of course properly chaperoned. On the other hand, he considered that it was just as well she had not joined the excursion. He wondered whether a man as notoriously prudent as himself would not best show his prudence by bolting off at once to the safety of London and his very domestic hearth. But he could not bear to go, because he could not bear the prospect of not returning to the yacht and Harriet.

Again, he wondered whether, as the safest measure of precaution, he ought not to telegraph to Mrs. Sutherland to come to Rome, bringing with her their daughters; he knew they would come like birds, and like tame birds settle on his shoulders. His anxieties as to his own behaviour would then be at an end. But no! He could not bear that prospect either. How terrible would it be if Lord Furber, fascinated by Rome, kept the yacht dallying at Ostia and invited the whole Sutherland family for a cruise! Lord Furber would be quite capable of the act, and capable further, of manœuvring his new housekeeper into comic and impossible positions for the mystification of the Sutherland ladies. And Harriet herself would be quite capable of casually addressing him in the presence of his family as "Sep"!

What was the sinister and delicious power over him of the piquant Harriet? Why had absence from her increased her power? If he dozed off he was sure to dream oı Harriet arrayed in one of the multitudinous dresses which Lord Furber had lavished upon her in his crude, millionairish way. Mr. Sutherland also passed long stretches of the night in reflecting upon his relations with Lord Furber. He ought to have detested Lord Furber. But he did not. He ought to have cursed their intimacy. But he did not. He constantly felt that sensation of having had a narrow escape in the Coliseum. And he foresaw that he might easily soon find himself in new danger. Lord Furber had mentioned the Coliseum and St. Peter's. He, Septimius, had come scatheless out of the Coliseum. If they went to St. Peter's, would he come scatheless out of St. Peter's? In the night Lord Furber's cleverness, his chicane, seemed to grow more and more diabolic and irresistible. Why was the fiend so set on buying Lallers? . . . Something dark at the bottom of all that! If in the morning Lord Furber suggested a visit to St. Peter's, what ought Septimius to do?

However, when morning tardily arrived, Septimius rediscovered his self-confidence. His brain had the hard and glittering brilliancy which comes of insomnia and fatigue. What precisely had he been fearing in the night? His fears had been absurd. Lord Furber could not force him to do anything that he wished not to do. The sun shone in at the bedroom window and completed Mr. Sutherland's restoration to sanity. He dressed himself unaided, and at nine-thirty precisely, the hour of the break-fast rendezvous, he appeared in the private sitting-room. Five seconds later, through the opposite door, Lord Furber also appeared, all fresh and diabolic.

"How did ye sleep, Sep?" said the baron cheerily.

"Fine," answered Mr. Sutherland.

Why this lie?

"So did I," said the baron. "And I don't often. It must be a great place for sleep, Rome must." Septimius knew that Lord Furber really had slept well.

"What d'ye think of the valet here?" Lord Furber demanded.

"Never saw him."

"Ye didn't! Well, Bumption has made me nearly help-less. I can shave myself, but I can't wipe my own razor. The dago here cut himself wiping it. Look at my only clean collar."

The baron pointed gaily to a blood spot on his only clean collar. He was enjoying the simple life. His eyes were full of laughter, innuendo, charming menace, chicane. His voice was rich with subtle significances.

"Hm!" murmured Mr. Sutherland, non-committal.

"Well now," said the baron, after the breakfast was brought in and they had begun to eat. "What d'ye say, Seppie? Shall we drive back to the yacht, or shall we see something else first?"

"Better see something else," said Mr. Sutherland, "as this is your first visit to Rome." He had meant to say "Go back to the yacht," but he could not. The baron was strangely putting words into his mouth.

"What?"

"St. Peter's, do you think?"

Madman! Ass! He might just as well have said the

Pantheon, the Forum, the Cloaca Maxima, or the Borghese Villa. But he had to say "St. Peter's."

"All right, if ye like," said Lord Furber, just as though he was politely yielding to a whim of his beloved crony's.

In the still, warm air they walked to St. Peter's—arm in arm. Mr. Sutherland in spite of himself enjoyed the pressure of the baron's arm. It seemed to him that the friendly intimacy of two boys of fifty or so was rather beautiful. On a thousand points the baron sought information from his crony, and listened to the replies with admirable respect. But no sooner were they actually within St. Peter's, having beaten off ten or a dozen guides, than the baron's demeanour changed, and St. Peter's became his, and not Mr. Sutherland's. He loosed Sep's arm, and, gazing around at the overwhelming yet austere interior upon which ten million pounds had been spent in three centuries, remarked:

"I like this place. It's a good answer to the Coliseum. Nothing dogmatic about it. It's as impartial as a railway station. Haven't you got the feeling that if we went down some steps somewhere we should come to the trains of the Pennsylvania Railroad—say the Chicago Limited?"

A bell rang. From some distant chapel they heard the sound of singing. They walked on for a few minutes over the marble floor and stared at the marble walls and the immense mosaic pictures, and stood under the dome; and Lord Furber raised his sparkling eyes to the skyey roof of the dome.

"Well," said the baron. "He could do it. He came across with the goods, no mistake."

"Who?"

"Michael Angelo. See here, Sep. I reckon we've got to climb up to the top of that contraption."

"Yes," answered Mr. Sutherland, weakly acquiescent; "you certainly ought to see the view."

In fancy he saw himself in the gallery at the summit of the dome, four hundred feet above Rome, in the compelling society of Lord Furber; and he said to his heart that he was undone. Why had he not replied that the view was not worth the trouble of the climb? They returned to the portico and bought tickets, for which Mr. Sutherland paid.

"A lift!" cried the baron with glee. "A lift in St. Peter's! I wouldn't have missed it for anything . . . I say," he said to the liftman, a rosy, fat man who seemed delighted to have company, "what would Clement the Sixth have said to this lift of yours?"

The liftman smiled uncomprehendingly, and Lord Furber, who for this trip had handsomely broken his rule against carrying money, made a present of ten lire to the official.

They ascended a chequered shaft, and the liftman bowed them out with zealous cordiality, and they were on the vast roof of St. Peter's, which is also the roof of Rome —a hill-town in itself, this roof! Little domes, shops, dwellings, girls selling picture-post cards, workmen, palisades, railings, roads, colossal statues. All Rome and the history of Rome beneath them. The Mediterranean on one side. The Apennines on the other. The rolling Campagna, on which here and there cities gleamed. The Tiber. The gasworks. And the wind blowing freshly across the plateau of the roof. In the streets far under was calm; but here half a gale. They turned. Michael Angelo's dome rose from the plateau apparently as high as when seen from the streets. And beyond the dome, in the clouds, the cupola, and beyond the cupola the ball!

"Come on!" said Lord Furber, and started off almost at a run towards the beckoning dome.

Mr. Sutherland followed as he had followed in the Coliseum, the kettle rattling after the dog. He knew that he was now in another and a morally dangerous world. He trembled lest he should be going to defeat; but he could not hold back. They reached the dome and climbed stairways and passed through a tunnel and entered a gallery, and they leaned forward dizzily, and the interior of St. Peter's was beneath their feet, with tourists walking like dolls on the marble floor. And all around curved thousands of square yards of glittering mosaic, every inch finished with the minuteness of a jewel.

"I give in," exclaimed Lord Furber.

Mr. Sutherland breathed relief. He thought that the baron would go no higher. But the baron was simply acknowledging in Michael Angelo a superior. They hurried out again, and broached another and a darker stairway, and at every turn an official saluted them, and in proportion as they rose higher the salutations of the officials grew more welcoming at the sight of these rare visitants from earth.

They passed through another tunnel, and had another view of the interior; and now the tourists had dwindled to beetles crawling over the marble floors. And then they engaged themselves in ladder-like twisting stairs that wormed their way between the inner and the outer domes; and breaths shortened and puffs quickened from *adagio* to *allegro*, and cheeks reddened. Higher, higher. The world well lost and sunken away. Higher, higher, and higher!

An official at the top of a staircase scarcely a foot wide seemed to be standing on Mars itself. He beamed at the adventurers who had arrived to mitigate by their earthly presence the tedium of his withdrawn and solitary existence. His smile rested lovingly upon them. They paused. He pointed reluctantly to a door. They passed. They were magically in the open. A gale, a great wind, smote their pink faces. They clutched at their hats. They were in the exposed gallery of the cupola, and the roof of St. Peter's lay thrice as far below them as the city lay below the roof.

"Yes," thought Septimius. "It is all over with me."

CHAPTER XXXII

THE INTERRUPTION

"This gives ye a better notion of Rome than any ye would get down there," said Lord Furber.

They had skirted round the gallery to the East face of it where an absolute calm seemed to obtain. They sat, side by side, in a niche in the sunshine. They had taken breath. Their cheeks were still pink, and their hearts still a trifle overworking at the great engineering job of circulating the blood. But they tingled with the unfamiliar sensation of perfect health, and suddenly comprehended the perilous foolishness and futility of all drug-taking. Further, they were as proud as boys, because they were two boys who had said they would climb the dome of St. Peter's, and had climbed it.

Much of the city lay directly in front of them, a criss-cross of streets dotted with a thousand towers. Two human beings like ants were traversing the vast Piazza exactly in front of them. They moved slowly, scarcely perceptibly, crawling.

"Ye see those two fellows crossing the Piazza?" said Lord Furber. "Look, they're just at the fountain on the left! That's you and me, Sep. I mean there isn't *that* much of difference between them and us. Nobodies. Insects. And they don't know it. And we only know it because we're up here. I feel like Jehovah laughing in his beard at Ralph Furber and S. Sutherland down there . . . Sep! Have ye got all ye want?"

A curious, benevolent, familiar, boyish tone, as though the baron was saying also: "I hope ye have. I want ye to have had all ye want."

"I should think so," Septimius replied placidly.

"I reckon ye have." The baron added, unable to bear the idea that Septimius had done fundamentally better in life than he himself had: "So have I, I suppose. But what does it all matter, anyhow? This perch is doing me good. Clears yer brain. Gives ye a sense of proportion. That's what it does. Eh, Sep?"

"Yes," Septimius agreed. "Yes."

"For two days past, I don't mind telling ye, I've been wanting summat. Terribly. I wanted it last night. Now I don't want it. No, I *don't* want it."

"Oh," said Mr. Sutherland blandly. "What was that?"

"Nothing. Only that Laller business. It got on my nerves. Funny thing, I was beginning to be a bit superstitious about it! Did *I* know there were any Laller frocks in that stuff that I had sent down to the yacht? Not me. And when Harriet said 'Laller' it gave me a regular turn. And yet I could have sworn there wasn't one iota of superstition in me. Upon my soul, I thought I was the only man in the world who wasn't superstitious." He laughed. "I can see now clear enough from up here. I thought it meant I was bound to get hold of Lallers. Fact! I was so sure of getting it I didn't care what tone I used to ye, Sep. Harriet had vexed me, and I let it out on ye. I never wanted anything as much as I wanted Lallers. And for very good reason. But it's all altered now. Now I don't want Lallers. I don't care who has Lallers. But, by G——d,

I wanted it yesterday and last night! I thought last night if I didn't get it I shouldn't ever be able to go home again and hold my blooming head up. I thought I should be humiliated for ever and ever. Comic, ain't it?"

"Very," said Mr. Sutherland calmly. He was relieved. He saw how wrong and entirely silly he had been to imagine that it was going to be all over with him when he reached the cupola. Lord Furber had abandoned his prey.

"Of course," the baron continued, "I know why ye wouldn't sell me Lallers. At least I think I know. Ye're going in for a combine of some sort, and Lallers 'll be part of it." Mr. Sutherland at these words had a slight recurrence of apprehension. Was the millionaire trimming round?

"You aren't so far out," Mr. Sutherland candidly admitted . . . "It'll be a two-million affair."

"Well," said the baron. "Yesterday, if I'd known that for sure, I'd have suggested ye let me take the whole affair off yer hands, and I'd find all the capital, and take all the risks, and give yer a hundred thousand for yeself. That's what I'd ha' been ready to do yesterday, or even this morning before we came up here," Lord Furber spoke sadly and courageously. He did not even glance at Septimius, but fixed his eyes in philosophical meditation upon the town of Tivoli glistening in the hills a dozen or more miles off. "And *you* don't want Lallers either, Sep," he added nicely. "Not really!"

"Well," said Septimius, not to be behindhand in true wisdom. "If you look at it like that, I don't. Everything's only an idea. I admit it."

He felt the stirring of an absurd impulse to relinquish Lallers and the entire scheme to his crony. It seemed to him that if he did so he would be rising superior to his crony. And beyond that, and purer than that, was an obscure motive of mere benevolence. What a gesture to say: "Lallers is yours, my friend"!

Then he stiffened suddenly. How clever the fellow had been to guess at the existence of a scheme for a combine! Yes, he was too clever. He was a necromancer; that was what he was. He was a fellow to beware of. Why should Septimius make him a present of anything at all? Besides, the fellow didn't want Lallers any more.

Lord Furber had been wearing his Homburg hat at the back of his head, so as to hide the white patch over the wound. He now tipped the hat forward over his brow, and deliberately felt his chin.

"My chin still look queer?" he inquired.

"No. Nobody would notice it who didn't know about it."

"It doesn't hurt nearly so much this morning . . . Of course," he went on dreamily, "I know I've been spoilt. I'm far too rich to escape being spoiled. If I want anything I'm always convinced I positively *ought* to have it. And when anyone stops me from having it I think I've got a genuine grievance against them. Funny, isn't it?" He smiled, half-wistfully. "I *should* ha' liked Lallers. I won't deceive myself. I *should* ha' liked to get it."

Then he gazed at Mr. Sutherland as if desiring to share with Mr. Sutherland the rich joke of a multi-million-aire's complicated psychology.

Mr. Sutherland was at last overcome. He knew he was about to behave like a grandiose fool, and that later he would regret his action. But the wish to hear himself, seated there in the skies on the top of St. Peter's, utter the wonderful words: "See here, old man, Lallers is yours"

—this wish was terrific in him. He could no more resist it.

"See here, old man," he started.

He was just plunging over the precipice when somebody walked round and faced them. And not an inebriated American! Harriet Perkins herself! Mr. Sutherland felt —and with awe—that some divinity was shaping his rough-hewn ends.

Harriet wore the yachting costume, hat and all, but with a different pair of shoes. And she was as bright as the morning.

"Now you needn't look so startled, you two. I'm not startled to see you here. Why should you be startled to see me here? Everything is simplicity itself. I had to come to Rome on professional business. I knew you'd be staying at the Paradiso. It's one of the very worst hotels in Rome, but it's the place where all your sort of people go, and so of course you couldn't be seen anywhere else. So I went to inquire for you at the Paradiso. You'd gone out, but the giant at the door told us he'd heard you tell your chauffeur to go to St. Peter's. I felt sure you couldn't possibly come to St. Peter's without making the ascent of this Matterhorn of a dome. At least, I knew that Ralph couldn't, and that Seppie would be forced to follow him—much against his will. I wanted to see you on urgent business, and here I am. I should have caught you at the hotel, but I absolutely had to get a larger pair of shoes to match this costume . . . Ralph, you must have wirelessed very good instructions to the dressmakers about my figure, but you went rather wrong on the size of my feet. They're larger than you imagined."

Not a trace of breathlessness in her: after climbing half a thousand stairs the girl was as fresh as though she had never left earth! This seemed wonderful to Mr. Sutherland who was still conscious that his heart was working under pressure. As he stood up and shook hands he was particularly conscious also of an unreasonable pleasure at the sight of her, and he definitely decided that he could neither leave Rome nor send for his wife and family to join him in Rome. He felt both happy and wicked: a sensation than which there is perhaps no finer in human life.

"I think I'll sit where you are, if I may," said Harriet persuasively to the baron, who rose, took her hand, and pressed her into the seat.

"And what's yer business?" asked the baron. "Why have yer deserted yer post as housekeeper of my yacht?"

"Ah!" exclaimed Harriet, with a teasing piquancy, "wouldn't you like to know!" She examined the baron's face, and concluded that his mind was far away on some matter of which she knew nothing. "But you must listen as if you were interested," she added, "not that you won't be interested. You will."

CHAPTER XXXIII

THE PRESS

"I came up in the launch," said Harriet.

"Not the flyer?" the baron demanded.

"The flyer. Why not? I'd a lot of important house-keeping to do."

"The caterer does all the buying—except the big things that the purser does. And he knows the whole job. I reckon he's marketed in pretty nearly every big port in Europe."

But Rome isn't a port," said Harriet. "And even if it was, your caterer wouldn't know how to market in it. I've seen yacht caterers at their deadly work in Southampton and Torquay. They go into shops like sheep to the sacri-fice. The tradesmen can sniff them half a mile off. No! But I brought the caterer with me, as well as the purser with his purse. Mr. Antinope informed me that he'd never known a yacht have a woman-housekeeper before. What fun he is—and doesn't guess it! They're waiting for me. I haven't begun to shop yet. But when I've finished with those two sometime this afternoon, they'll be worth a great deal more to you than they used to be. It's fortunate for you that my mother put me through a stiff course of housekeeping when I was young. Also, among other things, I speak Italian—and not like an Englishwoman either."

Lord Furber curtly asked:

"And have yer climbed up here just to sing yer own praises and show off yer frock? Or is there anything else?" He had ceased to be an insect crossing the Piazza of St. Peter's, and was once more a full-sized millionaire.

"Plenty else," Harriet replied. "What I've told you is only the overture. I've sent a doctor down to the yacht by car."

"Anybody ill?"

"Depends what you call 'ill.' Mrs. Bumption's ankle was about a yard in circumference this morning. She didn't sleep all night. And Bumption didn't sleep. Bumption foresees himself a widower, and Mrs. Bumption is terrorizing the stewards, so that I thought I'd better wait on her myself. I told her if she wasn't quiet I should pour some water over her face. She would not lie quiet. I got the water all ready in a jug, and held it over her . . . And she was quiet. We now understand each other. She is an old dear. Nobody's ever handled her before."

The baron laughed.

"Harriet," said he, "I can see ye're destined to make some good man unhappy for life. But it isn't going to be me—I can promise ye that. What else have ye for me?"

"Bravo, Harriet!" said Mr. Sutherland, blandly and daringly.

"Oh! I've hardly begun yet. Mr. Robbington came on board at seven o'clock this morning in a great state."

"Who's Mr. Robbington?"

"Don't you know? You ought to. He's the Rome correspondent of your paper, the *Courier*."

"Of course he is. Well, I can't be expected to remember the names of all the foreign correspondents of my newspapers, can I? What was he after? He wasn't supposed to know that I was anywhere near Rome. Nobody was supposed to know. Smart fellow, Robbington! Smarter than I thought."

"He didn't know you were near Rome. At least he didn't know last night when he was telephoning his message to the *Courier*. He only found out after the message had gone."

"What message?"

"About a strange English yacht being at Ostia, and sensational things going on on the yacht. Women being entrapped from launches and swung on board against their will like cattle. And all that kind of thing. He'd got wind of it. He knew it all except the name of the yacht—and that seems to have gone wrong on the Italian telephone."

"Who told ye?"

"He told me himself. He saw the captain first. He didn't say much to the captain. The captain sent him to me—everybody seems to come to me. He was very confiding to me, Mr. Robbington was. An artless young man—quite the journalist. He rushed back to Rome in his car, and I dare say he's now trying to find your lordship."

Lord Furber walked to and fro in the gallery of the cupola.

"What *was* there in the darned message? D'ye know?"

"Oh yes. He showed me a copy of it, and then forgot to take it away with him. Here it is." Miss Harriet Perkins opened her bag and produced a paper.

Lord Furber read (to himself):

"Ostia, which is the port of Rome, was to-day thrown into feverish excitement by the doings of a mysterious large and luxurious yacht flying the Blue ensign of the British Naval Reserve, which dropped anchor there this morning. A considerable number of beautiful and handsomely-dressed young Italian women came down in a procession of motor-cars from Rome at an early hour to meet the yacht, and were taken on board from launches. A little later one of these ladies, apparently not satisfied with what was going on, escaped back into a launch. She refused to return, and was ultimately forcibly taken and strapped into a box, which was hoisted on board, the lady still courageously struggling. It is impossible to obtain further particulars yet; but the local authorities have been informed of the affair and doubtless more will be heard of it within the next twenty-four hours."

Lord Furber put the paper in his pocket. Then he took it out again and showed it to Mr. Sutherland.

Said Harriet:

"You can imagine that on the front page of your lovely *Courier*, and the sort of headlines it will have, can't you? Well, this is the brand of news you instruct all your men to look out for, all over the world, I expect; and now at last you've got some results."

Mr. Sutherland and Harriet regarded one another cautiously.

"When did the fellow find out the name of the yacht?" demanded Lord Furber.

"About midnight," she said. "Long after his message had gone."

"Oh well. We can let it die. Nobody ever remembers these things for more than a day," said Lord Furber grimly.

"I don't think it'll die as quickly as all that." said Harriet maliciously. "It was the correspondent of one of your rivals, the *Evening Telegraph*, that told Mr. Robbington, and a message with full particulars will appear in the *Evening Telegraph* this afternoon, he says. What fun for Fleet Street! Your large and luxurious yacht will be the talk of all England by to-morrow morning. No wonder Mr. Robbington rushed down to Ostia to see you. He was in a very peculiar condition. I gave him some breakfast."

CHAPTER XXXIV

THE PRESSMAN

THE facial expressions of Lord Furber became so multitudinous and fearsome, the glitter of his eyes so formidable, and the movements of his legs so antic, that Harriet Perkins walked away, disappearing round the curve of the gallery. Mr. Sutherland followed her.

"It *is* a bit of a blow for him," said Harriet smiling. "Do you think it's safe to leave him?"

"If you ask me," said Septimius, "it's a great deal safer to leave him than to stay with him."

"Not with you there!" said Harriet. "Seppie! Never shall I forget you knocking him down! That was the most wonderful thing that ever happened to me or ever will."

Septimius unsuccessfully tried to hide his satisfaction at this statement so deliciously made by the bewitching creature, and to hide also his consciousness of the facts that he was a seventh child, had stroked the Cambridge boat, and had conducted himself heroically in dramatic circumstances on the yacht.

He said blandly:

"Anyhow, I don't think he'll do anything very serious without an audience."

"That's the cruellest remark I ever heard. Your fist may be a man's, but your tongue is a woman's, Seppie."

Mr. Sutherland smiled mysteriously to himself.

"But I like him," he added. "He's the cleverest man in my experience—and—you're the cleverest woman, Harriet."

At this moment the high wind carried off Mr. Sutherland's hat, which, being somewhat of the shape and lightness of a parachute, sailed away clear of the dome, sank slowly, and vanished, seemingly determined to examine for itself the privacies of the Vatican gardens.

"No importance," said Mr. Sutherland blandly. "It isn't mine. I took somebody else's from the Paradiso this morning." The wind made waves on his sparse, short hair, as on a field of young corn.

Then a man came puffing out into the gallery through the orifice which led to the five hundred stairs. A very fair, youngish person, with a short, fair beard and a nervous demeanour. You would guess at once, from the beard and the demeanour, that he belonged to the British colony of a foreign city.

"Oh! Mr. Robbington!" Miss Perkins greeted him. "Then you called at the Paradiso, and they gave you the message I left for you in case you did call!"

"Thank you, I did. The janissary at the concierge's counter failed you not. Of course, he knew me."

"Yes," said Harriet. "He told me he knew you. This is Mr. Septimius Sutherland. Seppie, Mr. Robbington, Rome correspondent of the *London Courier*."

Septimius and the journalist bowed to each other, and Mr. Robbington's bow was the courtlier. Mr. Robbington also had the advantage of being able to raise his hat in token of polite deference.

"One of the hatless brigade," said he, with such a charming and humorous smile that nobody could have been offended by it. "Lest I should be misunderstood," he continued, "I ought to tell you that an average of seven hats are lost in this gallery every day of windy weather. Then Lord Furber is not here after all?"

Harriet explained that the baron was round the other side of the circular gallery.

"I'll go to him. I feel quite ready for him," Mr. Robbington concluded.

And he went.

"You'd better come, too," Harriet murmured to Mr. Sutherland. "You might be needed." She laughed.

The baron was staring over the parapet. He had not quite ceased laughing at the spectacle of the voyage of Mr. Sutherland's hat. He turned sharply at the sound of Mr. Robbington's footsteps, and frowned, because Mr. Robbington, whom he did not know and had never seen, evidently had the intention of addressing him, and the baron hated to be addressed by strangers.

"Have I the honour of speaking to Lord Furber?" Mr. Robbington cermoniously inquired, again bowing and raising his hat.

"Ye have."

"My name is Robbington, and though personally unknown to your lordship, I am the Rome correspondent of the *London Courier*. An unfortunate thing has happened, and I have come to inform you. I was quite disturbed about it up to a couple of hours ago, but now I am strangely calm. The truth is that it has occurred to me that if I am to be hung I may as well be hung for a sheep as for a lamb."

The baron pierced every portion of Mr. Robbington's body with darts from his homicidal eyes.

Mr. Sutherland and Miss Perkins had gone round the curve the opposite way from Mr. Robbington; they had gone round quietly. Lord Furber, facing Mr. Robbington, did not see them; neither did he hear them; moreover they half hid themselves in a niche, like Sir Toby Belch and his companion hiding to watch Malvolio.

"I know what's happened," said Lord Furber.

"Miss Perkins told you?"

"What the devil has it got to do with you who told me?"

"Just so," said Mr. Robbington, with surprising imperturbability. "Nothing to do with me. Still, it must have been Miss Perkins. I'm sure she told you much more concisely than I should have done. I'm apt to be a little long-winded, especially when I'm excited. Well, Lord Furber, the first thing I want to say is that I resign my post on the staff of your esteemed, sensational rag, or, more properly, newspaper. Nobody shall ever be able to say that I was dismissed. I am also preventing you from doing something which in calmer moments you might regret."

He drew down the corners of his lips sardonically.

"I cannot imagine why I ever took on the job," he continued. "The money, though it doesn't amount to wealth, is useful, but you can pay too high a price for money. My new-found leisure will enable me to get on with my handbook to Rome, which, perhaps I may be allowed to mention incidentally, is conceived on an entirely new plan; and also with my translation of Dante, which will bring in less money than prestige. I have reason to believe that my translation of the great mediæval poet is better than Carey's. Not that that is saying much. I have always thought that Carey has been grossly over-praised. However, possibly you will say that all this is beside the point. I will only add that, being not entirely bereft of the milk of human kindness, I feel a certain sympathetic sorrow for your lordship in the predicament in which providence, through my unwitting agency, has placed your lordship."

Mr. Robbington then drew breath, still amiably, yet sardonically smiling at the speechless baron—and waited.

"Why don't ye verify yer facts?" the baron at length asked, in a voice terribly calm and quiet.

"Yes," said Mr. Robbington. "I was expecting that question. But supposing I had stopped to verify my facts, and supposing some other paper had got hold of the same incomplete facts that I got hold of, my editor would have been wanting to know by cable what the deuce I meant by not getting in first, and what the deuce I thought I was in Rome for. Perhaps you don't know the side of the *Courier* editor that I know. I'm not stating my position very clearly, but your lordship has brains enough to catch my drift. And I should like to ask what the deuce your lordship means by coming to Rome without letting me know. I am the finest guide in the world to Rome. I could have put you wise on lots of things. Here you are, for instance, wasting your time on this hackneyed panorama, while I should have taken you to see Hadrian's villa—a private country house—it would give you millionaires something to think about. You think you understand luxury, whereas you simply haven't begun to understand luxury. In the matter of luxury you are about eighteen hundred years behind the times."

"Ye shall show it me, young man."

"Oh no, I shan't. I'm no longer at your beck and call. And I'll tell you another thing, since we're talking. You make a fuss about verifying facts. But the *Courier* doesn't want its facts verified. It never prints facts, save by accident. I except the racing tips, which I admit are rather remarkable. Have you ever considered how humiliating it must be for a man of my tastes and ambitions to work for a sheet like the *Courier?* No, you haven't. Of course you haven't. I have the honour to wish your lordship good-day."

Lord Furber stuck his hands into his pockets and approached Mr. Robbington, who involuntarily stepped backwards.

"Say," said he. "Say, my friend. Do ye live in Rome for choice?"

"No," answered the journalist. "I live in Rome because it's cheap, and because I just happen to be in Rome and haven't the enterprise to leave it."

"Where should ye live if ye could choose?"

"What a foolish question! London naturally! There's no other place."

"Well," said the baron. "Ye're the best highbrow and brow-beater I've struck yet. I'll give ye a job in London—editor of the literary page of the *Evening Mercury*. Thousand a year. Start at once."

"Thanks," said Mr. Robbington, with a most expansive smile. "I'll take it. I think I could help you there. You might write and confirm. Good day."

He turned away and then came back.

"If there's anything I can do," he suggested in a relenting and benevolent voice, "to clear up this *Vanguard* mess, I'll be glad to do it."

"We'll just let that alone and sit tight," said Lord Furber.

"I think you're very wise," said Mr. Robbington. "Let time do its healing work, my lord."

And he departed.

CHAPTER XXXV

THE WATCH

LORD FURBER was in many respects rather old-fashioned. In the matter of watches, for instance, he adhered to the ancient chain or cable principle, as opposed to the new bracelet principle. When he wanted to know the time he drew his watch from the depths of his waistcoat pocket by hauling in a chain or cable whose other end lay in the opposite pocket of his waistcoat. He held that bracelets were proper for women only, and, moreover, he did not care to have to twist his forearm and crick his elbow-joint in order to look at his watch.

The baron's umbilical region was crossed by an exceedingly thin gold chain, at one end of which was the thinnest gold watch ever constructed and at the other end a flat gold pencil.

Now immediately upon the departure of the newly-appointed editor of the literary page of the *Evening Mercury*, Lord Furber snatched at the middle of the chain and dragged out both watch and pencil. His fingers slipped down the chain in the direction of the pencil, and the next instant the watch was whizzing with incredible velocity round and round in thin air and forming the circumference of a circle of which the centre was the pencil and the radius was the watch-chain. His features were contorted as if in anguish, his teeth set, his head sunk, his shoulders lifted, and all the muscles of his right arm strenuously taut, in the effort to get the very maximum of speed out of the revolving watch. And the watch made a hissing sound as it whizzed in its orbit.

Such, on this occasion, was Lord Furber's method of relieving his feelings after a period of undue and unaccustomed strain. The watch, in fact, was suffering in place of Mr. Robbington. Suddenly the chain parted at its jointure with the pencil, and the watch, like a shot from a howitzer, described a marvellously beautiful parabola in the air, the chain rushing after it as the tail rushes after a comet. The watch and chain travelled an immense distance ere they disappeared somewhere beyond the back of the dome of St. Peter's.

Lord Furber, as soon as he had recovered from his astonishment at the celestial spectacle, dashed the pencil furiously down on the ground and attempted to stamp it with both feet into utter shapelessness and uselessness. However, his feet being inaccurately aimed, and the pencil very small, the pencil escaped destruction. Whereupon the baron with extraordinary calmness stooped and picked up the pencil and put it back into his pocket and seemed to pretend that nothing had happened. The crisis was passed. The baron's reason was restored. The baron had conquered himself. He breathed and smiled softly as a babe.

"Come out o' that. Come out of it," the baron said, agreeably inviting, "I knew all the time ye were there spying on me."

And Harriet and Mr. Sutherland came out of it.

"I say, Sep," said the baron. "He was a bit like yeself. He attacked me before I was ready for him." Septimius only smiled, for he could think of nothing to say in answer to this allusion to the prize-fighting episode.

"And he was a bit like you as well, Harriet," said the baron. "He was all for bullying me and teaching me how to live." And Harriet also smiled.

"But," said the baron, "he was ready enough to take my money. They always are."

"I don't know that *I* am," Septimius put in blandly. The baron stared at him darkly.

"But why did you throw the watch away, Ralph?" Harriet quizzed.

"I didn't throw it away. It's a hunter, and I sent it to track down Mr. Sutherland's hat."

"Well," said Harriet, "you kept your temper very wonderfully. And we congratulate you. You're making progress, Ralph."

"Now listen here," said the baron. "I don't want any sauce. And I warn ye I'm still dangerous. I *did* keep me temper. But I only kept it because I thought I'd disappoint ye. And it might ha' been better for ye in the end if I hadn't kept it."

"Don't boast, Ralph," said Harriet. "We're proud of you—at least I am; Sep doesn't know you as well as I know you. But you can't frighten us any more. We can see now you're a Christian after all. Be good, and tell us like a man how you do intend to get out of that hole that Mr. Robbington has put you in."

Lord Furber said:

"There is no hole. So I'm not in it. I'm not going to do anything at all. I told yer already. The thing 'll be forgotten in three days, and I shall get square with the *Evening Telegraph* pretty soon; you may bet I shall. I shan't laugh it down. I shall live it down. Anyhow it's a good joke, and if the joke's on me it's still a good joke."

At this point a man in wide knickerbockers with green

tabs at the tops of his patterned woollen stockings, appeared round the curve. He was the first stranger to visit the cupola since the baron and his friends had taken possession of it, for the hour was still early. The man stared around, murmuring half-audibly in a pleased tone: "The Woolworth has this beat." Mr. Sutherland made a sign to the baron. The visitor was he who had disturbed their colloquy in the Coliseum on the previous evening. Lord Furber went up to the stranger.

"No," said Lord Furber to him. "This isn't the golf course. It's the dome of St. Peter's."

The stranger regarded the baron uncertainly, and then, no doubt, concluding that lunatics might be unsuitable company at a great height, hurried away.

"I told ye I was dangerous," said Lord Furber to his friends. "But if that chap had had his deserts he wouldn't ha' got off so cheaply."

"I don't quite understand why you should go and behave like that to people you don't know," said Harriet correctively.

"I do know him," said the baron. "We both know him, don't we, Sutherland?" He related, in somewhat exaggerated terms, the incident of the Coliseum, and continued in a louder and an excited tone: "That chap cost me a 'deal' last night. I'd just got Sutherland into the right mood for closing the 'deal.' He was just ready to give way to me against all his instincts. I'd put the evil eye on him. And then this half-tipsy feller butted in and broke the spell, and I was done down."

The baron gave Mr. Sutherland a humorous glance and Mr. Sutherland, absolutely amazed at such singular, shameless candour from the master of chicane, merely coughed.

"And that's not all," the baron proceeded. "I brought yer Seppie up here this morning and began it all over again, and everything was going fine when my new housekeeper romps in and bursts up the spell a second time. Well, I give it up. I won't try any more. It wouldn't be any use trying any more. Fact is, I was surprised that this here Seppie stood for it a second time."

The baron stood there like a great professor of sleight who had only been defeated by pure hazard in the performance of a dazzlingly brilliant trick. He could well afford to confess defeat. Mr. Sutherland coughed once more and Harriet thought he was a darling, and a very clever darling, to do nothing but smile. The smile was more effective than any formula of words. It was not a victorious or vain smile, but a modest smile, as of one whom destiny has let off and who calmly intends to remain let off.

"But what did you want our Seppie to do for you?" Harriet asked.

"Shall I tell her, Sutherland?"

"If you like," said Septimius. "Why not?"

And indeed Septimius didn't care who knew the circumstances. He held a firm option on the thing he would in all probability want to buy, and no publicity or gossip could deprive him of the option.

So the baron told a flattered Harriet, who had never before seen big business in the making.

"And I offered him a hundred thousand for himself," the baron concluded. "And he won't have it."

"*I*'d have it!" she cried. "Wouldn't I just!"

"Now look here, Harriet," said the baron. "I've stood a lot of d—d cheek from you. And I've turned ye the other cheek. And ye've finished up by spoiling my deal. Ye'd better put it right for me. Sutherland 'll do anything for ye. He'd murder for ye. He nearly did. I don't know why, for he's a respectable married man. But he would. See how he's blushing. Ask him to let me have Lallers, and he'll let me have Lallers. He couldn't refuse ye."

"But why are you both so keen on buying Lallers?" Harriet asked, prouder than ever.

"I don't know why Sutherland's keen," replied the baron. "But I know why I'm so keen. And I'll tell ye. I want to own the business that made those clothes ye're wearing. They're the finest clothes I ever saw on any woman. Call it sentiment. Call it silly. But that's why I want to own Lallers, and as soon as I own the business I'll give orders that they supply ye with frocks free of charge for the rest of yer life, my dear."

Then the baron laughed very loud.

"It's a good reason, isn't it?" he wound up.

"But it isn't the real reason," said Harriet.

"No, it isn't. But I couldn't honestly say it isn't one reason."

"Well," said Harriet. "I won't ask Seppie to sell to you."

"Why not?"

"Because I know what the real reason is."

(But she did not.)

In her tone was an accent of perfect assurance which visibly disturbed the baron.

"Ye don't."

"Yes, I do. So there."

"Tell me what it is."

"I won't."

"Who've ye been talking to? Who've ye met this morning?"

236

"I've met Count Veruda—in the Corso."

"Veruda doesn't know the reason. Nobody in Italy knows the reason."

"I didn't say Veruda does know the reason. You asked me who I'd met and I said I'd met Count Veruda. But I know the reason, and I suppose I'm in Italy!"

The baron glared and glowered and frowned and flashed. It was plain that he utterly refused to credit Harriet's boast, and yet somehow he was being forced to credit it.

"Now, now," Harriet warned him. "You behaved beautifully under the fearful strain of Mr. Robbington. Don't go and spoil it all with one of your frenzies, my little Ralph."

The baron bit his lip.

"When did ye find out," he growled.

"This morning."

There was a pause, indicating drama.

Said Mr. Sutherland blandly:

"Shall we go down to earth? I want to make Lord Furber a present of a new watch."

The baron again laughed loudly. They went down to earth.

CHAPTER XXXVI

MONTE CARLO

Lord Furber had said:

"There's more *fun* at Monte Carlo."

This was at Ostia, and it had ended the discussion between Harriet and Mr. Sutherland and the baron as to their next port of call. Genoa had been ruled out at once, as having no diversions worthy of voyagers in a two-thousand-ton yacht. The baron had affirmed that the famous Genoese palaces could be seen in a couple of hours, and that the Genoese restaurants were less inviting even than those of Rome, and that the opera house was too large for the singers therein, and that the municipal authorities had not yet had the wit to create a Casino.

The argument had lain between the rival claims of Monte Carlo and Cannes. Harriet had upheld Cannes, saying that everybody knew that Monte Carlo no longer counted, and that nobody pretending to be smart could possibly be seen nowadays at Monte Carlo. Lord Furber had replied by reading the list of guests at the Hotel de Paris and the Hermitage at Monte Carlo. The baron was ever inclined to conservatism. Mr. Sutherland knew little of either town, save the strictly bourgeois side; but the legend of Monte Carlo appealed to him more strongly than the legend of Cannes, which indeed was still in the making of Monsieur Cornuché, the regretted Aladdin of continental gaming resorts. Lord Furber had said that if they cared not for Monte Carlo they would proceed to Cannes. The question was settled.

Mr. Sutherland declared, and declared again and again, that he really ought to return to London instantly, by the night express from Rome; but he used no effort to depart, the fact being that he could not nerve himself to face the wrench of quitting any yacht made heavenly by the presence of Harriet Perkins. Mr. Sutherland was in a sad happy way.

The sailing of the yacht had been delayed by Harriet. Count Veruda, informed by wireless of the early arrival of the *Vanguard* at Ostia, had travelled to Rome from Naples, bringing with him Miss Perkins's luggage. At the last moment, and after the decision for Monte Carlo, Harriet discovered that Count Veruda had not brought with him all her luggage, and she must telegraph herself to Naples, whither the Count, under orders, had returned. (Lord Furber had said privately that the pleasant Count would only be an encumbrance at Monte Carlo, a city as to which the baron considered he had nothing to learn.) Harriet insisted on going ashore to dispatch the telegram herself. She would not trust it to an English-speaking "runner" at Ostia, nor would she permit it to be wirelessed from the high seas. Her excuse was that it contained details of an intimate nature unsuited to any English-comprehending male eyes. Harriet had spent more than an hour ashore.

Then, at sea, Harriet had suggested that the yacht should pay a call at the island of Elba. Lord Furber had embraced the scheme with fervour. He had his weaknesses, and one of them, which he shared with all millionaire newspaper proprietors, was an excessive admiration for Napoleon, and a naïve but unspoken conviction that the resemblances between Napoleon and himself were extremely striking.

They had dropped anchor outside the little futile harbour of Portoferraio at midnight, and the following day had examined in detail the miserable little Napoleonic home and haunts, and Lord Furber had delivered the verdict: "Well, it was a d—d shame to put him in a hole like that."

Heralded by wireless messages, the tremendous *Vanguard* had arrived at Monte Carlo on the next afternoon, amid much public excitement and marine pother. For no such majestic craft as the *Vanguard* had been seen within the Monacan port since the vast *Lysistrata* belonging to the deceased proprietor of the *New York Herald*; and in size and style the *Vanguard* yielded nothing to the vessel which had been the home of James G. Bennett.

The marine pother had been the result of the operation of the rule that the largest yacht must always have the best berth. Other important yachts belonging to other important persons had been shifted about by the harbour-master to make right room for the *Vanguard*, but as evening fell the other yachts, one of them a thousand-tonner, had begun to compete in other ways, and in particular in the burning of electricity. Never was such a display of illumination. Decks were like the rue de la Paix at night, and the lighting of the stern gangways on to the quay dazzled to blindness the eyes of beholders. The *Vanguard* won in the contests.

The hour was ten-thirty. The lamps of the ancient city of Monaco, with its standing army of two hundred warriors, shone on the hill over the *Vanguard's* stern. Trams were running round the rim of the harbour to the north. Monte Carlo itself was shut off from the harbour by an intervening hill, and no sign could be seen of its casino, its hotels, its restaurants, its cafés, its theatres, its dancing-establishments, its night-clubs, or its parterres of flowers.

But high in the westward, free of the intervening hill and visible from the yacht, were the sheeted lights of the most significant, the most fashionable, and the most discreet building in Monte Carlo—the International Sporting Club—an establishment devised and arranged to the end that the richest people could lose more money in less time and in a more quiet luxurious environment than in any other spot on the Mediterranean coast.

A Hispano-Suisa car, blazing to emulate the yacht, stood waiting at the shore end of the long glittering gangway.

Lord Furber and Mr. Sutherland emerged from staterooms on to the *Vanguard's* main deck. They were attired for a great nocturnal occasion; that is to say, Mr. Sutherland had achieved the very plenitude of correctness, while the baron, somewhat snobbishly relying on his incomparable wealth and his power in the world, had limited himself to the least possible correctness: the baron regrettably wore neither a crush hat nor patent-leather shoes. Harriet's dictum that he had never left the Five Towns seemed to be not untrue. He was, however, freed now of the surgical patch on the back of his head, and his chin also was natural.

"Ye see that," said the baron, pointing to the sheeted lights on the hill.

Mr. Sutherland admitted that he did.

"That's the International Sporting Club. That's where I'd thought we'd go. It's always best to begin there. Then ye know where ye are, and where other folk are, too."

Mr. Sutherland, who was always apt to be ingenuous when he found himself in centres of fashion and expensive wickedness (for he had religiously given his life to the tenth muse, whose temples are in London, E.C.), inquired what the International Sporting Club might be. Lord Furber, delighting as every man does in the rôle of cicerone to an innocent, explained the attributes and aim of the I.S.C.

"Then why do they call it the International Sporting Club?" said Septimius.

"For the same reason as the Casino Company is called the Baths Company," answered the baron.

"I see," said Septimius; and he did see.

"I wonder how long that infernal girl's going to keep us waiting here?" exclaimed Lord Furber, stamping impatiently on the deck. His justification for impatience in a situation which any other man would have accepted as the most natural in the world, was that he had never in his life permitted any woman to keep him waiting.

"Tunnicliff!" he called sharply.

The blond secretary stood attendant near the head of the gangway. He had had an arduous late afternoon organizing, under Lord Furber's direction, the social side of the visit.

"Sir?"

"Just find out how long Miss Perkins is going to be."

The Honourable Luke disappeared without a word. Presently Harriet came up. She was wearing a black frock and her keys.

Lord Furber noticed the insignia of office, but remained calm.

"We're waiting for ye."

"Why?"

"Ye're going with us to the International Sporting Club."

"I'm not."

"But ye knew we were going."

"Yes, I knew you were going. But I never said I was going. I've got a lot to do. It's no light job, mine isn't."

"But ye never said ye weren't going."

"My life's too short to say all the things I'm not going to do. I never said I wasn't going to jump into the sea to-night and swim to Cannes. Now, did I?" She laughed amiably.

Lord Furber knew that she was challenging him not to lose his temper, and since he meant to win, he miraculously contrived to remain calm.

The relations between the two had shown an undercurrent of hostility ever since the scene in the gallery of the cupola of St. Peter's. Harriet had deliberately and irritatingly intrigued him, and the baron with much histrionic skill had hidden every symptom of being intrigued. Nevertheless, he was ever suspecting her of conspiracy against him with some person or persons unknown. She would come in to meals; she would not come in to meals; she would vanish for hours at a time; and no reason given except the foolish reason of her housekeeping. In the baron's opinion her housekeeping, though very efficient, was absurd, and he wished her to abandon it; but she would not abandon it.

"Do come, Harriet," Mr. Sutherland entreated.

Harriet shook her head.

"Well, look here," said the baron. "Come later, will you? Say eleven o'clock." His tone was a marvel of reasonableness.

With an equally marvellous (and dangerous) reasonableness, Harriet replied:

"All right. I'll come later. Eleven o'clock. Mr. Tunnicliff will bring me up, won't you, Mr. Tunnicliff?"

Mr. Tunnicliff stiffly gave assent.

CHAPTER XXXVII

LUKE IN THE CAR

"Oh!" cried Harriet Perkins, "I do believe I've brought two right-hand gloves! Yes, I have. *Would* you mind running down to my cabin, Mr. Tunnicliff? You're bound to see two left-hand gloves at the top of the left-hand top drawer in that funny little wardrobe by the side of the bed—I should say, the bunk."

For the Honourable Luke, on this occasion, at any rate, to hear was to obey. Was he not acting in a professional capacity?

As Harriet made the request, the other Mr. Tunnicliff was walking up the glittering gangway from shore to yacht. Harriet, standing at the head of the gangway, turned to face him, just under one of the constellations which lit the incline. She wore the green evening dress recently bestowed upon her by the largesse of Lord Furber, with her old olive-tinted cloak negligently thrown over it, and she was full of the sweet consciousness of looking very well in an environment of gigantic expense. Full, also, of the consciousness of being femininely equal to any number of men friendly or hostile. She was, and had been for some days, the only effectively functioning woman in the great yacht; for Mrs. Bumption was still set aside, and nobody, except her husband, had laid eyes on her since she had been put to bed. Mrs. Bumption was indeed forgotten by the world of the yacht.

Harriet had plainly begun a new life, far more exciting and agreeable than that of hotels. Not only was she active in the control of a complicated domestic organism; not only had she the sense of semi-tyrannic power—she was a queen among several score of male beings. She had electrified the social atmosphere of the whole vessel. Every man on board was aware of her, and felt the propriety of flattering her, and most of them found pleasure in flattering her, even in speaking to her and being spoken to by her. And had not the mightiest insisted upon having the advantage and tonic of her society in the selectest haunt of Monte Carlo? The Honourable Luke was her obedient errand-boy.

And now the wireless-operator, grandson of an earl, and with the most disdainful nostrils in all Monte Carlo, was approaching her, and she wondered how he would greet her. The young man was handsome and handsomely clad, as became one who in port had nothing to do but to exist beautifully. He halted at the summit of the gangway with a mien which, quite undesignedly, might have given to the unwary the impression that he was the owner of the yacht. He raised his hat in a manner unsurpassably graceful and impertinent; the curve of the arm which lifted the hat must obviously have been inherited from his late grandfather.

"Good evening, Miss Perkins," said he, in a low, caressing voice. "I see that your evening is about to start."

"Yes. And if you'd been a minute later you'd have missed the start."

"And you are still vamping, I perceive." His tone was impeccably courtly. "The way you asked my poor cousin to fetch your glove—a masterpiece of the vamping art. I needn't ask if you've been to Hollywood, Miss Perkins. You must have spent arduous months in the film studios of that astonishing city."

"Mr. Valentino, I believe," Harriet responded, bowing. "But haven't you got anything more to tell me?"

The wireless operator replied quickly and with relish: "I certainly have something more to tell you, and I promise you I won't tell anyone else, because I feel it's a piece of information which you and I ought to share with nobody. I've just been to the Café de Paris, and in passing the Hôtel de Paris on my way home, who do you think I saw looking out of a second-floor window and sort of hiding?"

"Give it up," said Harriet promptly.

"Lady Furber."

Harriet quite failed to control a movement of extreme surprise.

"You may well jump," said the speaker. "I dare say you will jump still more within the next few hours. Look at this."

He drew from his hip pocket a folded copy of a London evening newspaper, and displayed the front-page, on which flared headlines relating to the *Vanguard* and to Lord Furber.

"Just come. And probably Lady Furber has just come, too. What wife in her position would not have come? The thing that surprises me is that the whole visiting population of Monte Carlo is not congregated around this notorious vessel. However, we may expect sightseers in plenty to-morrow morning."

"Do you know Lady Furber?" asked Harriet.

"No. How could I aspire so high? But I know her by sight. Her red hair is unmistakable. And you may take it from me that the lady I have seen is the wife of the Baron Furber, owner of this yacht and of all our immortal souls. I expect she's come to reconnoitre for herself—

to see whether all those vamps from Rome are still on board. When she finds that only one vamp is on board, she may decide that even one vamp is more than is strictly necessary."

"I think I ought to call at the Hôtel de Paris," Harriet smiled.

"Yes, and leave your card."

Harriet thought she heard a footstep on the stairs below, and she waited impatiently for the Honourable Luke to reappear. But the Honourable Luke was dilatory. At length he came, with a long white scrap in his hand. She took the scrap, examined it, and thanked the bringer with an exquisite smile.

"Well, your news is very interesting," she said to the wireless operator, who was standing silent. "Good night."

"Good night," said the operator. "And good luck— at the tables—and elsewhere."

He hurried away with an unexampled bow, and at the same time, not troubling to conceal the gesture from Harriet, winked at the Honourable Luke.

Seated in the car by the side of the Honourable Luke, Harriet ought surely to have been in meditation about the disturbing arrival of her old friend, Lady Furber. But, in fact, she was at first occupied with thoughts of the Honourable Luke.

Was there anything in the charge just brought against her by his cousin? Had she been vamping Luke? She was interested in this question only in so far as she wanted to understand herself. What the possible consequences of the alleged vamping might be to Luke himself did not trouble in the least. She had a suspicion that she liked Luke. He had been very rude to her; he had rebuffed a friendly advance from her; but she liked him. He had neither the magnificent style nor the magnificent figure of his sinister cousin; but she liked him. He was moody and reserved; his manner of putting her into the car was strangely reserved; he sat down by her as though she had the plague; but she liked him.

The point was, would she have dispatched any other man on board to retrieve the glove? Well, she admitted that she would not. Nor would she have used to any other man quite the tone she had used to Luke. That tone was in all probability a challenge to resume intimacy. All which possibly did amount to what the wireless operator would call "vamping."

The car, which made no more noise than a cat purring, mounted the steep hill on third gear, it being one of those cars for which gradients have no significance worth mentioning. In a few seconds, as it seemed, the machine had arrived at the doors of the club. An attendant opened the door. The Honourable Luke stepped out. Harriet remained seated. The Honourable Luke impassively waited.

"Mr. Tunnicliff," said she at length, "will you get in again, and ask the driver to move on a bit and then stop. I should like to have a little chat with you, if you don't object."

"As you wish," said the Honourable Luke.

Harriet was obeyed.

"We're cosy enough here, aren't we?" Harriet observed.

"Yes," said the Honourable Luke.

The car had come to a standstill in the shadow of some trees which overhung the road. A tram, descending the hill, deafened their ears, and shook the foundations of the earth.

Harriet turned her head to see Luke's face.

"Do please look at me," she asked persuasively, but with a touch of warning impatience.

Luke obediently moved his head and looked at her, in a strictly non-committal way.

"I'm going to ask you to do me a favour" said Harriet. "Will you?"

"If I can."

"But naturally you can."

"Conscientiously?"

"Of course."

"You surprise me."

The fair-haired, slight, nervous, timid, easily-flushing young man offered this piece of insolence in a gruff, half-inarticulate voice. Harriet smiled as though he had paid her a compliment. The Honourable Luke glanced away.

"I promised to be at the Club at eleven o'clock," said Harriet. "But now I find I must pay an important call at the Hôtel de Paris. I might be kept there half an hour, even an hour. I want you to say nothing about it. You could wait in the car. Lord Furber will expect you to see me into the Club, though I've got my ticket all right. I'm a member there every season. And if his lordship asks why we're so late——"

"*You're* so late," the Honourable Luke corrected.

"*I'm* so late," Harriet agreed, "say I insisted on going for a drive first up to the Corniche road to look at the scenery."

"But you can say that for yourself."

"I can, and I will, but I want you to back me up. See?"

"I see. But I can't do it conscientiously."

"Why not?"

"Because you're evidently up to something that you think his lordship wouldn't care for. And it's no part of my job to deceive him. I know you're a regular con-

spirator, like he is. But I'm not a conspirator, except
under his orders."

"Then you won't oblige me?"

"Oh, yes, I will. I didn't say I wouldn't do it. All
I said was I couldn't do it conscientiously. But I'll do it."

"You're a dear," said Harriet. "I knew I could
trust you. Tell the driver to go on to the Hôtel de Paris,
will you?"

"Not yet," said the Honourable Luke. "You say
you knew you could trust me. But you aren't trusting
me."

"Yes, I am."

"No, you aren't. You haven't told me what's at the
bottom of all this. You must."

"But I can't possibly do that."

"Then you don't trust me, Miss Perkins. I'm not
going to trouble to tell you that I shouldn't breathe a word,
or that I should be like the grave, and so on. Because
you ought to know all about that. You *do* know. But
the fact is you're too proud and stuck up to tell me everything. You think you'll tell me just as much as you think
you will, and I shall accept it. But I shan't. Either I'll
be trusted entirely or I won't be trusted at all. Take it
or leave it."

For an instant Harriet suspected that somehow the
Honourable Luke must have overheard her own ultimatum
to Lord Furber a few nights earlier, so exactly was he
adopting the attitude which she had adopted. But she
dismissed the silly suspicion, perceiving that the attitude
was exactly as natural to Luke as it had been to herself.
In other words, in one matter, at any rate, they were kindred
minds: they had the same pride and the same obstinacy.

She put her hand lightly on his arm and, moving her

head, looked into his eyes in the gloom of the limousine, and smiled.

"You're quite right," she said. "Confidence is either complete or it's nothing. And now I come to think of it, I should *love* to trust you completely."

She removed her hand from his arm, and he immediately put his hand on her arm. Assuredly they were very cosy in the car, whose interior was like a tiny but utterly comfortable boudoir—and safer than any boudoir from interruption.

"I must make it short," said Harriet, "because we haven't much time."

"Pooh!" said Luke. "The boss won't be leaving the Club until two in the morning! Go ahead!"

"You're very autocratic," Harriet murmured.

"It's the only way to treat some people," said Luke, at the same time gazing at her in a manner which was not in the least in the world autocratic.

CHAPTER XXXVIII

HARRIET IN THE CAR

"Of course, you know Lady Furber?" Harriet suggested.

"There's not much 'of course' about it," said the Honourable Luke. "Furber's a rather independent sort of a fellow, and he has his own rooms in their house in Belgrave Square; so that even if I go there, which I don't often, I needn't necessarily see her. Still, I do know her."

"Well," said Harriet. "It doesn't really make any difference whether you know her or not. But she's a great friend of mine—an old friend."

"That's very odd."

"Why is it odd? Anything the matter with Lady Furber, or with me?"

"It's odd because she isn't your class at all. She's *his* class. His cousin, I think . . . And only a few years ago she was living in the provinces—Five Towns— Council school teacher or something. So I was wondering how she could be such an *old* friend of yours. I swear she couldn't have met anybody like you before she came to London."

"And what class d'you suppose I belong to?"

"Same as mine. The old High-and-Drys. County seats, Tory. Ruined by death duties, the war, and super-tax."

"You're not far out," said Harriet. "Except that I'm not quite ruined."

"Well, that's where you've got the pull over me. My lot were quite ruined—and no mistake about it. So I took service under the new Huns."

Harriet proceeded:

"Moreover, I haven't had a great deal to do with my class for years . . . I've been travelling—alone. When I was living in Paris, I don't remember exactly how long since, there was a party of teachers from the Five Towns on one of those cheap excursions—you know, 'a week in Paris, six guineas inclusive.' And I was asked to give up one day to showing them around. Some of those excursions are rather well managed. Ahem! It was then that I met Lady Furber. But of course she wasn't Lady Furber, then, and never expected to be, either. I needn't tell you all the details; but we became great friends. It isn't that I see her very often; I don't; only we're always corresponding. You may believe me she's no ordinary woman."

"I do believe you," said the Honourable Luke; "no ordinary sort of girl would have married *him*."

"But she was tremendously in love with him."

"Yes, I dare say."

"And he was with her."

"Was he?"

"Yes, he was. And there was the baby."

"Then she had two children—the baby was one and he was the other."

"Quite. Well, they've had a terrific quarrel. Of course this is strictly private."

"It isn't what I should call strictly private," said the Honourable Luke. "I knew about it. At least, I heard about it. We all heard about it. They were always having shindies. But this last one was about ten sizes larger than usual."

"And I suppose you know the cause of it?"

"No, I don't. I doubt if anyone does—really. If you understand me. Do you?"

"You mean they don't quite know themselves? One cause as good as another?"

"Something like that. They're of the same blood. She's fiery. He must have been hopelessly spoilt long before he'd any idea of marrying either her or anybody else. Both as proud as the devil. Ding-dong. That's what it's been, all through, you may bet your life. The cause, whatever it is, isn't a cause—it's only the occasion."

"Yes," Harriet thoughtfully murmured. She was thoughtful, not by reason of her concern for Maidie Furber, but by reason of the grasp which the Honourable Luke showed of the fundamentals of human nature. She had not guessed that the timid and ferocious boy had in him such wisdom.

"I suppose *you* haven't heard the cause?" Luke demanded negligently.

"If I had, do you think I should be asking you, my young friend," Harriet replied. "I haven't had even a glimpse of her for over a year. But I can promise you this. You're going to witness the most superb scrap of all your career as secretary to a volcano . . . I mean, you mayn't actually witness it, but you'll feel the effects of it. We all shall."

"Here?"

"Yes. Here."

"In the yacht?"

"Probably. Lady Furber has just arrived in Monte

Carlo. She's staying at the Hôtel de Paris, and I shall see her to-night—while you wait for me in the car."

"You've seen her already, then?"

"No."

"You've heard from her?"

"Not a line."

"Then how d'you know she's here?"

"I was told."

"Does Lord Furber know?"

"He certainly does not. If he did he wouldn't be amusing himself at the Club this moment."

"Does Sutherland know?"

"Nor him either."

"Why has Lady F. come to Monte Carlo just now?"

"Because of the scandal in the London papers about the yacht."

"Scandal?"

"Haven't you heard?"

"Not a syllable."

"And yet you're supposed to be a private secretary! My poor friend, what have you been doing to let yourself be kept in the dark like this? Surely you owe it to your self-respect to be aware of every mortal thing about your soda-water bottle of an employer!" And Harriet informed him of the enormous *gaffe* perpetrated by Mr. Robbington, and the journalistic performances thereafter of the rival *Evening Telegraph*. "You now have in front of you nearly all the raw material of the thunderstorm that will soon be breaking over our unprotected heads," she added.

"There's another point," said the Honourable Luke.

"What? Haven't you finished cross-examining me yet?"

"No; I haven't. I want to know this. You say

you're an old friend of Lady Furber's. Then how is it that Lord Furber hasn't recognized you—I feel sure he hasn't."

"Of course he hasn't. But then, you understand, he'd never met me before."

"But he must have heard his wife talking about you. After all, they aren't always quarrelling—not by any means. I've seen them myself on the most affectionate turtle-dove terms. He must have known your name at least."

"How insufferable you are with your disgusting suspicions!" Harriet exclaimed. "I'm not in the witness-box, and you aren't a K.C. Anyone would think you wouldn't believe a word I said until it was proved to be true." Then she laughed. "Still, I'll tell you, though you're as big a bully as Lord Furber himself. I got a new name at the beginning of last year. A cousin of mine left me the whole of her fortune on the condition I changed my name to hers. She was extremely rich—until about a year before she died. Then she lost most of her money—not that I knew! So that she only left about sixty pounds a year."

"And did you change your name for a rotten sixty pounds per annum?"

"Sixty pounds isn't rotten. Six pounds wouldn't be rotten. No money is rotten." Some heat here in Harriet's tone. "Besides, the poor old thing fully meant to be generous. I think it would have been dreadfully mean of me to refuse her merely because she'd been done in by investment-agents when she was too old to look after herself. And what's more—I enjoyed changing my name. A new name gives you a new outlook. And you have to learn to answer to a new name—that's good exercise for the brain. I call my new name my 'hotel-name.' Has your highness any objection?"

"How like a woman!" said the Honourable Luke superiorly.

"Oh?"

"Hasn't it occurred to you that you're in the yacht on false pretences?"

"Indeed, I'm not in the yacht on false pretences."

"Yes, you are. You come on board and worm yourself into all his secrets. First you're his confidential secretary, then you're his housekeeper. And God knows what you'll be next! D'you imagine he'd have behaved to you as he has done, if he'd had the slightest notion that you were as thick as thieves with his wife? Of course he wouldn't! No *man* would have done what you've done. A man would have been ashamed to do it."

Harriet felt insulted, and the more so because she knew that the accusation against her was not an unjust one.

She had, in fact, several times in the watches of the night brought the accusation against herself—and tossed it away again. Naturally, therefore, she was furious with the Honourable Luke, and warmly desirous of crushing him for an insufferable, interfering and pharisaical jackanapes. Said she:

"Will you please have the goodness to remove yourself from this car at once, and tell the chauffeur to drive me to the Hôtel de Paris. And, for all I care, you can run along and tell Lord Furber everything I've told you."

Without a word the Honourable Luke sat up out of the cosiness of the upholstery and turned the handle of the door. At the same time he switched on the interior lamp, illumining Harriet's face and his own. But neither could see the features of the other. It may be stated, however, that both were indignant, offended and angry. Harriet showed her feelings in the eyes. The Honourable Luke showed his in the hanging of his lower lip. Harriet was the first to resume some sort of self-possession. It may seem strange that something in the gloss and curves of Luke's light brown hair moved her in the direction of common sense and good manners (and perhaps also of good nature), but so in truth it was.

"I say, Luke," she addressed him, in a queer, strained voice.

"Well?" he questioned darkly, putting one foot on the step.

"Come back and shut that door—it's terribly cold—and sit down a moment. I want to ask you something."

"Well?" Luke sighed and sat down.

"Switch that light off, please. There's no need for us to advertise ourselves to the whole of Monte Carlo."

"No," Luke agreed with sadness, and he switched off the light, and sighed again, the reluctant and resentful martyr of impossible women.

Silence within the car. Not a sound in the utterly deserted street.

"Why are you so rude and unpleasant to me?" Harriet demanded.

"I'm not," said Luke. "I was only telling you the truth. And, of course, like all women you hate the truth." He raised his voice suddenly. "Come, don't deny it. Was I telling you the truth or wasn't I?" He glared directly at her now.

Harriet laughed as easily as if Luke had been his cousin the wireless operator.

"I don't object to the truth. What I object to is the tone you use." A good-natured appeal in her voice.

She said to herself, strangely alarmed:

"I've got on to some very thin ice . . . It's cracking under me."

But, contradictorily, perversely, she enjoyed her alarm; she would not on any consideration have had the ice thicker than it was.

"The point is," Luke countered, copying the good-nature in her appeal, "do you want me to take you seriously or don't you?"

"Why should you take me seriously?"

"I'm hanged if I know!" said Luke, and smiled savagely.

Harriet proceeded, pouting:

"Perhaps I *ought* to have told Lord Furber about his wife and me. But I didn't tell him instantly, in the first few words, and even you must see that I couldn't tell him later—it was too late then. And I can't tell him now, can I? He must be left to find out for himself. Besides, why should I have told him? If he's got himself into difficulties with his wife it's his own fault. And women have to stand together. If they didn't, where would a girl be —in these days?"

The implication in her latest tone was that society had arrived at such a pass that innocent and defenceless women, surrounded by an inexorable pack of unprincipled wolves in the guise of men, had to protect one another by fair means or foul—or resign themselves to the terrible disaster of being devoured alive and *en masse*.

"It's just occurred to me why I take you seriously," said the Honourable Luke, quite ignoring Harriet's arraignment of society. "The reason is that I hate, detest, and loathe you. You're a heartless flirt, an abandoned female, and a positive danger to the public." And with these words he leaned towards her and squeezed her wrist in his cruel masculine grip.

Odd, most odd, divinely odd, that for Harriet those brutal words had in them an angelical quality, soothing, uplifting? She was leaning back; he was leaning forward and sideways. She glanced at him from under her half-closed eyelids. And the boudoir in which they were enclosed together was so small, so cushiony, so impregnated with her perfume! Never before, despite sundry previous adventures of a not uninteresting nature, had she felt as she felt then. Timorous! Daring! Ready to swoon! Ready to sing songs of triumph! She noticed the expression on his face: at once honest, wise and masterful. Curiously there was something touching in the very bow of his black necktie, something intimidating in the sheeny convexity of his white shirt-front. She thought: "I'm seeing him now for the first time. He's all new to me. I've been blind."

He murmured:

"I shall have to kiss you in one minute—or less."

"Indeed you won't!" said she lazily. She was thinking: "I must be several years older than he is."

"Why not?" he asked.

She said:

"It's not done." And she was thinking: "He isn't even quite as tall as I am. And he's so shy. Not now, of course. But generally."

He said:

"But the other night you told me yourself that a kiss was nothing."

"Ah!" said she. "That was because I was offering it to you. Now you're asking for it."

"And I told *you*," said he, "I told you you'd see what a kiss was."

"Yes," she agreed. She was thinking: "This is a ridiculous situation. I can't possibly have my beautiful, solitary existence complicated in this way." She said aloud, but not very loud: "I absolutely forbid you to kiss me. And if you try to I'll never speak to you again."

"Of course I submit," said he.

And he kissed her on the cheek, softly, softly. Had he touched her or had he not touched her?

"I needn't tell you *that* isn't a kiss," he explained. "The time hasn't come yet for you to see what a real kiss is."

He shifted away from her.

"But," she protested, "we've only known one another a few days."

"I don't see what the point of that is. What on earth has that got to do with it?"

"But it's absurd!"

"Yes. Quite. Shan't you be a bit late at the Hôtel de Paris?"

CHAPTER XXXIX

TWO FRIENDS

To an acquaintance of hers, the omniscient negro who swayed the portals of the Hôtel de Paris, Harriet Perkins suggested:

"Lady Furber is here, isn't she?"

The negro shook his head with a benevolent and indulgent smile, after asking for the repetition of the name.

"She didn't arrive after lunch?"

"No, madam."

Harriet passed within, thoughtful, and found the concierge.

"Mrs. Flinders is in, I suppose?" she demanded with nonchalant assurance.

"Yes, madam. She is in her apartment."

"Please inquire if she can see Miss Harriet Perkins at once. Yes, Perkins."

The concierge told somebody else, who told somebody else to telephone upstairs. In two minutes Harriet was in the lift.

"I ought to have known she wouldn't have registered in her own name—as things are," Harriet said to herself.

When the lift stopped, Lady Furber stood waiting at the gate of the cage.

"My dear, how clever of you!" said Lady Furber, in a state of considerable joyous excitement. And Lady

Furber showed also that Harriet's swift discovery of her had somewhat taken her aback.

"Of course," said Harriet, as they entered the privacy of the apartment, "I guessed you'd use that incognito we invented for that week-end of ours in Flushing once. I admit it *was* rather clever of me."

"But——"

Maidie Furber was a woman of medium height and age; that is to say, she was a little shorter and a little older than Harriet. A verdant negligée well set off her coppery-reddish hair. She had a fresh complexion and her demeanour was vivacious. You could see instantly that she belonged to the category of what, in the Five Towns, and no doubt elsewhere, are called "downright" women. No airs. No pretence. "This is just me, and here I am." Slightly nervous. But dignified and feeling confidence in her own common sense and force of character. "I've been in tight places, but I've always come through." And withal, a sturdy habit of command. And an eye, a snub nose and a mouth that could not be trifled with. In short, a complete individual.

"But what's happened to you, Harry?" cried Lady Furber.

They were shaking hands again on the hearthrug, in front of a speck of fire. They had not kissed, and did not kiss. Lady Furber was not a woman-kisser. Since she was grown up she had kissed only two human beings; one was a man, and the other his child.

"Happened to me?" said Harriet. "Nothing. What do you mean?" She blushed.

"You look so—kind of radiant," said Lady Furber, discovering traces of a local accent.

"Well, isn't seeing you enough?" said Harriet, still blushing; she foresaw the moment when it would be her

263

duty and diffident pleasure to confess to Maidie "all"—or most of it.

Women doubtless exist who, in similar circumstances, would not have known "where to begin." But Maidie knew precisely where to begin, and though she was always conscious (not without an agreeably snobbish satisfaction therein) of Harriet's superior birth and distinction of carriage, Maidie began. After all, she was the older, she was a mother and not a spinster, and she had the disposal of mints of money.

"Now how did you find me out, my dear? You've given me a regular shock, you know."

"But you couldn't hope not to be seen and recognized," said Harriet.

"Why not? People often aren't. Indeed they generally aren't. It isn't as if I was a Monte Carlo kind of a woman. I'm not. I shouldn't know any of the folks here, and they wouldn't know me. I said to myself I'd take my chance. How was it?"

Harriet explained.

"And this other Tunnicliff, the wireless man? Is he all *right*?"

"He's horrid, and yet he isn't. Yes, he is. But he won't say anything. Nobody knows but him and me—up to now."

Harriet was forgetting that she had told the Honourable Luke. But then her recollection of her talk with this young man was extremely confused.

"So you're not surprised at me coming, are you?"

"No; I'm not exactly surprised. But why did you come?"

"Well, it was all in the papers about the goings-on on the yacht, so I thought I was entitled to have a look for myself."

"But you got my cable, of course?"

"I got it twelve hours late, and by the time it came I'd fixed everything to come straight off to Ostia, or wherever it might be. I'm like that, you know. Picked it up from Ralph—not but what I had it before I married him. Your cable made me change my ticket, that was all."

"I'm surprised you could get a seat in the Blue Train at such short notice."

"You wouldn't be if you knew a bit more of Ralph. He's got a lot of shares in the Sleeping Car Company. Besides everybody always does everything he wants. You simply say: 'It's for Lord Furber—or Lady ditto,' and the thing's done! Convenient, my dear . . . I don't quite understand, even now, about those women being on board."

"But I told you in my cable it was all owing to me—just me."

"Well, you know what telegrams are."

"I spent 225 lire on mine, anyhow," said Harriet. "Why! It was the longest cable I ever sent or ever heard of."

"It was fine," said Maidie.

She was standing up, and she put her podgy little hands on Harriet's shoulders for half a minute. Harriet had sat down on a sofa. "Now tell me all about how you came to be in the yacht at all. It was just like you. Just!"

Harriet told. Now and then she laughed hesitatingly, and Lady Furber laughed hesitatingly. Then Lady Furber took a chair opposite to Harriet. And Harriet refused a cigarette, and Lady Furber smoked a cigarette, though very amateurishly. And they laughed more freely and more frequently.

"We must have some tea," said Lady Furber suddenly, and rang the bell. "Tea for two, please!" She turned curtly to the bowing waiter. "Here! Here's the tea to

make it with. Three teaspoonfuls. Bring me back the
packet, please." She handed over a small packet which
lay on the mantelpiece. "Has he understood me?" she
asked Harriet when the man had gone.

After the tea interval, Lady Furber said:

"And this Mr. Sutherland? I know *her* a bit. She's
fluffier and more girly than her daughters. What was
Ralph after with him?"

"Oh!" Harriet replied. "Some deal. Buying a
business. Trying to buy it. Several businesses. One of
those city deals. Millions in it, I gather."

"Oh, millions? Really?"

"Yes," said Harriet. "Millions."

"And Mr. Sutherland won't?"

"No."

"Well, if he stands up to Ralph and sticks to it, he's
somebody—I'll say that for him."

"He'll stand up to him, *and* stick to it," said Harriet,
as if proud of her Septimius.

"I'm not so sure," Lady Furber murmured reflectively.
And then very vivaciously, and with a certain constraint:
"Well, you've made the acquaintance now of my man.
What d'you think of him? I mean really."

Her smile was sincere, confident, and an invitation to
sincerity and confidence. The pair, helped by tea, were
on the terms of two men rendered intimate by long
unclouded friendship and mutual esteem—or as near thereto
as a pair of women could ever be."

"Oh, well! I like him," said Harriet, easily.

She felt, and they both felt, that they had safely passed
the dangerous stage of the interview.

"You think I don't quite appreciate him properly,
eh?" said Lady Furber.

"Not at all," Harriet answered. "I'm sure you appreciate him. I admit he's a little spoiled."

"A little, my girl! I used to think that no man could be as difficult as he was when he lived in the same house with his father and his sisters in Bursley, and the menfolk always sat down to meals in their shirt sleeves! Seems a hundred years ago! But truly, he's more difficult now. Much more. And yet he's learnt a lot since then. So've I! . . . Funny that if I'd thought to tell you the name of his yacht you mightn't ever have gone on board, and all this wouldn't have happened!"

"But nothing's happened, Maidie. I mean so far as you and he are concerned. Seems to me the point is what happened before he joined the yacht—seeing that we're talking."

"Seeing as how we're talking," Lady Furber repeated the phrase musingly, in the idiom of her youth, "I'll tell you. It all came out of a row I had with one of my tradesmen. It wasn't anything and yet it's everything. I owed them about a thousand or eleven hundred pounds, and I said I wouldn't pay it because I reckoned I was being swindled, and nothing would make me pay it and I never would pay it as long as I lived. Of course, Ralph said I was wrong—you know how a man simply loves to take the opposite side. He said if I'd been swindled it was my own fault, and I'd gone into it with my eyes open and so on and so on. And I must pay it. He hates haggling over bills. I remember he once said to me, when I thought we were being done in over a hotel bill, he said: 'Maidie, d'you know what I do when I'm being robbed like this? I've only one rule,' he said. 'I pay. Saves so much trouble, lass,' he said. Well, he said about this other bill; he said they'd make me pay, and he didn't want his name in the paper over tradesmen's bills. I said they wouldn't make me pay. He got out of hand—you know. So did I. Neither Ralph nor anybody else can make me do anything I've made up my mind I won't do. And he knows it, really; only he always thinks *he* can, and nothing will cure him. He kept on at me. I said: 'Pay it yourself, then.' No. That he wouldn't! He said he'd see me at the devil first. So while we were having it out, I just sat down and wrote to 'em that I'd never buy another thing from them—from the firm I mean; and not a word did I say about paying. I read him the letter. He tried to snatch it off me. I told him if he did I should only write another one and a worse one. That calmed him a bit; but it made him angrier."

"You must have some lively times, you two," Harriet put in.

"Well, haven't I always told you so?"

"And how did it end, you terror?"

"It didn't end. It hasn't ended. He said if I didn't do as he told me, he'd never speak to me again. I said, I didn't care, and he couldn't browbeat me. And he can't, either! Only you see the mischief is that if he says a thing he'll never unsay it. Never! I never told you about that time when I persuaded him with a lot of trouble to go with me on a motor-bus. The bus didn't come for ages, and I said we'd take a taxi. And he said: 'No, you made me promise to take this bus, and I'll stay on this pavement till it comes along.' Well, it didn't come along, and a policeman told us that that service had been taken off. Would Ralph give up? Not he. He'd have stayed there till he dropped down dead, if I hadn't gone away and hired a private bus with the right number on it. That's the sort of sublime idiot my man is. And I expect it's that that has helped to make him a millionaire. So now you see."

"And there's nothing to be done?"

"Well, I did do something. I went quite half-way to meet him. I said if they'd issue a writ for the money I'd pay up at once. Well, they haven't issued a writ, though it's my belief he did get someone to urge them to do so. They haven't issued a writ, and they won't. He'd give the eyes out of his head if they would. But no! They know better. And he knows I was in the right, right from the start."

"And do you mean to say he hasn't spoken to you since?"

"Oh! He plays the game, Ralph does. He speaks to me when other people are there. But never when we're alone. Never! Funny tale, isn't it?"

"It strikes me as a terrific deal of a fuss over nothing at all," Harriet ventured.

"That's how it strikes me, too," Lady Furber agreed with an uncomfortable smile. "But that's how things happen in married life. It's the principle, my girl. It's a question whether I'm going to be able to call my soul my own, or not. I know all Ralph's good points as well as anybody. I think there's no one like him—perhaps it's a good thing there isn't." She smiled again the uncomfortable smile. "But my end has to be kept up as well as his."

"Jewellery, I suppose?" said Harriet.

"Jewellery? What jewellery? Oh, you mean the bill. No. It wasn't jewellery—it was frocks. Just frocks."

Harriet rose up from the sofa.

"What firm?" she cried.

"Lallers," said Lady Furber. "What are you laughing at, Harry?"

Harriet was indeed laughing.

269

CHAPTER XL

THE WAGER

WHEN Harriet returned to the waiting car, Luke was fidgeting about on the pavement, with one eye on his watch and the other on its large competitor, the Casino clock; they both showed ten minutes to twelve. He did not see her at first, and she had time to observe a grave dissatisfaction in his mood. But the moment he caught sight of her a transfiguration occurred in the demeanour of the exasperated youth. She saw heaven in his rapturous glance. Mr. Sutherland, with all his chivalry and passion, had never been able to look at her like that. Nor had the glance of Mr. Sutherland, with all her liking for him, ever affected her as she was then affected. She thought how wonderful it was that Luke and herself could have such a magical influence the one upon the other. Only a few evenings earlier, and he had been naught to her but a timid little boyish secretary who could not say Bo to a goose. And now——!

She opened her mouth.

"Let's give the old Club a miss and run up to La Turbie, and look at the sea and the hills from there," she might have said; she wanted to say it; she was on the very verge of saying it. But, as she was a woman who knew that she was loved, she did not say it. Instead, she said, to herself: "It isn't a minute to the Club, but if I get into

270

that car he'll be kissing me again and I shan't have the nerve to stop him, and it wouldn't be good for him, because he'd be getting a bit above himself."

Hence she put on a negligently smiling and most deceitfully calm demeanour and addressed him:

"It was fearfully hot in the hotel. I think I'll sit by the driver. I couldn't bear being inside. Do you mind?"

Whereupon the Honourable Luke fell straight out of heaven into the devil's clutches.

"That won't do," he said grimly.

She pretended not to notice the savagery of his tone.

"Won't it?" she smiled. "Then let's walk down."

And she moved forward, and then waited while Luke gave an instruction to the chauffeur. For Luke's practical purposes she might just as well have been by the driver and he within the car as he by her side and she by his in the street. Still, Luke considered that the distance between the hotel and the Club was horribly short. Moreover, he had the illusion that they covered it in two seconds, in no time at all. No sooner did they start than they arrived.

And Harriet said to herself:

"How cruel I am! How exquisite he is when he pouts!"

At the Club doors she had another narrow escape of suggesting a drive to La Turbie. They entered the Club. The attendants recognized in them frequenters of the Club. They ascended the stairs.

At first sight the chastely decorated gaming-saloons (intentionally so different in style from the gaming-saloons of the Casino, whose ceilings are supported by throngs of inadequately-clad wantons of solid gold) seemed strangely deserted. Harriet looked to the right, where baccarat is played with Roman profuseness by Greeks, and, beyond a judge of His Britannic Majesty's Supreme Court of Judicature, the aunt of a British Cabinet Minister, a British Labour M.P., said to be studying the vices of the British rich, and the editor of an American religious weekly, the gamblers were limited to a mere handful of nonentities. Certainly neither Lord Furber nor Mr. Septimius Sutherland was there.

To the left, at the roulette tables, a few British and American subjects were admirably collaborating to maintain the atmosphere of ennui which is the chief and most essential characteristic of the cushioned, glittering dens where congregate the wealthiest victors in the struggle for life.

Within the bar, half a dozen French cocottes and several London marriageable maidens of high social distinction (with attendant swains) were gloomily smoking, and imbibing all the colours of the spectrum.

Then, from round the corner, Harriet and the Honourable Luke heard a sudden loud murmurous hum of Anglo-Saxon voices, and hurried towards the enheartening sound. Five-sixths of the nightly company of the Club were seething about the four sides of a roulette table! An exceedingly odd spectacle, to the initiated, for in the International Sporting Club roulette is held to be the pastime of neophytes and cowards and quite unworthy of the general attention! Baccarat alone commands the respect of the truly enlightened.

The solution of the enigma was immediately plain. Lord Furber sat on one side of the table and Mr. Septimius Sutherland on the other. And obviously the identities of the two were known to the watching crowd. But the solution, though in one sense it did solve the enigma, in another sense only deepened its mystery. For millionaires and prominent financiers never unbend themselves to the childishness of roulette. They play baccarat or they play nothing.

Not a soul in the watching and participating crowd could guess why the principal players had so far forgotten what was due to their plutocratic rank as to sink to the miserable level of the spun ball and the thirty-six numbers. Nevertheless, the explanation was simple. Mr. Sutherland knew not the principles of baccarat, for in youth his education had been neglected.

The croupier at one end of the table had little to do, whereas his partner at the other end, at which the baron and Septimius were playing, had rather more than he could manage, with the result that the spins were delayed. At this end the numbers were thickly covered with token money of the highest denominations, which both the opulent ones put down carelessly, rapidly and quite unsystematically. The onlookers, according to the wont of onlookers, would have followed the baron's leads, but it was almost impossible to do so, owing to his deplorable lack of system. If he consistently won, and he did, it was not from any merit, but because fate had decided to reward the rash. If Septimius consistently lost, and he did, he was only getting his deserts.

The baron was excited and apparently displeased; Septimius achieved and kept a marvellous bland tranquillity. Once the baron staked the maximum on Zero, and Septimius plastered half the numbers with plaques. Zero was thrown. The croupier swept a fortune off the numbers in a single swoop of his rake, and then swept half of it towards the baron. A second time the baron staked the maximum on Zero, and Septimius plastered half the numbers again. Zero was thrown.

"Confound it!" muttered the amazing baron, while the audience thrilled to the unique strangeness of the sight.

"Lend me another hundred thousand, will you?" asked Septimius agreeably and placidly. "That will make three hundred and fifty thousand, won't it?"

The baron in gloomy silence passed a great pile of tokens to the croupier, who passed them to Septimius, who counted them with the rapid precision of a bank-cashier, and went on playing anew.

Then the great calm of Septimius was broken. His eyes gleamed; he waved a hand. He had seen Miss Harriet Perkins. Placidity had vanished from his features, but it had given place to ecstasy. He lost and lost with rapture. Among the audience the suspicion began to take shape that Septimius was a lunatic. How could the poor dull souls divine that he was enjoying the rich and novel sensation of utter recklessness under the gaze of a woman who for him was peerless. For a few minutes he had been staggered at the amount and the swiftness of his losses; he was far on the way to dropping half a million francs. But he had soon recovered his perspective. Half a million francs came to less than four thousands pounds, and though he was hardly a millionaire, he could well afford to squander four thousand pounds once in his life for the sake of an unexampled intoxication of bliss. He knew that he was alive. He glanced at his watch.

"Three minutes past the half-hour," he said across the table to the baron.

They had arranged to play till twelve-thirty.

"And a darned good thing, too!" growled the baron, gathering up his multitudinous tokens and walking away.

"Change these for me," said the baron, noticing the Honourable Luke in the crowd.

The evening's entertainment was nearly at an end; but there remained the pleasing agitations of rumour. Before the players had got ten yards away from the table the quidnuncs were asserting that in their opinion—and they had watched the table closely—Mr. Sutherland had lost not far short of a million francs, and Lord Furber won as much or possibly more. Being every one of them Anglo-Saxon, they might have stated the sum in pounds or dollars, but they did not do so, because if they had done so they would have been deprived of the magic word "million," which was honey to their tongues.

They also pointed out to one another that, had Mr. Sutherland not been playing, Lord Furber would have broken the bank, and that Mr. Sutherland's presence was therefore to be regretted. What a drama missed; the breaking of the bank by a millionaire!

Lord Furber stopped.

"How much have ye there, Sep?" he asked, indicating the paltry store of tokens which Mr. Sutherland held in one hand.

"Two thousand and ten," said Mr. Sutherland, without counting.

"Give me the two thousand, will you? We'll reckon up afterwards."

The baron took the two thousand and returned to the table. A dozen quidnuncs returned with him, in the sure expectation of seeing the fatal results of chance upon a fascinated fabulous winner who thought that he might as well win a little more. Lord Furber handed the two thousand to the head-guardian of the table.

"Change these," said he. "And divide the money among the table-staff."

The head-guardian, who had been feeling depressed, brightened.

"Thank you very much, my lord."

"Seems to me it's I who ought to do the tipping," said Septimius gaily; and the audience was confirmed in its conviction that the man was a perfect lunatic.

"Why! There's Count Veruda!" murmured Mr. Sutherland. And indeed the tall, full figure of the Count was approaching, with all the old air of superiorly enjoying a secret joke which nobody else was capable of perceiving.

Harriet, who had moved aside, out of the questing vision of Septimius, wondered what would happen at this the first meeting of the two men since the dinner given to the guests of the Splendide. Her own encounter with Veruda, in Rome, had not been satisfactory to her because somehow she had not succeeded in mentioning their previous meeting at all, and Veruda's bearing had given no sign whatever of the constraint which usually follows a misdemeanour found out.

She advanced towards the three men, speculating as to the nature of the business which had so quickly brought Veruda from Naples to Monte Carlo. But she realized that all suspicions, if she had any, were absurd; Veruda was now merely resuming duty as one of the baron's private secretaries.

The baron nodded to his minion as negligently as though they had not been parted by a monstrous and inexcusable event for which they were equally responsible.

"Ye know Count Veruda, Sep?" said the baron.

"Indeed I do!" Septimius blandly exclaimed. "And I'm delighted at this opportunity to apologize for an omission. I never thanked you, Count, for the really marvellous banquet which you offered me, with others, of course, in your magnificent yacht. I don't think I ever enjoyed a dinner more." He shook hands with the host of the historic repast. That was all.

Count Veruda blushed. His face was ruddy as always; but the blush was marked enough to intensify its glorious carmine. At this juncture Mr. Sutherland's eyes at last discovered Harriet.

"I've had the time of my life," he said with enthusiasm, turning eagerly to her. "The time of my whole life!"

"I'm so glad," said Harriet simply; she was touched by his extraordinary naïve enthusiasm.

And then the Honourable Luke appeared with a wad of French bank-notes as thick as his arm.

"These right?" Lord Furber questioned, taking possession of the wad.

"Yes, sir."

Lord Furber stuck the bundle into his pocket.

"Don't let me keep you here," said he gently to the Honourable Luke. "You've had a heavy day."

It was an order of dismissal from the rooms. Luke glanced at Harriet, a glance of supplication and despair. But Harriet was devoting herself to Septimius; she seemed to be absorbed in Septimius. The Honourable Luke waited, hesitated, scowled, and departed.

"Hello, Harriet!" the baron greeted his housekeeper casually, as if till then he had been unaware of her presence.

"Hello, Ralph," she answered in kind.

Did he know that she had been nearly an hour late at the rendezvous? Or didn't he? Not equal to the feat of looking at him without any self-consciousness, she went on with her talk to Septimius. And Septimius, by his mood, provided a magnificent distraction, a distraction so complete that Harriet failed to notice the dejected vanishing of the Honourable Luke.

While the baron and the Count chatted together, Septimius led the way to the rooms where multi-coloured beverages were served to visitors without any inquiry as to their winnings or losings or their pasts or their moral characters. Lord Furber, from behind, demurred to Mr. Sutherland's plan for taking refreshment, but Septimius came back to him and took him irresistibly by the arm.

"My dear fellow, you must give me my revenge."

The baron had to yield; he did not, however, yield very gracefully; somehow his demeanour gave the impression that Septimius was his master, always had been and for ever would be.

Three Parisian beauties having just quitted a table, Mr. Sutherland took the same, called a waiter, in a voice like the snap of a toy-pistol, to clear away the glasses and dry the marble, and himself placed a chair for the occupancy of Harriet.

Count Veruda hesitated.

"Count," said Septimius grandly. "I beg you to allow me to return, in some very slight degree, your glorious hospitality."

The Count bowed, waited for Lord Furber to be seated, and then sat down.

"We will have champagne," Septimius announced.

He did not ask whether champagne chimed with the desires of all or any of his guests—he blandly and firmly stated an intention regarding the immediate future. Mr. Sutherland had evidently decided to go the pace. He had probably never before gone the pace, and was therefore acutely inexperienced in the operation, but he held fast to the great leading principle that you cannot properly and effectively go the pace without consuming champagne— and at one o'clock in the morning. He examined the winelist with a tremendous air of connoisseurship, and ordered a magnum of a celebrated and costly brand dated 1914.

"I hear you've cleared in the neighbourhood of a couple of million francs," said Count Veruda to Lord Furber.

"Who did ye hear that from?" the baron somewhat pugnaciously demanded.

"My old friend, the doorkeeper."

"It'll be five millions in London by to-morrow night," said Lord Furber grimly. "Sep, what about a cigar?"

Mr. Sutherland was thunderstruck by this question, which amounted to a terrible demonstration of his short-comings as a host in a tabernacle of the vices. In two minutes he had a pile of cigar-boxes a foot high on the table, together with various sorts of cigarettes suitable to the rouged lips of ladies. The splendid chained waiter poured out into five glasses some of the contents of a titanic gold-headed bottle.

"And now," said Septimius, when Count Veruda and himself had plenteously quaffed and Lord Furber and Harriet Perkins had sipped, "we will just go into our accounts, my dear Furber."

"Not to-night! Not on your life!" Lord Furber gloomily objected.

"We will go into our accounts," Septimius repeated calmly.

A strange kind of a host—but a host, and therefore not to be contradicted, even by such a baron as Lord Furber.

"Let me see," he proceeded, drawing a fountain-pen from one pocket and a note-book from another. "You found three hundred and fifty thousand for me. I gave you two thousand afterwards. I have ten here." At this point he slipped a token gaily on to the table. "I had ten thousand two hundred and forty seven before I started, and of that I now have——" He pulled out of a third pocket a confused mass of small French notes and francs.

"What ye've got left hasn't anything to do with me," Lord Furber growled. "Ye owe me three hundred and forty-eight thousand."

"True," said Mr. Sutherland. "I have that figure clearly in my head. I was merely going to calculate the total of my losses."

And he proceeded to count the money on the table, very carefully; after which he mumbled figures inarticulately between his lips, and wrote in the note-book.

"And now let me see," said he. "The rate of exchange is——"

Count Veruda named the rate of exchange, and with the gesture of a conjuror Mr. Sutherland drew a cheque-book from a fourth pocket. He filled up first a counter-foil and then a cheque, and then wrote on the serrated end of the cheque, "Under three thousand pounds," and waved the cheque like a flag in the air, to dry the ink, and handed the cheque to Lord Furber.

"Take charge of this, will you, Veruda," said Lord Furber, indolently and disdainfully. And the Count took charge.

"Well," said Mr. Sutherland, having pocketed money, note-book and pen, emptied his glass, and refilled it. "I never signed a cheque with greater satisfaction. And I'm quite sure that I never got better value for my money."

He poured more champagne into the glass of Miss Perkins. She protested. He ignored the protest.

"I suppose you can solve the mystery, Count," Harriet ventured.

"What mystery, dear lady?" The Count smiled enigmatically.

"Why Mr. Sutherland is so riotous at losing, and his lordship so tragic at winning?"

The Count kept silence.

"Harriet," said Lord Furber suddenly, and as it were menacingly, "ye were late to-night. Ye said ye'd be here at eleven."

"I was a little late," Harriet admitted, uneasily, in spite of herself. The man had noted the hour of her arrival after all!

"What were ye doing?"

"Oh!" she answered shortly. "I had one or two little affairs of my own to attend to."

"What's the matter with ye?" the baron inquired pertinaciously.

"What d'you mean—what's the matter with me? Nothing's the matter with me."

"Well, I don't know," said the baron. "Ye look as if ye've just paid a visit to paradise and come back to tell us all about it."

"That's a very good description," said Mr. Sutherland. "She does." The simpleton was under the delusion that the enchantress was finding joy in his joy.

"Perhaps I have," said Harriet, as enigmatically as Count Veruda himself could have spoken. "But all this is no answer to my perfectly serious question."

Mr. Sutherland was biting the end off a cigar. He finished the amputation quickly in order to reply to the enchantress. This was a Mr. Sutherland whom nobody on earth had ever seen before—a Septimius careless, indiscreet and unprecedentedly communicative; a Septimius tasting the full savour of life.

"I'll tell you," said he. "Somehow or other when we came into the Club, Lord Furber and I settled on a strange wager—a wager such as has probably never until to-night been made in these rooms. He said that if you tried to lose it would be just as difficult to lose as to win. I said no. We laid a bet—who would lose the most. And the one who lost the most was to have Lallers. You know how set he's been on getting Lallers from me. I thought I might as well give him a chance. Well, he hasn't got Lallers. I keep it—definitely."

"Um!" murmured Lord Furber, musingly.

Count Veruda glanced away, and shared the joke with the rings of a curtain-pole near the ceiling.

As for Harriet, she could not decide whether she was glad or sorry.

CHAPTER XLI

THE DECK AT NIGHT

LATER in the night, Mr. Sutherland was escorting Miss Harriet Perkins back to the yacht. Lord Furber, who had gone off with Count Veruda, had confided Harriet to Mr. Sutherland's efficient care. The baron's final glance at Harriet had been quizzical.

Now the way, and the only way, from the Club towards the yacht, was to turn to the right immediately on coming out of the Club. But Mr. Sutherland and his charge had turned to the left, up the incline, and somehow they had reached the Terrace in front of the Casino, whose windows were now all dark. Mr. Sutherland had suggested that, as the spring night was warm (it was not), and as after the carbonic acid gas of the stuffy rooms their lungs needed the air of heaven, they should enjoy a little stroll. Harriet could not deny him. It was Mr. Sutherland's hour, and she felt towards him as she had felt in the *Vanguard's* engine-room on the evening of the banquet: namely, that as she could give pleasure to the innocent and rather wistful man at no inconvenience to herself, she might as well increase the sum of human happiness by so doing.

Mr. Sutherland did not take her arm, nor even make the least gesture indicating a desire to take her arm. He was ever prim. Yet adoration for Harriet burned softly in his eyes and gently throbbed in his voice.

The Casino Terrace, which a few hours earlier had been, and a few hours hence would be, thronged with some of the smartest frocks and uneasiest consciences in Europe, was as deserted as a thoroughfare in an abandoned city. They stood and gazed: no moon; no stars; but plenty of diffused light on the rippled, enchanted surface of the sea beneath their feet, as they leaned against the parapet. Mr. Sutherland had quite recovered from the champagne. To such an extent, indeed, that he could not think of anything to talk about. He was in bliss; he would fain have said brilliant, sincere, unforgettable things to Harriet. But the arts of conversation failed him. It was Harriet who had to save both of them from the constraint of utter muteness.

"So you're going on with Lallers yourself," she said, after a longish silence.

"Yes," said he. "It will be a big deal."

"He wanted it badly," said Harriet.

"Who? Our friend? He certainly did. But why should he have it? I'm not absolutely devoted to it myself. And once or twice I've been on the very point of letting him have it, because I felt like letting him have it." His voice was liquid with benevolence; then it changed: "But I said to myself, 'Why should I?'"

"D'you know why he wants it?"

"No. Novelty of it, I expect. Nothing but a whim —say a morbid longing." He smiled.

"Sep!" she said suddenly, raising a little in the scale her low, rich voice. "I suppose you wouldn't like to let me have the option on Lallers for a few days, perhaps a week?"

"Yes, I would!" he replied with vivacity. "I'd do anything for you. And I won't ask any questions either."

"It might be useful to me," she said, dropping her tone again.

They discussed the notion, which, now that it was uttered, seemed absurdly wild to Harriet.

"It would be very unusual," she laughed.

"What does that matter?" Septimius heartily protested. "Unusual or not, if you want it, it's yours."

In the end he said: "I shall write the moment I get home."

"Write me . . . when you get home? Are you going then?"

"Yes," he answered. "I must go. I must leave. I must return to my family. Life on the *Vanguard* is too dangerous for me." He gazed at her courageously, brazenly, for a moment. "Too dangerous," he repeated, and gazed at her again.

"So it would be!" thought Harriet, frightened, and yet amiably amused in her alarm.

She perceived that if she was not as impassive and unyielding as the parapet, Mr. Sutherland might leap. . . .

"Shall we go home?" she said, firmly prosaic. "It's been a tiring day." Mr. Sutherland moved, sighing as though with relief at a tremendous peril escaped. They went home, over the brow, down the steep hill past the Club. The Club was still illuminated; the doorkeeper was still at the door; one or two automobiles were still waiting there with the everlasting patience of automobiles in the night . . . .

"Fools!" exclaimed Mr. Sutherland, himself again, sententiously, as they passed the building.

"Yes," said Harriet, absently.

Her mind dwelt upon a vision of the Honourable Luke tossing lovelorn on his bed. But perhaps he was asleep. She knew that he had a great reputation in the yacht as a sound sleeper. When would he fulfil his threat to make her see what a kiss really was? . . . .

The quay was quiet and uninhabited. None of the gangways showed a light except that of the *Vanguard*. Mr. Antinope was standing in the middle of the *Vanguard's* gangway—a tall, muscular, overbearing, spectacled figure. He withdrew respectfully, but without abating his dignity.

"Oh, Mr. Antinope," Harriet greeted him, "one moment."

"Yes, miss."

"Good night, Sep," she said laconically to Mr. Sutherland.

"Good night, Harriet," Septimius responded, laconically also. And descended into the arcana of the yacht, carrying with him a heavy, hidden load of emotion, together with the calm strength to bear it.

"You got that file of bills I sent you by Fenton, Mr. Antinope?"

"I did, miss, thank you."

"Did you look through them?"

"Thursday is my day for checking the bills with the chits," said Mr. Antinope, politely but with finality.

In the tone of those few words Mr. Antinope reminded Miss Harriet Perkins that he was no ordinary purser. And in fact he was not. Mr. Antinope, in his time, had been just as much a certificated master-mariner as Captain Joe Slapser himself, and had commanded a yacht—not as fine as the *Vanguard*, but still, very fine. His eyesight had failed him, and he had been obliged to retire from the bridge to the office in order to earn a living.

"Of course!" Harriet agreed. "I'd forgotten."

"You couldn't be expected to know, Miss," said Mr. Antinope coldly.

"His lordship returned?" Harriet inquired.

"I think his lordship has turned in, Miss."

"And Count Veruda? Of course you know he came back to-night?"

"Yes, miss. He was on board before you left with Mr. Tunnicliff. But he didn't come back aboard with his lordship."

"Oh!"

Harriet's brain had received a fillip, and the fillip was intensified by the fact that at that very moment she espied in the middle distance of the deck, on the port side, Captain Slapser himself and the Chief Engineer himself, in converse. What were those two doing abroad in the middle of the night? Suddenly she recalled the sound of a footstep which she had heard below during that talk with the wireless operator. Could it have been the footstep of Count Veruda? Had Count Veruda overheard? If he heard, had he communicated the news about Maidie to Lord Furber? Had Lord Furber decided to fly? He would have had plenty of time to come aboard and rouse his skipper and give secret instructions for flight. Why had he looked at her and spoken to her so strangely? Had he somehow learnt at last that she was Maidie's friend?

She resolved to risk a throw.

"See," she said very casually to Mr. Antinope, "what time did Lord Furber say we should be leaving?"

Mr. Antinope was caught. He had been enjoined to secrecy, but now he could only assume that Miss Perkins was in the secret.

"Six-thirty, miss," he answered.

Harriet sat down in the shadow of the boat-deck, in one of the wicker fauteuils which stood at the end of the stairs, and lit a cigarette. When she had smoked it, she reconnoitred. Nobody was about; the three mandarins of the yacht's personnel had retired for a too brief night. Harriet ran ashore. In less than a quarter of an hour, a little breathless from hill-climbing, she was within the Hôtel de Paris and demanding urgently Mrs. Flinders. Fortunately in such places, half past two a.m. is not quite an unusual hour for visits.

CHAPTER XLII

FLIGHT

CAPTAIN SLAPSER was on the bridge, drinking thirstily at a cup of tea which had just been brought to him by an early-rising steward. A mate was at the wheel. A deckhand stood by. Another mate leaned on the rail right forward. With one exception all the boats were swung in and made fast. They had indeed never been swung out during the call at Monte Carlo. The exception was a dinghy, in which were two men bending over a mooring buoy from which a hawser held the *Vanguard* by the head. At the stern a couple of men were standing by to haul in the two hawsers which held the yacht by the stern.

On the quay stood, solitary, a splendid middle-aged marine individual with a short beard—the Harbour-Master. This official had had a disturbed night, for Captain Slapser had roused him at an abnormal hour in order to get the yacht cleared. He was not accustomed to abnormal hours and in the ordinary way strongly resented them; but the skipper of a ship owned by a millionaire has at his command a sovereign method of soothing harbour-masters, and the harbour-master of Monaco was proving his goodwill by personal attendance at the departure.

One of the men at the mooring-buoy waved a hand and blew a whistle. The engine-telegraph rang out sharply. The harbour-master grandly lifted the stern mooring-ropes from the bollards on the quay; they splashed into the water and were pulled out dripping into the ship.

The sun had not yet visibly risen, but the great affair of dawn was in fact begun, and there was light on the sea and gleams of sunshine on the pale summits of mountains above La Turbie. The air was fresh, chill, tonic. Captain Slapser, thinking that at that hour no drink, not even beer, could rival tea, experienced the thrill of British satisfaction which was always his on quitting a foreign shore.

The first delicate throbbing of the propellers vibrated through the ship. The harbour-master saw the space between the ship's counter and the quay widen—oh, so gradually, scarcely perceptibly, but inexorably. The water under the counter was churned white. A hawser which had slackly held the stern to another buoy further up the harbour lifted itself out of the water, grew taut till it strained and cracked as if in pain. The men in the dinghy raced away to the distant buoy. The ship swung round by the stem. More whistling. More engine-telegraphing. The ship, with infinite, cautious, creeping deliberation was heading for the open Mediterranean. An electric donkey-engine hauled in, with a fierce rattle, the long rope from the distant buoy. The dinghy flew after the end of the rope, like a man striving to catch a train which is already in motion. The dinghy overtook the yacht, and clung to her mighty side. Falls were lowered, and the dinghy snatched up out of the sea to the very top of its davits. The severance from the shore was complete.

A few sailors who were swabbing the decks of the other yachts gazed curiously at the slow-gliding ship. Captain Slapser waved a negligent hand to some dignitary of equal rank on one of the other yachts. The *Vanguard* slipped between the breakwaters and began to pitch indolently to the swell of the Mediterranean, described a curve, and then began to roll. The twin squat towers of the Casino showed themselves astern. The engine-telegraph rang once more. The propellers revolved more rapidly and the ship spread a white, streaming tail. The sun, appearing from its secret lair behind Mentone and the Italian frontier, struck the ship in full force and clad her in bright glory. Lastly, Captain Slapser lit a cigarette.

Lord Furber ascended out of the bowels of the ship, and fixed himself in the very easy-chair in which Harriet Perkins had sat awhile during the dead of night. He wore his splendid dressing-gown, an aggregation of colours which seemed to meet the sunrise on almost equal terms. He spoke to none of the men engaged in making the ship's toilette; and nobody ventured to accost him, for it was plain that, as not infrequently happened, he desired mental solitude. He had asked for nothing in the way of food and drink; he had not even rung for Mr. Bumption. His mien was calm, conquering, grim.

There he was, borne along in the vast and self-sufficing organism which he had brought into being for the extension of his own individuality and the extinction of his ennui. With him on board were near upon eighty other individuals, and they were all (except Septimius Sutherland) his servants and the subjects of his whim. He had his cooks, his bedmakers, his cleaners, his washers, his technicians, his experts of varied categories; and his desires were their law. The cooks cooked the dishes that he desired in the fashion that he desired. The beds were made as he desired. The ship was cleaned (within limits) as he desired. The men were dressed as he desired. The ship was steered as he desired at the speed he desired. Not a soul (unless it might

be the transient Harriet Perkins) could or would say him
nay. He was absolute master. The Mediterranean itself
seemed to be his; for not another craft could be descried
upon its surface. The sunrise had obviously been engine-
ered by nature specially for the completion of the phenomenon of his pride. And he had naught to do but give
orders. He rarely even signed the cheques, the magic
oblongs of twisted paper which rendered possible the enormous and complex miracle; the cheques were signed on
his behalf by the secretary and a director of a limited
company which in its turn was but another manifestation
of his individuality.

Thus he lolled autocratically in the wicker fauteuil,
while the organism functioned in perfection, and his mind
went back to the years when he had thought out his earliest
inventions in a ramshackle shed in the narrow garden of
his father's cottage, and washed himself in a tin can in the
scullery sink, and never worried about his finger nails and
very seldom had a bath (for in those days no cottage had
a bathroom).

He had the right to marvel at his own gifts and force,
and he did marvel at them, as his eye roved around the
beauty and the efficiency of the moving *Vanguard*.
Nobody could be more free than he was, and few could
enjoy a more assured and agreeable dominion.

Nevertheless, in those moments he was aware of a
sensation of danger escaped, and a sensation of running
away from acute discomfort, if not of wrath. But that
he had indeed successfully fled beyond any risk of pursuit
caused a sardonic and victorious smile to lighten his face.

"Hello, Sep!"

Mr. Sutherland had ascended also, and Mr. Sutherland's demeanour, as well as the fact that he had forgotten

himself so far as to affront the yacht's public in a dressing-gown, indicated that Mr. Sutherland was in no ordinary mood.

"Good morning," said Mr. Sutherland. "But what's this?"

"What's what?"

"We appear to be at sea."

"We are."

"But you never told me you were leaving Monte Carlo."

"I only decided after I left you last night."

"My dear Furber, I wish to God you had warned me."

"Why?"

"I was intending to go back to London this morning."

"But you never told me!" the baron exclaimed.

"Still, you knew that I couldn't stay on board with you indefinitely. And I should have thought that as a mere matter of courtesy—where are you bound for?"

Strong words for Mr. Sutherland!

"Oh! Depends on the weather. Perhaps Algiers."

The baron did not argue; he bluffed it out. But he was a little afraid of Mr. Sutherland. He could have wished that he had had the wit to warn Mr. Sutherland and put him ashore.

CHAPTER XLIII

THE MAGNET

ABOUT this time of the early morning Harriet rushed into the sitting-room of Lord Furber. She was dressed in black and the keys of office jingled at her waist. She looked and felt tired; which was not surprising, since she had had scarcely any sleep—after an emotional evening and two quite full glasses of champagne. Also, she was in a state of considerable excitement, which fatigue was intensifying.

"Oh! It's you!" she exclaimed, and stopped.

The Honourable Luke was lolling in the baron's armchair. He, too, seemed to be rather exhausted, and his fine, fair hair was less smooth and glossy than usual. But to Harriet, with his blue yachting suit, club necktie, and virginal white plimsols, he presented an agreeable, even an adorable spectacle—a spectacle which appealed to her in the most disturbing manner, perhaps partly because of his evident forlornness. He did not move at her entrance —merely gazed at her like a melancholy child.

"Do you know where Lord Furber is? Is he up?"

"I think he's on deck," Luke wearily answered.

"Oh!" Harriet was rushing away again.

"I say," he stopped her.

"What's the matter?" She spoke as to a boy.

"Did you know we were leaving this morning?"

"Of course I did."

"Well, I didn't. Hadn't a notion of it. They wakened me at six o'clock with a message that *he* would want me at seven-thirty. As if I should take an hour and a half to dress myself!"

He yawned. He was ineffably attractive, and not unaware of this important fact. Harriet knew that she ought not on any account to linger. But she lingered.

"The poor little thing's knocked up," she gently teased him. "What time did it go to bed?"

"Not till long after one."

"Why not?"

"Well, if you really want to hear, I waited outside the Club for I don't know how long."

Harriet was delighted.

"But why?" she innocently asked.

"I thought you'd be coming out."

"How silly of you!" she commented, with superiority.

"Instead of that I expect you preferred to go on gallivanting with that fellow Sutherland."

His jealousy filled her with bliss.

"I do hate jealousy—and jealous people," she said firmly. "There's nothing I despise more."

"Oh! Isn't there! Well, it's your fault. And I should like to know what time *you* went to bed. You weren't in your cabin at half-past two."

"Who told you that?"

"Nobody. I knocked at your door at half past two, and there was no answer. So I peeped in. The place was empty."

"A nice thing!" Harriet said. "Supposing I'd been in bed and asleep."

"I shouldn't have minded."

"No doubt. But I should. What did you want with me in the middle of the night?"

"To talk to you. I felt I must talk to you."

He made this plaintive moan with a naïvely insinuating air that was irresistible to Harriet—or nearly so. Never had she beheld a male creature looking so nice.

"You don't look very nice this morning," she observed judicially. "It's your hair. You've forgotten it. And as for that necktie you've chosen——"

"Harriet!" He stood up. "When *can* I talk to you?"

It was of the highest importance that she should hurry off at once, for much depended upon her promptitude of action at this juncture. But she was held within the room by an invisible power. She simply was unable to depart, though invaluable moments were flying.

"What do you want to talk to me about? What was it that was so desperately urgent that you wanted to see me about it in the middle of the night?"

"You know."

She did.

"I don't."

"I thought we understood each other."

"Look here," she said. "I've no time to watch you beating about the bush in this style. Why can't you say what you mean? Did you want to talk to me or to kiss me? Let's get at it."

"Both."

"As a preliminary to marriage?"

"Of course." Luke's glance lightened, and he blushed deliciously.

"I see. How old are you?"

"Twenty-eight. At least, I shall be next month."

"You don't act as if you were a day older than eighteen. How old do you imagine I am?"

"About the same."

"Oh! Well, I'm exactly a hundred. Have you any private means?"

"No. I can't say I have."

"Don't say it then. What salary do you earn?"

"Five hundred a year."

"I've got more than twice as much as that myself," said Harriet. "I suppose you'd expect me to keep you."

"Harriet!"

"Any prospects—of coming into a title for instance?"

"Not a bit. My eldest brother, Amberley, has four sons."

"I see. Of course you're an honourable, but we couldn't eat your 'honourable' for breakfast, could we? . . . Yes, well. Anything else to say?"

"Harriet, you're awful!" Luke pleaded.

"I doubt if I am," she said, as if impartially weighing the charge against her. "I'm only looking the facts in the face. I question whether you've ever tried to look a fact in the face in all your life. You'd make a splendid, reliable husband, wouldn't you? The sort of rock-man that a woman could always count on for support!"

Luke continued to gaze at her. His eyes shone— mere morning humidity, nothing else. Only a table separated them. Harriet saw the precise locality on the Persian carpet where, kneeling, and she kneeling, he had mentioned to her that his thoughts dwelt upon the pleasures of kissing her. The way round the table was extremely short. Harriet's keys clinked. She was moving. No, she was not moving—something was moving her in spite of herself. Luke was not Luke, he was a magnet.

"I am about to be ridiculous," she said to herself.

But just then she heard a cough—of the kind generally described as "discreet"—beyond the double doors, one of which was ajar. It was a feminine cough. Luke started violently.

"Doesn't it occur to you that you are ridiculous?" Harriet murmured in a half-whisper. And hastened jingling out of the room, and shut the door after her with a great bang. Immediately he was alone, the Honourable Luke became a man, and began to swear in the most objectionable, coarse fashion, and stamped about, and then fell to cursing not merely Harriet but the whole of her sex.

CHAPTER XLIV

THE MEETING

WITHIN the next minute there was enacted, on the promenade deck, one of the most sublime and terrible scenes that ever happened, either on board a yacht or in the entire annals of domesticity.

Mr. Septimius Sutherland, in his dressing-gown, had nervously walked away from Lord Furber to the extreme after limit of the deck. The distance was perhaps less than twenty-five feet. Lord Furber, in his dressing-gown, had risen from his chair, irresolute for once; he was in half a mind to go after Septimius and square things up, and in half a mind to stay where he was and let things rip. Septimius as usual had many minds, each independently functioning; but the minds of Septimius had little or no bearing on the crisis at hand.

Three seamen had begun to polish the brass in the neighbourhood of the togas. The baron would have shooed them away violently in no time, but not the baron himself dared disturb the order of the *Vanguard's* working day, which, as with all self-respecting vessels afloat, was as unalterable and implacable as a succession of astronomical phenomena. Brass had to be polished, and it had to be polished at a certain hour—yes, even though the ship went down—and until the signal sounded for the crew's breakfast the cleansing and the rubbing must continue, at no matter what cost of inconvenience and constraint to the piper-paying owner.

The baron was indeed moving towards Mr. Sutherland, and facing the rising sun, when he heard footsteps behind him on the stairs, and turned sharply, and his eyes beheld the form and likeness of Maidie his wife, Lady Furber.

At first he thought his eyes, those generally truthful witnesses, were lying to him; but he could not distrust them for more than a moment; he indubitably recognized his wife's hair, nose, glinting glance, her dress, and the shape of her muscular ankles.

Never had Lord Furber been so surprised, startled, shocked, overset, bewildered and infuriated. Maidie had got the better of him—he knew not by what chicane and conspiracy and deceit!

He had in truth heard of her arrival in Monte Carlo; and as he very particularly desired not to meet her at that delicate juncture of their conjugal relation, he had fled; his fleeing would serve her right, but, more important, it would avoid a battle on ground which was not of his own choosing. He had decided on flight in an instant; he had taken measures to keep secret the preparations for the flight.

The departure had been effectively achieved long before any guest in any hotel could possibly have left his bedroom.

And yet here the woman most brazenly was. The impudence of the dangerous creature! Come to obtain personally, had she, some explanation of the singular incidents on board which had been described in his own morning paper, and super-described and embroidered by other newspapers? No doubt she intended to use those incidents as a lever for forcing him to yield in the matter of their quarrel!

Well, she had asked for trouble, and she should have trouble, and more than she wanted. He would destroy her, annihilate her. His marital prestige was at stake, and in comparison with that, what else could count? He clenched his fists; his face was contorted. A hurricane, a tempest, a typhoon was about to descend on the devoted yacht. The baron cared for nobody and nothing save the satisfaction of a tremendous instinct.

"Pass us that tin of Brasso," one deck-hand murmured to another nonchalantly, all ignorant of the cataclysm which was ripe and ready to engulf him for evermore.

The baron heard the mild, ordinary words, and in some strange way they brought into his brain the memory of his first conversations with Harriet Perkins and of his masterly self-control in the interview with Mr. Robbington at the summit of the dome of St. Peter's. In a flash he saw a better way—the only effective way. The four-wheel brakes on his newest automobile presented themselves to him in the guise of a symbol; he applied the symbol, and happily the brakes acted simultaneously, or there might have been a disastrous skid.

"My dear!" he exclaimed charmingly—and none could be more charming than the baron when, rarely, he chose to be charming. "Of course I gave ye up last night, and so I was going on to Cannes to meet ye there—as we arranged in case ye couldn't get that train, the night before last. Ye had my cable?"

He saw that Maidie was thunderstruck and thoroughly nonplussed for a second by his gambit, but the next second she had appreciated his admirable scheme for saving appearances at all costs. Clever woman, curse her! And she must be admitting now that he was the cleverer. She should suffer for this. Never, never, would he abandon the point upon which they had quarrelled. What he had said he had said, though he died for it.

"Yes, darling," she replied a bit weakly, though with considerable histrionic skill.

He advanced as she reached the top step. The encounter of their eyes was formidable, nerve-shaking. The deck-hands at the sight of their mistress sheepishly raised their white hats. The baron shook hands with the baroness. It would have been bad acting for him to kiss her; for they were Midlanders and they were cousins, and they had grown up together in a house where it was held to be bad southern form to kiss or to show any undue sign of deep affection in the presence of any public, however limited. As a fact, no living person, save only their child, had ever seen Ralph and Maidie embrace. So the baron quite rightly refrained from kissing the baroness: which did not prevent him from giving her hand such an excruciating squeeze as would have made an ordinary woman faint from pain. (This was his warning of what was to come to her later.)

"Here! Sit down, my girl," said he, benevolently. "Ye look tired."

"Well, I am," Maidie admitted.

The baron thought rapidly.

"Women 've no business to travel alone," he went on, as she sat down. "I ought to have fetched ye myself. And if I'd known in time I would have."

After this enormous whopper he paused to recover, afraid lest he might be going too far. But only Mr. Sutherland and the deck-hands were there to overhear.

"I had a sort of notion you might," said Maidie, gazing steadily at him.

The baron quailed; then continued intrepidly to invent:

"I suppose ye missed the Blue Train, and took the night express to Marseilles, and then the afternoon train from there.   Get's here about three a.m., doesn't it?"

"Yes, that was it," Maidie calmly agreed.

"Well, I didn't hear ye come aboard; I must have just gone to sleep.   I hope there was somebody on deck."

"Oh yes."

"And ye brought yer luggage?"

"Oh yes."

"And gave orders ye weren't to be disturbed this morning?"

"Yes; but the starting off woke me up.   I went into your room, but you weren't there."

"No; I've been up here ever since we left harbour. Ye might have wakened me when ye came," said the baron.   "But I reckon ye thought ye'd give me one o' yer dramatic surprises, eh, this morning? Well, ye managed it very well, and I'm proud of ye, wench."

Thus the improvised play proceeded, until suddenly the baron, who was still most actively cerebrating, rang the bell, and at the same moment cried:

"Rayner!"

"Yes, my lord."

"Good morning, Rayner," Maidie greeted the magic servant.

"Good morning, my lady."

"Rayner. Tea for her ladyship."

"I've had some, Ralph, thank you."

"Ye'll have some more then, my girl.   And I'll have some as well. Tea for two, Rayner."

"Very good, my lord."

"And Rayner."

"Yes, my lord."

"Ask Miss Perkins if she can oblige me by coming up here at once."

"Yes, my lord."

"Sep!" called the baron. "I want ye."

Mr. Sutherland had been in misery lest, wearing his dressing-gown, he should be summoned to a lady's presence. He was now put out of his misery. He thanked heaven that he was not as Lord Furber, unshaved.

"This is my friend, Mr. Septimius Sutherland, my dear. My wife, Sep. She's stolen a march on us. I didn't expect to see her till this afternoon at Cannes."

"Lady Furber! Delighted! This is indeed a pleasure," Mr. Sutherland murmured, speaking and bowing elaborately in order to minimize as much as possible the fact that he was in a dressing-gown, with his neck bare.

Maidie, seldom very apt at conversation with entire strangers, said nothing; she smiled.

"I thought you said we were bound for Algiers," Mr. Sutherland remarked to the baron.

The baron had quite forgotten this detail: a flaw in the wonderful realism of the play!

"Get on!" said the baron, employing the Five Towns idiom. "Ye know I was only getting at ye."

And he laughed rather satanically, and Septimius tried to laugh.

"I think, if Lady Furber will permit me, I'll just finish dressing," said Septimius; and without waiting for permission, he vanished.

"Funny chap, Sep!" observed the baron lightly to the baroness. "Ashamed of his dressing-gown!"

"You needn't be ashamed of yours, me lad," said Maidie.

"No," agreed the baron. "I lay it was my dressing-gown that brought ye to the Riviera."

Miss Perkins appeared, not up the stairs, but from the other end of the deck.

"Yes, Lord Furber?" she questioned primly.

"This is my wife. I expect you've met already this morning, but I wanted to introduce ye formally. Maidie, Miss Perkins, my housekeeper—temporarily—filling up a gap. She's leaving to-morrow."

The ladies bowed.

A whistle went, waking the ship. The deck-hands gathered together their tins and engine-waste and hurried off towards the forecastle.

The baron stood silent for a few seconds, while he surveyed in retrospect his own performance as a comedian. He frankly admitted to himself that it was marvellous, perfect, and far better than Maidie's performance in the same vein. He decided, in view of the self-consciousness of the two women, that the time had come to strike.

"Yes," he said, in a wholly new tone, "and ye can't put it across, either of you! Because I've tumbled to it! Ye were at the Hôtel de Paris last night, Harriet—that was it!"

Harriet hesitated, and then burst into a laugh. The baroness burst into another laugh. The baron grinned menacingly. None of them knew what the immediate future held. Certainly the baron did not know.

But in order to reflect further upon what the immediate future ought to hold for himself, if justice was done, he walked defiantly down the stairs to the masculine privacy of his own state sitting-room.

CHAPTER XLV

LUKE'S CABIN

"COME on!" murmured Lady Furber lightly, to her companion in peril.

Harriet nodded, and the pair followed Lord Furber into the masculine privacy of the owner's state sitting-room. They also sat down.

Lord Furber moved towards the door which led to his bedroom.

"Come now, Furby," Harriet enjoined him. "Don't run away again. You've run away once; hasn't he, Maidie?"

"That he has, the poor darling," Lady Furber agreed, smiling very amicably.

Lord Furber, somewhat shaken at being addressed, for the first time in his life, as 'Furby,' turned and faced his pursuers. He had decided that on the whole this was the wisest thing to do. He faced them warily, for he knew that in Maidie he had a handful, and he knew further that in Harriet he had a handful. And he divined that the pair must indeed be very deeply leagued together, for otherwise Maidie could never have thus openly divulged to Harriet the fact that she was at loggerheads with her spouse.

"And when did I run away before?" he asked with sinister calm.

"Why!" Harriet exclaimed; "you've just run away from Monte Carlo because Maidie was there and you were afraid."

"Not at all," laughed the baron. "I merely left Monte Carlo because I shall have to come to an understanding with yer friend Maidie, and a yacht is not a suitable place for coming to the sort of understanding that I intend to come to. It's too public. In a yacht everybody knows everything—sometimes before it's happened. Everybody's on the top of everybody else."

"Tell us, Rafie, how did you find out that Maidie and I are such friends? I'm sure you didn't know yesterday."

"I'll tell ye," said the baron to Maidie. "Veruda found out ye were at the Hôtel de Paris."

"Of course he did," Harriet put in. "And he found out by eavesdropping. Veruda all over!"

"And when ye were so late last night," the baron glanced at Harriet, "and Veruda gave me the news, I began to think. And I remembered how a long time ago Maidie 'd told me about a friend of hers I'd never seen who'd had to change her name to get hold of a fortune, and she'd showed me a photograph . . . It came over me all in a flash. I admit it never occurred to me when ye came aboard my yacht that ye were a spy—and a spy of Maidie's! Yes, that I do admit."

"I didn't come as a spy. I didn't even know it was your yacht I was coming aboard of. But when I discovered it *was* your yacht, naturally I had a good laugh to myself. Not that Maidie had told me anything about any quarrel—she hadn't. But I'd picked up from her letters that domestic life with you was a bit lively, and I thought I'd like to see for myself what kind of a husband Maidie's was, and so I lay low."

The baron spread his legs.

"And when ye'd seen Maidie's husband for yeself, what kind of a feller did ye think he was—in yer wisdom?" he demanded grimly.

"I thought he was the goods all right—but the rough stuff," said Harriet enigmatically.

"Oh!"

"And then ye sent for Maidie?"

"What do you mean—I sent for Maidie?"

"Didn't ye cable to her from Ostia?"

"The man is a marvel," cried Harriet. "A marvel! Nothing can be hidden from him. How did you guess I cabled?"

"I just guessed—this morning."

"Well, I did cable. But only because I thought my name might be getting into some silly newspaper, and I wanted to keep straight with Maidie. I didn't tell her to come, I only told her the yacht was going to Monte Carlo, didn't I, dear?" Harriet's eyes twinkled.

"That's right," Maidie concurred, and Maidie's eyes twinkled also.

"Well," said the baron, with much dignity, "I'm glad I'm the goods."

At this point Maidie sprang up, and, outraging their common code of deportment, kissed Lord Furber. She might as well have kissed a milestone for all the response she got.

"So you *are* the goods, you great ninny!" said Lady Furber. "And he's so quiet and so calm! He's having a most trying time, and he hasn't broken any furniture yet! Somebody's been doing something to him. Is it you, Harry?"

"I dare say it is," said Harriet.

Maidie kissed the milestone again.

"When you've quite finished," said the milestone, moveless and granitic.

"Now, my lord," Harriet resumed, standing up, "you're beaten. You know you're beaten. Be a man, and tell us you're going to give in."

"I'll tell ye something else," said the baron. "I'll tell ye I'm not going to discuss my private affairs with anybody but my wife."

"Then why did you begin to?" Harriet retorted. "You started it upstairs. You told us both we couldn't either of us 'put it across.' Wasn't that discussing your private affairs—your most private affairs?"

"All right," said the baron. "If ye must have it— both of ye!—I'm not beaten, and nothing can beat me, and I'll never give in." He paused and rubbed his chin. "It's all nowt but a lark, of course; but what I've said I've said, and I wunna give in."

The atmosphere was changed.

At this very moment the Honourable Luke had the misfortune to enter the room. Strangely enough he was carrying a tray with a teapot and other matters, including three cups and saucers.

The baron turned ferociously on the Honourable Luke. He knew not that his secretary's nerves were suffering from a short night and an attack of Harriet. Nor did the Honourable Luke know that the baron's nerves were suffering from a short night and an attack of Harriet.

"What's that?" the baron demanded, challengingly.

"Tea."

"Why isn't Rayner serving it?"

"I took the tray off him."

"Why?"

"Because I thought you wouldn't like to be disturbed by a servant," answered the Honourable Luke, a little curtly. The curtness was due to the baron's tone acting on Luke's frayed nerves.

Luke set down the tray. The baron gazed at it.

"I told Rayner tea for two."

"And I told him tea for three," said the quickly-awakening aristocrat in Luke.

"What the devil did you mean by telling him three?"

The Honourable Luke, flushing, burst out:

"What the hell do you think I meant? . . . Excuse me, ladies."

He departed.

The baron's cheek was blanched by this staggering defiance. He dropped into a chair. He had been defied in the presence of women.

"Well, Ralph, you asked for that," said Lady Furber, sweetly and philosophically. "Only now, of course, the poor lad will have to leave."

"He will," said Lord Furber, briefly.

"Lord Furber," Harriet exploded furiously. "You put Luke into an impossible position, and he'll lose his place through it. But you'll give him another one I hope. You can make him a secretary of one of your companies or something, where he won't always be under your orders and seeing you every day. And you'll make his salary at least a thousand a year. It's the least you can do—after this. After all, you're a gentleman!"

"Heaven forbid!" sighed Lord Furber, sardonically.

"Then you won't!" Harriet glared over him.

"Yes, I will. I'll give him anything ye like. I'm rag. I'm putty. I'm chewed string."

"Thank you," said Harriet, stiffly.

"But I'll never give in to Maidie," the baron added.

Harriet ran out of the room. That is to say, truthfully, she did not in fact run, but she moved over the Persian carpet at an astonishing speed. The lounge was empty. The double-doors of the dining-saloon were open, and the sound of voices proceeded therefrom. Two stewards were laying the table for breakfast, under the supervision of Mr. Bumption, who gave her a bow in which were mingled benevolence and a nice regard for the dignity of his superseded and suffering wife. Rayner, the deck steward, was casually seated on a chair in the corner, and taking a cigarette from a yellow packet.

No professional prestidigitateur could have caused a solid object to vanish more quickly than Rayner hid the yellow packet: and no acrobat could have used more agility than Rayner used in springing from the chair; and no sergeant-major could have looked more disciplinary than Mr. Bumption looked as his eyes gazed at Rayner thus trapped in flagrant delinquency. For Harriet had already established her authority.

"D'you know where Mr. Tunnicliff is?" she asked, her agreeable tone indicating that officially she had seen nothing wrong.

"I don't know I'm sure, miss," said Rayner earnestly. "He's most likely in his cabin."

"Where is his cabin?"

Although Harriet had established her authority, she had not yet completely acquired the complex geography of the ship.

"I'll show you, miss."

Rayner led the way out on to the deck, down a secondary stairway, and along a corridor, and pointed to a door at the end.

311

"No. 8, there, miss."

"Thank you."

Harriet stood hesitant at the door of No. 8. Then she knocked. Then, getting no answer, she cautiously turned the handle, pushed against it, and peeped within, very quietly. A bold action, she thought! She saw the Honourable Luke's home afloat, his domestic interior.

It was remarkably different from that of his cousin, the wireless operator. As tidy as a hive. No pictures cut from *La Vie Parisienne*. No pictures at all, save a photograph of a middle-aged lady. Very few books. Indeed, no book except a Spanish grammar, and a copy of a work by Blasco Ibañez. On one side-wall, the bunk (of which the bed had been made). Under the bunk the usual drawers. On the other side, a desk, with a type-writing machine and a telephone and an assorted supply of stationery in a rack; the telephone was hung on the wall immediately over the desk. In one corner a lavatory basin, with towels carefully folded on a different kind of rack. One easy-chair, and one deck-chair. Harriet instantly loved the interior, which gave her a feeling of security and tranquillity. Still, perhaps she would have preferred just some little symptom, somewhere, of untidiness, for the perfect man ought surely not to be perfectly tidy.

The Honourable Luke was lounging in the easy-chair, his head averted, his eyes shaded from the world by his left hand. He looked up, and saw that the invader was Harriet.

"Go away," he adjured her, and gave a tired scowl.

Harriet obeyed him by slipping in and shutting the door. A still bolder action, she thought! He said nothing for a moment, but glanced out through the thickly-glazed porthole. The sea was rushing past the little circle of light at a tremendous rate, and every now and then it curved

upwards and the stout glass was covered with solid water.
Somewhat stuffy in the cabin! Harriet perched herself on
the bunk, which was so high that her short-skirted legs had
to dangle and did dangle.

"Go away, I tell you," the Honourable Luke repeated
—one might say savagely.

"All right," Harriet soothed the dejected savage, and
tattooed with her heels against the mahogany fronts of the
drawers. Never had she felt happier or more angelical
than she felt then.

The Honourable Luke suddenly fronted her.

"I don't need anybody to come here and tell me I've
made a fool of myself," he said gloomily. "But I was
tired, and my nerves were all gone. Besides——" He
stopped.

"So were the panjandrum's nerves all gone, and he's
an older man than you, old as you are. 'Besides'? Besides,
what?"

"The fellow has no right to speak to anyone like that,
and I won't stand it."

"Still," Harriet argued, "it *was* a bit annoying for
him when you said you thought he wouldn't want to be
disturbed by a servant, wasn't it? It showed you knew there
was domestic trouble about."

"So I did know."

"Of course you did, practically, but not in theory."

"I don't care. I know I'm ruined. I know I shall
never get another place. He'll never give me a character.
And my people will never forgive me for taking this place."

"Who's that?" Harriet asked, pointing to the photograph.

"That's my mother."

"And she won't forgive you? A woman with a face

like that couldn't *not* forgive you anything. So you needn't pretend."

Although the Honourable Luke was in the easy-chair and Harriet was on the bunk, their heads were not more than a couple of feet apart. Harriet leaned forward, and smiled. She felt that she was more angelic than any angel could ever be.

"Luke," said she, "you never did a finer thing. And what you did you did perfectly. It couldn't possibly have been better. It was worth being ruined for."

"Do you think so?"

"I was so proud of you I had to run out and come and tell you how proud I was. I bet by this time the whole ship knows I'm in here. Not that I care!"

"I say!" said Luke, with an air of discovery. "You're an angel!"

"How true!" thought Harriet. She said aloud: "Stuff!" Then she thought: "Why am I here with this young man with no prospects and not a cent of his own? But I was forgetting. He has prospects, or I'll never speak to the panjandrum again. Only he ought to be eight or ten years older than me, and he's a year younger. And he's an inch shorter. He'll never be able to thrash me, and I should so like to be thrashed, just once. And I've known him hardly a week. It's all wrong. No, it isn't. It's all absolutely right. Especially as he's certainly got a dickens of a temper! If ever there was a blooming idyll on this earth, I'm in the middle of one now at this minute."

Luke leaned forward and raised his face and his arms.

"It's his eyes," Harriet thought. "It's his eyes when they're sad. Now I shall know what he really means by a proper kiss."

She was correct in her vision of the future. She did immediately learn what the Honourable Luke really meant by a proper kiss. And she was well satisfied with his meaning. Precisely how the wonderful thing happened she could not have said; nor could he. But there the thing was: his arms round her neck, his lips on hers, hers on his. Life! He loved her. She sat upright again, smiling. He stood, not smiling.

"Is it true?" he murmured doubtfully.

She nodded, and laughed.

"But I've nothing to offer you."

"Yes, you have," she said. "Everything."

"But I can't keep you. I shan't ever be able to keep you."

"Yes, you will," she reassured him: the angel once more. "The panjandrum's all right. He's sorry. He'll give you another job—a much better one."

"But I won't take it," Luke cried. "Nothing would induce me——"

"Well," she said calmly. "We'll see. We'll see."

The telephone gave a little tinkle. But their heads were together again, and Luke was stroking Harriet's hair. The telephone gave another tinkle . . . And a third.

"Is that the panjandrum?" Harriet asked.

"What if it is? Let him go to the deuce!"

A minute later steps were heard outside, and a deep voice. The fortress was endangered. The Honourable Luke jumped up to defend it, and decided that he could more effectively do so from outside. He dashed into the corridor, and banged the door behind him.

The baron was in the corridor. The baron had actually come to seek his unresponding serf. Luke clenched his fists.

"I say, Luke, my lad," said the baron, with a self-conscious laugh, "it's all right. I'll apologize to you first, and then ye can darned well apologize to me afterwards. But I'm bound to tell ye, ye aren't cut out to be a private secretary—at any rate not mine. I'll find ye a job in London—something worth having."

And the baron hurried off, as though he had committed a crime.

CHAPTER XLVI

THE OPTION TRANSFERRED

EARLY afternoon. Sunshine. Smooth sea, with delicious Mediterranean dapplings of its surface. The incomparable Riviera coast on the starboard beam. The sun ahead, and a long, straight, white wake astern.

The baron sat alone at the after end of the topmost deck. The wireless operator popped out of his shanty at intervals for a breath of air; he had been very busy, sending and receiving. Several figures stood motionless on the bridge. Not another soul in sight. Only the Honourable Luke and Harriet knew where the Honourable Luke and Harriet had hidden themselves; all that could be said was that house-keeping and secretaryship were not their chief interests. Mr. Septimius Sutherland was understood to be packing.

Mr. Sutherland and the baron had breakfast alone together and they had lunched alone together; the ladies not having appeared, and not having been inquired for, save in a perfunctory manner. The relations between Mr. Sutherland and the baron had quickly been restored to their original excellent amity; and the baron had undertaken to land Septimius at Marseilles, where he would have a better chance than at Cannes of securing a seat in some sort of express for Paris and Calais.

The baron was apparently reading *The Decline and*

Fall of the Roman Empire, by Gibbon. But what he actually read was "The Decline and Fall of the Furber Empire," by himself. For, if a two-thousand-ton yacht can indeed be dust and ashes, the *Vanguard* was then dust and ashes to its titanic owner.

Lady Furber somewhat surprisingly joined her spouse. She drew a chair towards the table on which was one of the baron's books, and she laid upon it some crochet-work. The habit of crocheting had survived from her Five Towns days. The baron ignored her. The baron furrowed his great, fringed brows in order to appreciate the full power of Gibbon. As for Maidie, she was exquisitely and most expensively dressed for yachting, and knew it, though she had never known how to make quite the best of her trouble-causing attire. Her little nose wrinkled itself up and down; her rosy cheeks dimpled with a changeful smile; her hair was magnificent. She began to crochet, and the superb rings on her chubby hands caught and threw back the sun.

Peace.

Then Maidie said:

"Ralph, you know you aren't reading."

Silence.

And Maidie said further:

"Ralph, you are an old idiot."

Silence.

And Maidie said still further:

"You know you haven't got a leg to stand on."

At this remark, the baron stood up, walked a few paces, remained for ten seconds also with his legs spread apart in view of Maidie, and resumed his seat, brow furrowed as before.

Maidie laughed low at such symbolism, and proceeded, in a very quiet voice:

"You've tried to beat me before, but you've never really beaten me, and well you know it! Over this Lallers affair I've met you more than half-way. I've said if they sue me I'll pay at once. I'll go further. I'll say that even if they threaten to sue me I'll pay up at once. You see, they won't sue me because they daren't. Then I've told you that if you're so desperately anxious for them to be paid you can pay 'em yourself. What's a thousand pounds odd to you? But no! You won't. You're just behaving like a child."

Silence.

Maidie started again:

"Of course, I admit it's a pity Harriet came into the business. She thinks so too. You and me don't want *anybody* butting into our private affairs. But it just happened like that. And it was all your fault. If you hadn't begun on her and me together this morning, you need never have known that she had butted in; or at least you could have pretended that you didn't know—and that would have been just as good. However, she's out of it now, I may tell you. She's got something much more important to think about."

Silence.

"I know you're dying to know what it is. I've a good mind not to tell you, but I will. She's engaged to Luke Tunnicliff . . . It's no use you pretending you aren't startled, Ralph. *And* furious. I know you are. I know you're simply dying to hear all the particulars. Well, you won't hear them. But this I will say—you're showing the most wonderful self-control. Yes. You've improved, Ralph. And I'm glad of it. I hope you'll keep it up, my lad."

Silence.

Lady Furber gazed with laughing eyes at the baron, while the baron frowned heavily at her. Gradually, as the silence persisted, Lady Furber's glance drooped and lost all its gaiety, and a tear shone where laughter had been.

"Ralph, you're awful," she spluttered.

Silence.

Then Mr. Sutherland appeared and came towards them. Whereupon Lord Furber smiled in his most enchanting style.

"Maidie, my dear," said he, "this news o' yours fair takes the cake. Yes, it's quite true—I'm startled right enough. What next? Have ye heard about Harriet and young Tunnicliff, Sep?" he asked Mr. Sutherland.

"No, what is it?" Septimius demanded. And was told.

Maidie, quite ignoring the bland Mr. Sutherland, jumped up rather violently and left the deck; the fact was that she did not feel herself able calmly to tolerate the difference between Ralph alone in her society and Ralph with her when others were present.

"Sit down, Sep," said Lord Furber glumly.

Septimius sat down in the chair just vacated. At this crisis he had only two minds, instead of half a dozen or a dozen. In one mind he was conscious of a prodigious relief at the astounding news, regarding it as a salvation for himself, a strong bulwark against conceivable folly. In the other mind he was conscious of terrible gloom, tragedy, the end of all things for him. But on the whole the first mind prevailed, though with difficulty, over the second.

"But it's impossible! Impossible!" he exclaimed. "Tell me about it, my friend. Tell me all about it."

Septimius, however, was destined not to learn the details immediately.

"Sep," said the baron reflectively, slowly, "I'm sorry ye couldn't let me have Lallers. I didn't want it for any financial reason."

"Then what for?" asked Septimius, almost welcoming the reprieve from the sad story of Harriet and the Honourable Luke.

"I wanted it for a domestic reason," said the baron, gazing seawards. "To fix up a certain difficulty with a certain woman. Well, ye may as well know—to get the better of her."

"My dear fellow," said Septimius, quick as ever to sympathize, and recalling many of the difficulties he had had with the fluffy Mrs. Sutherland, "why in God's name didn't you tell me this at first? Of course I'll let you have Lallers. I'll transfer the option to you now."

They talked a long time. The name of Lady Furber was not mentioned, for the baron was inclined to be ashamed to mention it, and Mr. Sutherland behaved with the height of discretion. They were merely discussing the business details of the transaction.

"It may be," said Septimius, rising to go to his cabin and write out the formal operative transfer, "it may be you won't want Lallers for ever. In that case, when it's served your purpose——"

"Seppie," said Ralph, "ye're a devilish clever fellow. I never thought of that. Ye shall have it back."

Mr. Sutherland departed.

And then Maidie returned. She had been crying and did not conceal the fact.

"I shall go back to London with Harriet and Mr. Sutherland and young Tunnicliff."

"Yes," said the baron. "That'll be all right about Tunnicliff. I've wirelessed Veruda to come on to Marseilles at once from Monte Carlo. So I shan't be absolutely without a secretary."

"So that's all you think of, is it?" Maidie whimpered. But she was astounded that her Ralph should address her with no other person present. Hope stirred in her breast.

"No, it isn't all," the baron continued. "It ain't all by a long chalk, my dear. Lallers is going to sue ye for that bill o' yours. And they'll threaten ye with proceedings inside three days."

"How do you know what they'll do?"

"I know because *I'm* Lallers now, and it's costing me a couple o' hundred thousand pounds, besides a contingent liability to find about a couple o' millions. But *I'm* Lallers." He laughed.

Maidie went away again, and came back with a bill, an envelope addressed to Lallers, Hanover Square, W.I, London, and a cheque for £1,113 4s. 6d. drawn in favour of Lallers. She displayed these papers to her spouse, and put the first and third into the second, and tossed the whole over to the baron.

"Here!" said she, between smiles and tears. "You can lick it and you can stamp it—I haven't got any French stamps anyway."

In silence Lord Furber obeyed the suggestion.

"And here!" said Maidie putting her right arm across the table towards her spouse, and dangling her right hand in front of him.

"What?"

"Kiss it."

"Why?"

"It's the hand you squeezed into perfect pulp this morning."

The most remarkable and improbable event in the entire history of the *Vanguard* and of Lallers then happened. The baron immediately kissed Maidie's hand. He did it clumsily, perhaps brutally; but he did it.

"I've won," said Maidie.

CHAPTER XLVII

LAST

THAT night the yacht was being manœuvred into the great basin at Marseilles. And the port of Marseilles is a most interesting and thrilling locality; but the most interesting and thrilling phenomenon lay within the yacht itself, and not outside it.

That phenomenon was the mind of Lord Furber. The baron, with his mind on board, wandered about alone. He could not stay at rest in one place. Nor could he carry on a connected conversation with anyone. He had the transfer of the Laller option, drawn up with all Mr. Sutherland's nice particularity, in his pocket. He knew that he could exercise the option at any moment, and from that moment could give orders at Lallers' establishment. Hence he knew also that if Maidie had not paid (but she had paid), Maidie at a word from him could be sued. Therefore he had won in the conjugal contest; and it was absurd of Maidie to assert that she had won. Nevertheless he was well aware, though he would not admit quite as much, that she had indeed won, for he had gained his end only by the main force of money; and Maidie had outshone him.

They were all leaving him. Harriet Perkins was going. Luke Tunnicliff was going. (By what magic had that mere lad established such an ascendancy over the